Sinister Journals

Joann MacLachlan

First published 2004
Revised 2019
Copyright © 2019, Joann MacLachlan, 1937-

ISBN 978-1-9991988-0-0

This is, above all, a work of fiction. It began in response
to an exercise in Julia Cameron's *The Artist's Way* and got
a little out of hand.

I dedicate this revised edition to my women friends.

CHAPTER I

FRIDAY, MAY 29, 1998

THERE WAS NOTHING VERY SURPRISING about Gertrude Moseley dying. The police certainly did not find the death out of the ordinary. An elderly lady [their words] lies down for an afternoon nap and doesn't wake up.

And Emma might have accepted her grandmother's death as natural were it not for two odd details.

The people who discovered Gertrude's body lying peacefully on the couch in her living room were friends, eight women, arriving for the 30th Anniversary of an annual trek to Oliphant. The fact that she was discovered by friends was not remarkable; however, more than one of the women had communicated with Gertrude earlier in the day, confirming what pots were available and what wines would be suitable. In none of those conversations had Gertrude given any hint of unease or disease. The weather forecast was favourable and she was expecting that together they could search the fen for wild iris and orchids.

Nonetheless, 85-year-old women have been known to die suddenly and of any number of natural causes. Therefore, the second detail was of some importance and contributed hugely to Emma's distress. In fact Emma couldn't see why everyone did not regard the second detail as proof of some kind of unnatural element playing fast and loose with her grandmother's mortality. Gertrude's aged dog, a twelve year old Doberman named More Sinister, was stretched out beside her, also dead.

*

Oliphant is less a town than a location on a map. North of Sauble Beach and directly west of Wiarton the houses straggle, perhaps 20 kilometers, the boundaries are unclear, along the eastern shore of Lake Huron, from the southern limits of South Oliphant to the northern limits of North Oliphant. Only where North meets South do the dwellings reach more than two lots back from the lake into a small settlement with attendant holiday trailer camps.

Oliphant has been home to a summer community for over a hundred years. A history of the area published in 1906 says:

"This town plot has been a disappointment, never developing even into a village. Being close to the Fishing Islands, hopes were entertained as to its becoming a business centre; when these failed to materialize after some thirty years of waiting, its numerous town lots were re-surveyed and made into park lots for farm purposes. The locality attracts summer visitors from Wiarton and other places, who have erected summer cottages in which they may enjoy the healthful breezes that blow over Lake Huron and the restful environment of the place."

Not much has changed since 1906, except that the automobile makes it possible for visitors to come from further away. The lack of development no longer disappoints. The majority of the visitors drive less than three hours and are happy to leave behind the development of Toronto, Cambridge, Guelph, Kitchener or Detroit. The more exotic visitors fly in. One cottage is owned by Germans and, presumably, rented out to fellow citizens of the New Europe. Another is guarded by two forlorn pink plastic flamingos; both flamingos and cottage belong to folks who spend most of their lives in Florida.

At the turn of the century prosperous farmers, retired prosperous farmers, from Paisley and Tara and Chesley, looking for places along the Huron shore where they could sit on folding wooden chairs and watch their grandchildren playing in the water, built summer homes in Port Elgin, along Sauble Beach, north up the shore to Oliphant and beyond. After spring planting was done, after the first hay was in, and

2

before the rigors of harvest began, the wagon, or Model T, depending on the era, would be loaded with extra bedding, food, children, essential crockery and pots. Then the family would leave the hired help, more plentiful in those years before the war, to milk the ten or twenty cows and feed the chickens. The rest of the family, or those who might be spared from the drudgery of chicken and cattle care, removed to the casual living of a cabin by the water - though laundry and baking and entertaining in the rustic circumstances may not have made cottage life so casual for the wives or hired girls. Sometimes the doctors, lawyers, or the owners of the local dry goods stores drove their wives and children to the cottage and left them there for a few weeks at a time; and the teachers who had nothing to do in the summer lazed around for maybe a whole month or two, usually at the retreat of a friend or relative because they couldn't afford their own. At the center of Oliphant the summer people built a small church and one of the early preachers, provided with a chunk of land to ensure his regular return, filled up a small peninsula with his progeny. Until recently most folks were related one way or another. That's what happens when generations of adolescents grow up dancing and boating and swimming together every summer.

By the end of the twentieth century, suburbia and retirees had invaded the summer world and many people raised their floors above the original concrete or brick piers, placed them on solid foundations and then they insulated walls and ceilings and covered their cottages with colored aluminum sidings, hiding the original construction. Brash new glass and plastic year-round homes shouldered in next to the weathered, uninsulated cabins built in the early years of the twentieth century.

One particularly charming relic sporting a stone turret is well over a century old. On a warm summer evening Gertrude discovered the fantasy castle resting on a rock outcrop toward the south of town. It faced west, dreaming of a hundred years of sunsets, and she also discovered that it belonged to distant relatives. Thereafter, she rarely let a summer go by without biking or driving that far south and then walking down the long winding lane to the shore and listening in her mind to voices from before the First World War, imagining long white summer dresses, feeling thick scratchy bathing costumes.

Her own cottage, a retreat bought not long before she retired from the Children's Aid, is also very old and had once belonged to those distant relatives. But it does not have a turret.

As the history mentions, a string of islands begins at Oliphant and marches north along the shore to Pike Bay. Like those islands, Lonely Island was once completely cut off from the mainland, but unlike them, it was easily accessible by rowboat or, when the water was low, by walking through the wetland. As the number of homes on Lonely grew, and the pressure of the automobile increased, gravel and rock were trucked in and a road was built – a causeway. Now several of the more modern homes on the island are occupied year around. The convenient isolation from the mainland, the ambiguity of its islandness, and the wonderful view to the west had attracted Gertrude some thirty-five years earlier, when she was searching for a place where grandchildren could attempt to catch frogs and water snakes and learn, often the hard way, to recognize poison ivy.

Gertrude's cottage embodied the range of building techniques represented in the town at large. The heart of the building had been fashioned of small cedar logs early in the century. With the advent of indoor plumbing in cottage country, a neat galley kitchen and a utilitarian bathroom were added. Eventually a dining room was patched on, south of the kitchen, and a second floor bedroom was superimposed. Above it all was a shiny green steel roof steep enough to encourage the winter snows to slide off.

When Emma's father, Mike, first visited his mother-in-law's cottage he was prevailed upon to add a screened porch to the dining room and living room side of the house. Gertrude provided the materials. Mike provided the labor. The porch became the major play area. In addition to a box of children's toys which sat in a corner all summer long, the porch was comfortably crowded with colorful lounge chairs and there, in the late afternoon sun, Gertrude usually took her book and teapot.

North of the screened porch the original front entrance had been enclosed, creating a sun porch. The house had been built facing the water and the sunset; consequently the enclosed sun porch had the best view in the house. It was Gertrude's room. A small desk for her computer and a large easy chair for reading, or comforting small people, squeezed in beside the huge bed. The bed had to be large for Gertrude rarely slept alone.

Traffic arrived at the rear of the house; a rustic sign suspended from a dying cedar pointed to the narrow lane leading in from the road which circled the island, one lot back from the shore. Hidden in the trees were several sheds, a tree house, and swings. Nearest the house was the bunky: overflow sleeping accommodation. Between the house and the road the incoming guest encountered, first, a high row of cedars, and then two large perennial beds, one of which, intended as a vegetable garden, had been fenced. As it turned out, it was the chipmunks who ate most of the strawberries and no fence deterred them. Meanwhile young bunnies, teasing the Sinisters – there had been a series of Dober-dogs, all named Sinister – were small enough to hop through the holes in the Frost Fence. The fence remained but served no purpose beyond supporting sweet peas and scarlet runner beans. Gertrude had long since given up on planting lettuce in favor of arugula and nasturtium which were either too spicy or too flavor-of-the-month for simpler rab-bit tastes. Chard, sorrel, rhubarb and a wealth of herbs remained in the enclosed garden. A parking area, roughly gravelled, and overgrown with golden birdsfoot trefoil and purple thyme, lay between the gar-dens and the house. Incoming visitors opened their car doors to the cool cedar smell of cottage country and their feet stirred up a warmly comforting smell of thyme as they crossed the drive. Everyone came in through the kitchen.

Given the startling discovery to be made by the first arrivals at the cottage that sunny Friday afternoon, it was fortunate that four women arrived together. In other years Edwina, who had a summer residence not far away, or Maude, who lived in Arthur, had arrived ahead of the others. Gertrude would go to the garden and gather bergamot, sweet cicely, and lemon balm to steep in her huge blue teapot. Then the two women would consume hot biscuits and sip tea while considering what the weekend would be like this time. While they waited for the rest to arrive, they would put on the soup and get out the fresh rolls and tear up greens for salad. Friday night's dinner varied little. A hearty soup would simmer on the stove, ready, no matter how long it took people to get away from their jobs or spouses and drive northwest into the spring sunset. Salad came from the garden. The women brought bread or rolls.

On this occasion, however, none of the women had arrived early. Margaret, Melody, Anna and Sarah arrived together at about 5. The four women began by unloading the van and carrying bedding and food to the back door; then two stood outside and handed bundles to the two inside who piled everything in the middle of the kitchen floor. The air was cooling at that time of day and they were mindful of Gertrude's admonitions to keep the warmth in and the cold out. Hence the strategy which got everything inside quickly and the door shut against the evening air and bugs.

Looking for Gertrude did not occur to them. She and the dog might be walking – slowly, for neither of them moved swiftly anymore. They made a dignified progress two or three times a day to the beach or along the road circling the island. Her old friends could be counted on to settle themselves. So, it was not until Anna had placed her cooler and bedding by the back door, inspected the garden, and sat a while on the bench behind the house, enjoying a cigarette, that she reluctantly went into the living room to put her blankets and pillow at the foot of the futon, which was her usual bed. It was as she turned from completing this final task that she discovered Gertrude.

At first, glancing across the shadowy room to where a huge rose colored couch partially blocked the view of the lake, she thought Gertrude was sleeping. It did not occur to her immediately that it would have to be a very sound sleep indeed which kept Gertrude from hearing their arrival, their many slammings of the door and flushings of the toilet and their good natured shouts issuing instructions for the storage of food and wine – there was always more food than there was space in the refrigerator and they always had to take the wine back outdoors for storage in the cool May air. When, as she moved to waken Gertrude, Anna tripped over the dog, lying between the coffee table and the couch, she had her first intimation of something troubling, something wrong. The coldness of Gertrude's hand was confirmation. She shook the arm gently. It did not respond.

Anna was a tall, strong woman with a beautiful face. She had grown up on a farm. As the oldest child with several siblings she had come to responsibility early and as an adult she had been principal for many years of an inner-city elementary school. She was not easily rattled. Thus, she did not scream, but the voice with which she summoned the others, the voice which had summoned thousands of boisterous students from recess, now brought her three companions crowding nervously into the living room. Anna pointed. They all stood and looked at Gertrude.

Into the silence, as each of the four was contemplating her own mortality, sang a cheerful yoohooing from the yard, announcing the arrival of more cars. The four women stood for a moment looking at Gertrude and then, without thinking or seeing much, found themselves back in the kitchen, calling out to the new arrivals to come in because there was something wrong. Then someone suggested they call the police and someone suggested they call the ambulance and someone remembered 911 and someone said it might not work up in cottage country and someone wondered whether they should call Gertrude's children and Melody found the phone book on the shelf under the bishop's bench and she notified the outside world.

While they waited for the officials to arrive, they dealt with death and surprise as well as they could. The hopeful ones wondered whether perhaps they had made a mistake and Gertrude was, for some reason, unconscious. Anna, who could still feel the touch of Gertrude's cool skin on her own, dealt firmly with that idea. Jean suggested that perhaps Gertrude had been murdered. There was a general shivering as everyone considered that if that were true the murderer might still be nearby, upstairs in the house even. But Gertrude's face was quite peaceful and no one was willing to get any closer to see whether there might be wounds or bruises. In fact they retired to the dining room to be in no danger of glimpsing the body which no one had thought to cover. Natasha and Melody wept quietly but freely. Others sniffed and blew their noses. Jean felt unwell and she and Margaret sat down rather quickly. Maude put water on to boil, and forgot what she had done until the kitchen filled with steam. Then she started over again and made tea.

As the surprise wore off they exclaimed and hugged each other and compared their own emotional and physical symptoms. Sarah was feeling rather nauseous; Jean was faint. Natasha said she felt as if she had been hit by a truck. They dwelt for some moments on the horrors of dying alone and the blessing of dying quickly and peacefully, as Gertrude appeared to have done. In their concern for Gertrude and, it must be said, for themselves, they completely ignored the dead dog. He had become invisible.

Natasha and Anna considered how to find Gertrude's children and came up with a chain of acquaintance who could find an appropriate phone number. The group had talked for years about the wisdom of creating a list of family phone numbers for each of them. The list might be useful for those planning special birthday or anniversary parties; and the list would certainly have been useful in this sort of emergency. Eventually they reached Gertrude's youngest child, Geoff, and left him to notify his brother and sister.

That done, the women gathered around the dining room table with coffee and tea and a huge tin of ginger snaps and chocolate chip cookies, which Maude had just brought in from her car, and they sat down to wait. As they waited they talked about Gertrude's memorial service.

At the group's first meeting, in Anna's living room many years earlier, someone, perhaps it had been Gertrude, had said that she needed a group who would care for her in old age and be there to bury her. In discussions held at various times over the following years Gertrude had been very clear about how her death was to be treated: the stipulation that 'Joy to the World,' not the religious one, but the exuberant one sung by Three Dog Night, be played at her final party was a clear indicator of the way in which she viewed death. The group had volunteered to sing another of her favourites, 'The Rose.' After considerable practice and due consideration, they all liked 'The Rose' well enough to agree that whoever was still alive might sing it upon the demise of most of them. They had laughed about not being the one who would have to sing a solo when all but one had gone – also about when it would be appropriate to record 'their song' so that it could be played for the last person. Someone, it might have been Gertrude, called it a musical tontine.

For thirty years they had met. They felt they had beaten some kind of odds. Gertrude was the oldest of them, the first to have grandchildren, the first to retire and now the first to require 'The Rose.' There was another song but none of them knew what it was. They would need to see whether her children knew. There was to be a party, not a funeral and Melody recalled that Gertrude's body was to be cremated. That much they were sure about.

So their discussion ranged over where and when the party might be, and more immediately over when they would rehearse. When they had been 30 years younger and death a remote possibility they had chosen their song and practised singing it in harmony. The words had been copied out for each of them and each was desperately trying to recall where the scrap of paper might have been put for safekeeping.

The vehicles bearing authorities presented themselves at the same time as Edwina, the last of the group to arrive. She was startled to be passed, just before she turned into the drive, by a marked car, complete with flashers on the top. She was further bemused when the officer showed no interest in her driving. In fact, he left his car with the engine running and the flashers going and moved quickly to the cottage door. Puzzled, Edwina swung around in her seat, used the remote to slide the van door open, shifted her wheelchair from its space behind her, positioned it, and swung into it with an ease which spoke of long practice. She was just rolling across the patio and calling out for someone to give her a hand into the kitchen when the coroner arrived, followed immediately by an ambulance and more police.

The constable who had so startled Edwina, had come out from Wiarton, the Sauble Beach office being but fitfully staffed until July. He had radioed for the coroner when he understood that there was a dead body. The new arrivals occasioned a good deal of confusion, renewed tears and anxiety on the part of the women, and routine questions and answers on the part of the officials. The newcomers had also to be offered tea, coffee, and cookies and informed of Gertrude's present physical location.

The constable, arriving first, had turned on the living room lights and begun a visual check of the space. The coroner remained for a moment with the women. The discovery had clearly occasioned quite a fluttering among Gertrude's friends, themselves no longer young, and the doctor, who had been a coroner long enough to be rather jaded about dead bodies, especially if they were not the result of violent deaths on the highways, looked at eight women, each old enough to be his mother, perhaps his grandmother, it was hard to tell, and feared that he might have to deal with several more deaths. He looked closely at each woman and assured himself that hysteria and heart attacks were not immediate threats before proceeding to deal with the real object of his visit.

The elderly women distracted his attention more than was wise from the situation of the body and his subsequent examination of it. It may also be said that he was unaware that the OPP constable had arrived only seconds ahead of him. Each of them presumed that the other would take note of the dog.

Leaving the coroner to deal with the body, the constable proceeded to deal with the witnesses. The policeman, a very young constable, who removed his hat respectfully and, despite the hour, was still very clean-shaven, asked how long the women were intending to be there. When faced with their confused faces and eight answers, he tore pages from his notebook and asked each of them to write out her name and home address. He seemed pleased that they had already notified Gertrude's family, though he did not call her Gertrude. He took down the deceased's name and her son's name and phone number. He asked who had found the body. His intention then was to interview the witnesses privately.

A quick look showed him a dining room where several elderly women sat around a long glass table, comforting one another, a living room where the doctor and attendants were maneuvering in a fairly small space, and a kitchen with only a small bench near the door as seating. He thought briefly about using the bedrooms which he presumed were upstairs. A another glance around indicated a wheelchair and two or three canes. He sighed, and invited Anna out to his car where he asked her to describe exactly what had happened when she'd arrived that afternoon. He wrote most of this down longhand; so it was a rather slow process.

The constable asked the same questions of most of the women, though the sergeant who arrived after the process was well under way, interviewed two or three of the women, just in case. This was after the sergeant had finished talking to the coroner and the coroner had finished saying that, given the angina and asthma medication in the bathroom and the age of the deceased, it looked like a natural death to him and had signed the papers releasing the body, and the ambulance attendants had switched from resuscitation mode to removal mode; the sergeant had also fetched his camera from the car and taken some pictures. He'd had one or two tricky situations in his career and liked to be prepared.

The doctor and the body and the police eventually rolled away. None of the women remembered when the ambulance had arrived for Gertrude's body but the attendants had left the door open for quite a long time as they went about their business. Thus the cottage had grown rather chilly and a few bugs fluttered around the lights when the last of the officials rolled out of the drive.

The eight women were left with the remains of their Anniversary Celebration. Their first thought was to pack up and go home. Jean had overheard the doctor tell the sergeant that, given the warmth of the afternoon, Gertrude could not have been cooling for more than a couple of hours. The medical confirmation of how recently Gertrude had been alive was somehow more disturbing than Natasha's personal anecdote about phoning Gertrude some time around noon, from the airport, to ask whether she should bring red or white wine. They shivered a little when Margaret remarked that the murderer might have been in the cottage at that time.

It was after nine o'clock when they reached this part of their deliberations and most of them had two or more hours to drive home in the dark. In these circumstances reaching a decision was remarkably easy; it took only an hour more of fervent discussion during which their reluctance to stay in someone else's home, especially one where a dead body, no matter whose, had so recently reposed, was rapidly overcome by their familiarity with the place and their extreme weariness.

At some point during the interviews with the police Sarah had warmed the soup, which she found ready in the refrigerator and they had eaten supper while they debated. Fires had been lit and the warmth of Stilton-potato soup filled the cottage. When they'd eaten, Margaret cleared up; she joined in the discussion from the kitchen while she dealt with the soup bowls and cutlery and as she moved about gathering and disposing of the cups and glasses which had been liberally scattered in most of the ground floor rooms. She hated cooking, or cooking under pressure anyway, so for each 'women's weekend' she packed her apron, rubber gloves, and dish detergent and arrived prepared to wash up for the entire weekend. The comfort which the women found in performing their usual tasks, and sitting around the usual table no doubt sped their decision making.

Their last request of the departing constable had been that he place More Sinister in a green garbage bag and carry his body to the back shed. Neither he nor the doctor had previously shown any interest in the creature. They had in fact shown every sign of leaving the dog's considerable bulk lying, in perpetuity, on the living room floor, in the corner to which the ambulance attendants had moved it when the coroner had difficulty examining Gertrude's body with More Sinister in place beside his dead mistress. The women on the other hand, once Gertrude's body had been removed, took notice at last of the dog. It was a notice that did not consider causes, merely results. They found More's dead body almost as unnerving as the body of their friend and discussed where they would bury him and how they would manage it.

There was no question in their minds that this was a task which required doing as early as possible the next day and with as much dignity as was consistent with eight old ladies getting a hundred pound body into a hole in the ground. Because of the bond between Gertrude and her dog they felt that some ceremony would be required. If they could recall enough of the words to their song they would sing that: it was as appropriate for the dog as for Gertrude; so was a song by Three Dog Night for that matter. Thus it was decided that Maude, who also had a dog, would say something and that Natasha would write something for Maude to say. They decided that, in order not to disturb the flower beds overmuch, but to protect the body from some of the wild animals, they would bury More Sinister inside the fenced garden but under the path at the farthest corner, next to the rhubarb. Rhubarb likes lots of fertilizer. All their decisions made, they settled themselves for the night.

*

Geoff had taken the phone call informing him of his mother's death at the end of a long day. He'd had to fire a young toolmaker and, since it was month end, he'd also had numerous calls from the accountant, who worked at home but was connected, both by computer and by speaker-phone, to the shop. Geoff's was a small, specialized business doing custom dies and he was foreman, supervisor and boss as well as chief designer. He had just parked his van in the driveway and was coming through the front door of his home; he raised his shoulders to release the tension in his neck and looked forward to a beer and a quiet dinner with his wife. The phone rang. He picked it up and a voice he did not recognize said, "Geoff, it's Melody, one of your Mom's group. I hate to be the one to give you this information," the voice paused as if waiting for him to ask something. Then it continued, "but when we arrived at the cottage this afternoon we found your mother. She must have died while she was having her afternoon nap."

Geoff was silent for several seconds while he considered that this might be some macabre joke. His mother had been fine the night before when they'd spoken about her plans for the weekend. How could she be dead less than a day later? "I'll be right up." He said when his mind began functioning again. "It'll take me a few minutes to get my things together and talk to Sue, get a bite to eat and then three hours to get there so I'll be there around... mmm.. 9.30 or 10."

Melody had repeated "No, no," a couple of times during this mono-logue but now she broke in. "No, Geoff. I don't think it's necessary for you to come tonight. The police will be here any moment and they'll want to talk to us and then I imagine they'll remove your mother to the hospital or a funeral home. You really may not be needed tonight and you do need to find out what happens next."

13

Geoff sighed in a way that suggested that what happened next might be a mystery taking some effort to unravel, that doing month end accounts or making a long drive through the evening of a stressful day might be preferable.

Melody continued. "Do you know where your mother's instructions are? Or who her lawyer is? Will she want the memorial here or there? I'm sure she wanted cremation and that might be done just as easily here. I'll give the police your number and if they want to talk to you they'll call. Otherwise, why not get some planning done and call me or come up in the morning." She was aware that she had taken over but she was also aware that Geoff, at least for the moment was happy to have someone else thinking for him.

"Thanks, yes, thanks. I'll drive up in the morning. I'll call before I leave here." He hung up and sat looking at the phone until Sue came into the living room.

"I thought I heard you come in. Was that the phone?"

"It was some woman in Mom's group. They found her dead when they arrived this afternoon."

"What do you mean 'they found her dead'? How did she die? What are they doing about it? I'll call them back and find out what's going on."

"She's dead Sue. What difference does it make how it happened? She's dead and there is nothing we can do about it. Those women don't need us. They're fine. They've got it all under control."

He held Sue for a long time, wishing that he had it all under control. Then he called his brother and sister.

Eric was sautéing garlic and onions for curry and Rowena had just changed out of her work clothes and was washing up that morning's breakfast dishes, when their phone rang. They were standing in the kitchen; so she heard him sighing a few times in various tones and then heard him sigh again before saying, "I have a set of keys. We can take a look at the apartment in the morning before we go. I'll be ready at about eight. Do you want breakfast here?"

"Where are you going?" Rowena asked when he'd hung up.

"Mom's dead. She died up at the cottage. All her women's group is there." His tone implied that each statement dealt him an additional blow. Bad enough she should die on a weekend but to have to go to the cottage and to deal with her friends was too much. After turning down the burner, he picked up a beer and went into the living room to think. He wanted to cry. He might later.

Marilla was at work. After work she'd met Mike and they'd gone out to dinner and a movie to unwind for the weekend. It wasn't until they got home that they found the message to call Geoff whenever they got in. Actually there were several messages. She called her brother; she lived on the west coast; so he'd been asleep for some time when the phone rang and he took several seconds to realize what was making that terrible noise in his ear. Sue rolling over onto her stomach reached across his body and grabbed the phone thinking as she went that, like the remote, the phone was always on the man's side and that it really wasn't much of an exchange for the wet spot which was always on the woman's side. She asked where Mar and Mike had been all evening and the two women traded information about their children as Sue punched Geoff awake. Then brusquely she said, "Geoff's got something to tell you," and handed the phone to her husband. Geoff was growing accustomed to the news now and told his sister quickly and clearly what he had heard and what would be happening the next day so far as he knew. He hung up and was asleep again in moments. Sue was not.

Marilla pushed the button on the phone down and grabbed the phone book. As Mike was sputtering and asking questions she found the number for Air Canada and dialed, thinking that perhaps at this time of night she might not have to wait, listening to Musak, for half an hour before speaking to a real person. She reserved seats on the first plane out in the morning and ran to the garage entrance. Mike thought for one startled moment that she was leaving immediately but she returned with his suitcase and her own and, carrying them both, ran down the hall to their bedroom. She flung his case toward his side of their bed and began tossing her underwear and socks and T-shirts from drawers onto the bed, folding them neatly and tucking them in rows along the side of the suitcase. She did this for two or three minutes before the tears that were running down her face required attention. Then she stopped her frantic activity long enough to blow her nose and explain her brother's phone call to Mike. They clung together sobbing. After a while they resumed packing.

"Aren't you going to call Dan and Emma?" Mike asked, carefully rolling his good belt and searching the corner of his suitcase for one of his good black shoes into which it would fit perfectly. Mar looked startled. She'd forgotten completely about her children, about their possible interest in their grandmother's death, forgotten anything but her own grief and her necessity to be where her mother was. She was the oldest child, and the only daughter.

"It's four a.m. in Kentucky. I'll call Emma in the morning just before we leave. We don't have a number for Dan this week, do we? Maybe we can leave a message on his e.mail but who knows when he'll be near enough to civilization to pick it up." They took a few more minutes to put the house in order, throwing out milk and lettuce which would go bad while they were away, placing garbage in the garage, writing a note for the neighbor asking her to feed the cats; then they set the alarm to allow themselves a couple of hour's sleep.

"I'll look like such a raccoon in the morning," Mar sighed, dabbing her eyes and blowing her nose on sodden tissue as they put out the lights and got into bed.

In Oliphant it was late when the women settled into the beds which they habitually chose, leaving Gertrude's little sun porch bedroom closed. Maude and Margaret retreated to the bunky, a one room cottage with its own toilet and sink and windows on three of its four sides. Sleeping in it was almost sleeping in a tent, but the large bed was more comfortable. The two women had shared this sleeping accommodation on retreats, for most of the 30 years; they sometimes slept there when they visited at other times too; it felt quite familiar. Melody and Sarah and Jean scrubbed their faces and teeth and took their nightgown clad bodies up the stairs. There had been a time when Melody and Sarah had brought a tent each year and slept out on the thyme beside the budding flowers in the backyard or, when the water was low enough, they'd pitched the tent on the flat stones by the beach. However, age had decreased their enjoyment of the setting up and taking down of tents at the same time that it increased their difficulty getting themselves up and down from sleeping bags on air mattresses. It was easier to climb the stairs which had a sturdy pine banister.

The upper floor of Gertrude's cottage consisted of one large room with windows only at the front, looking out over Lake Huron. It was the room usually favoured by parents with children when there were family weekends. The kids could be put to bed up stairs and then later their parents would creep up quietly in the dark, tripping over plastic lizards and little metal cars. The sole disadvantage for parents was the bright light that flooded the room in the morning despite the west facing exposure but the elderly women loved the view, especially if there were a thunder storm in the west, over the lake. Gertrude had covered all the walls with paintings of the flowers in her garden. One wall was May, one June, another July and the last was aflame with fall flowers. The painting was worn in places, where cots, or playpens had rubbed the walls; so she had often threatened to paint over the decorations, done many years before. Her guests and family had been shocked at the idea and the flowers remained.

Edwina said goodnight, wheeled out to her car, and drove up the road to her own cottage. Natasha unrolled her sleeping bag on the bed in the little room off the living room. She said she was nervous about sleeping so close to the room where Gertrude had died. She had considered sleeping in her rented car, but that would be uncomfortable. She was unwilling to leave the others, either to go home with Edwina or to drive to Sauble beach and look for a motel. She also reminded them that she had flown in that afternoon from Vancouver and she was not only very tired but also jet-lagged. Melody and Sarah offered to help her drag another mattress up the stairs where she could join them, but in time Natasha's exhaustion had increased and her reluctance had failed until at last she made up her bed, closed her door and was miraculously almost at once asleep.

Anna pulled out the living room futon and made it up. She missed Gertrude, missed her especially at this hour when they were accustomed to being the last to go to bed, talking late into the night about their most recent discoveries. Anna slid out onto the back patio and smoked three cigarettes in a row, the first she'd had since the one she had smoked before she'd gone in and found Gertrude almost seven hours earlier.

*

The next morning Maude woke about 6 and slipped out, trying not to wake Margaret. Maude was a tall, spacious, charming woman who had spent her life teaching kindergarten. She said that she'd never grown up, and certainly her eye retained the innocence of a child's. She took photographs that captured shape and color in their most elemental forms. She still lived on a few acres not far from Arthur, though she'd been intending for years to move closer to town. Now she hooked her camera around her neck and took her black Lab for a walk along the causeway and down to the beach where he was soon far from shore, chasing seagulls, startling the carp from their mating rituals.

The beach curved along the south side of the causeway between the Oliphant shore and the island. It was protected and shallow, perfect for small children who could walk a long way out before the water reached their bathing suits, well, could if they didn't sit or fall or push each other. For adolescents and adults the long walk out to water deep enough for swimming was less inviting; so families with teenagers usually tavelled the ten minutes to North Sauble for swimming. At this hour of the morning the beach was deserted. In May it might be deserted all day, except when the spawning carp churned in the shallows. Even in July people did not arrive until the sun was well up. The birds and fish, the occasional fox and water snake had the expanse of grey-blue water and its adjoining fen all to themselves.

Eventually, her feet icy from trying to capture the patterns of fish and reeds, Maude, straightened slowly, put the lens cap back on, settled the Canon around her neck, rinsed her feet, struggled into her damp socks and shoes, and whistled Foggy Dog in. He came ashore and shook that luxurious full-body shake which starts at the head, snaps the lips and ears and travels the length of the animal, ending with the haunches and a final rattle of the penis and tail. His owner sighed

18

and went west along the causeway, back to the cottage to make breakfast: scones and fruit salad.

Margaret heard Maude and her dog leaving the bunky. She snoozed
for a bit, enjoying the sound of birds. Then she read for a while. For
many years her mornings had been a rush to get herself ready for work
and her son off to school. Neither of them were morning people. When
she retired she promised herself that never again would she rush in the
morning. So she stretched her long slim body across the whole bed and
read for perhaps half an hour before enjoying the luxury of a bathroom
of her own. They had not been able to persuade her to come to the first
weekend in Oliphant until they promised her she could have her own
bathroom in the bunky. Later she had invited Maude to share the space
with her, but Maude was always up and out so quickly that Margaret
said it was like having the place to herself. She did not join the others
until there were already several women in the dining room devouring
scones.

Jean, small and, even when swathed in a plaid dressing gown, porce-
lain delicate, tip-toed down the stairs and used the bathroom. She slid
past the living room without glancing at the couch on the far side and
went out to the garden. This early in the year it was hard to imagine
the riot of color and greenery that took over in July and August. Inside
the fence only the grape hyacinth and narcissus flowered in the early
light. The lilac was in bud and in the shade of the cedars the daffodils
were nodding gently. The lovage was already waist high and the rhubarb in the back corner was lush and ready to pull but just the tips of
asparagus poked up along the fence, while the bergamot and yarrow
grew only to her knees. In the centre of the enclosed garden was an
Inukshuk which the group had built on their fifth anniversary and next
to it was a log wall, perfect for resting when she was weeding in the
long summer afternoons, Gertrude said. There Jean sat like patience
on a monument and watched the hummingbirds at the feeder until she
heard Maude's dog snuffling through the brush. Then she realized that
her bare feet were icy cold, and shuddering a bit she went back into
the cottage.

Sarah and Melody had come down stairs just as Maude was putting
the finishing pats to the scones. The kitchen was warm with heat from

the oven and steam from the water which was boiling for coffee. As she flipped the oven door closed Maude grasped the large pot and poured the contents quickly over the filter containing freshly ground coffee beans. Gertrude had resisted all offers of coffee makers, saying they did not make good enough coffee, and had resisted also all offers to buy her a kettle. The truth was that she felt both appliances, being things with only one function, took up too much space. As the smell of fresh coffee filled the kitchen Melody realized that what had wakened her was the noise of Maude grinding the dark beans which Gertrude favoured. Maude had been converted to Gertrude's method of making coffee not long after the group had started. Maude was the group's most creative cook but Gertrude had made good coffee.

Melody was the tiniest of the women but athletic still. Her quick mind and grasp of detail had made her a formidable Justice of the Peace and now made her an avid herb gardener; the weeds in her garden were not granted bail. Sarah, vivid and voluptuous, had begun as a legal secretary and in retirement she still revelled in cleaning out attics and basements to prepare estates for auction. Melody and Sarah had shared far more than an interest in things legal. Indeed, that was the least of their shared interests. The two of them, with their partners and sometimes with their children, or grandchildren, had travelled together, biked and hiked together, taken up Oriental medicine together and shopped for clothes together. Sarah could be counted on to wear underwear which matched her socks. Melody could be counted on to wear lace. No matter what the occasion, they could be counted on to be perfectly dressed. This morning Melody was still in a long white embroidered nightgown. Sarah wore brightly colored pyjamas with matching socks. As well as taking turns in the bathroom the two of them pulled the long glass table out from the wall and set it with cutlery and plates.

The dining room was yellow. Not a pale pastel yellow but an eye-searing color which gave the impression that the sun was rising inside the room, not out beyond the driveway. It had been a brilliant stroke, painting it that shade the first summer she'd owned the cottage, Gertrude remarked, if a new-comer commented on the color; she'd raise her left eye brow slightly so that the hearer was uncertain whether she was being ironic or merely enjoying an oft uttered pun. People loved sitting there, despite chairs which were none too comfortable, despite the narrowness of the room which meant that people could not move around easily once they were at the table, despite the fact that the windows were small and looked out on the driveway. There were many coats of yellow throbbing on the walls now, Sarah supposed. She and Melody each sat for a while talking to Maude who had proceeded to peeling and cutting the fruit for breakfast.

Natasha slept late. When she finally appeared she said that the death of a close friend coming after a long day – hideous traffic and lack of a simple way to get to Vancouver's airport, an in-flight movie about gang warfare, and then two hours in Toronto's rush hour – probably put her over the top on any stress scale. Her horoscope for the day had not been propitious. Natasha was an astrologer, had made a good living at it for several years, giving personal consultations and selling astrological crafts: anything with a sun, moon and stars on it would sell, she said, and some of it for very high prices. When her second husband died and her three daughters were well launched she had begun writing books. The books had taken her on long tours, though the rest of the group said she wrote the books so that she could take the long tours and write them off as expenses. They were jealous of her hotels and banquets and TV appearances, and they missed her when she missed group meetings. Natasha had, in the course of her travels, fallen in love with the west coast and to the horror of her women friends had moved herself to B.C. the year before.

She woke in total darkness in a room with no windows, disoriented and feeling hung over. It took a few moments of lying, steadying her heartbeat and breathing deeply before she got up and hurried through the living room to the bathroom, taking her clothes and makeup with her. She was aware that she did not want to make many trips through the room where Gertrude had died. It had a bad feeling about it. She noticed that Anna had already tidied up her sleeping bag and put the futon back in place.

Anna, opening her eyes much earlier in the morning, had realized she was facing the couch on the opposite side of the room which had lately been her friend's last bed. Nonetheless, she lay there a while, luxuriously stretching across the huge futon and smelling the coffee from the kitchen where Maude was making breakfast. There shouldn't be coffee; Gertrude makes the coffee, Anna thought. Then she smiled and stretched and began to hum, not the song they had rehearsed the night before but a song she had written for Gertrude's 60th birthday. Maybe they could squeeze that into the service too - and then she realized that she had no idea when the service would be and that they'd need to speak to Gertrude's children soon. So she got up and cleared her bedding away and wondered what those children were doing and thinking this morning.

CHAPTER II

SATURDAY, MAY 30

"On MAY 29, 1998 THE BODY of Gertrude Moseley was discovered at her summer residence in Oliphant." That was roughly what Emma recalled seeing in the clipping which her mother sent her when it was all over.

At the time, at least on the morning after her grandmother's death, she was delivering a young mare of a particularly reluctant baby and the phone rang for a long time before anyone paid any attention. It was early Saturday morning, the stable had been mucked out and along the tracks, beside the white fences, strings of horses were frisking towards their morning exercise. Emma had been wakened early, just as the first grey of dawn was streaking the sky, by a stable hand who thought she should know that her mare was down and struggling. It wasn't her mare, really. It was the mare of a consortium which bought up good mares and bred them to renowned stallions, but all horses brought to the clinic became hers as far as the hands were concerned. As far as she was concerned too, she thought, if she had ever had time or inclination to reflect on it.

Emma could hardly make out the voice or the words when, after wiping her hands and giving a reassuring pat to the mare whose foal was now nursing contentedly, she closed the box gate and loped down the long aisle to answer the phone. "It's Mom," the sobbing voice repeated over and over until Emma worked out that the person on the line was her mother and that her mother was talking about *her* mother. Now you are as confused as Emma was at the time.

"She's dead."

There was a long silence suddenly on both ends of the communication and Emma understood.

"Where?"

"The cottage."

"I'll try to be there tonight. Might be tomorrow by the time I can get a flight and arrange a ride."

"Try to get away by noon today. If you can get to Toronto airport by 3.30 this afternoon we could drive up together. Our flight arrives in Toronto at 3.15. We're just about ready to leave for the airport." Her mother's voice had become steady now. Dealing with practicalities had always been Marilla's strong suit. No doubt, thought Emma, correctly picturing the scene the previous evening, her mother had already had her clothes for the funeral and her cottage clothes, and her casual clothes neatly folded into one under-the-seat bag, even as she was making the phone calls for tickets and coercing Mike into moving more quickly to get his own slower brand of packing finished. It was talking to Emma that had shattered her morning composure, taken her past her initial shock and opened the door to memories of her Mom and a deeper realization of the size of her loss.

"I'll see what I can do. How will I reach you?"

"Leave a message at the Pearson Information Desk when you know your flight and time of arrival. We'll check there. Got to go. Mike's honking will wake the neighbors." There was a click and Marilla was gone, leaving Emma to check the mare again, organize the morning's work, call her assistant, and find the earliest and least complicated flight from Blue Grass Field to Toronto. It left in just over an hour and if she missed it there wasn't another until the same time the next day. Emma scarcely had time to think about her grandmother until she was eating lunch on the plane.

It seemed like a long time ago, it had been a long time ago that Gertrude had persuaded Emma's parents to let her spend two weeks of her summer alone with her grandmother. Emma had lived in Ottawa then. Gertrude had driven to Marilla's and Mike's, picked up Emma and her horse books and her collection of toy horses and her clothes too, of course, and they had driven to Oliphant.

Gertrude and Emma had sung all the way. 'Down by the Station' with all the silly rhymes they could think of. They'd been methodical and followed the alphabet from 'Did you ever see ants wearing purple pants' through to 'Did you ever see a zebra kick a cobra.' They'd also discovered that a conscientious singing of 'One hundred bottles of beer on the wall' took at least half an hour. They had sung it several times.

When they arrived, tired and hoarse, Emma had been assigned the upstairs bedroom. She'd displayed her toy horses on the shelves and gathered wild flowers for decoration. Later in the week she and her grandmother had painted the walls of the room a soft sage green and then Gertrude had begun to paint the flowers which Emma had picked, paint them hugely and directly across the surface of one wall.

Every morning after breakfast they let Sinister jump into the back seat and then the two of them drove to Owen Sound and Emma had riding lessons.

The summer before that long ago idyll Emma had had her first riding lessons. She'd been seven and one of her friends had been going for a week to ride ponies. They went together. Emma said at the end of that week that she would never again ride a horse if it meant that her feet could touch the ground on both sides. The visit to Oliphant, the trips to Owen Sound, all of it was a plot of Gertrude's to see whether Emma really loved horses when she couldn't keep both feet on the ground. Gertrude wondered whether grooming and tacking up an animal so huge might cool the child's enthusiasm.

Emma had visited Gertrude each subsequent summer for several years. After that, except for the time when she was glued to school desks, she rarely kept her feet on the ground. Veterinary College was squeezed in between competitions in dressage and show jumping; hours of grooming and mucking and training paid for her lessons and her horses' keep. She'd had her own clinic in Kentucky for several years now, had lucked into it while she was doing graduate work in the University of Kentucky's animal science department, but she still rode every day and competed in local competitions. She loved flat racing but had known since she was ten that she would be too tall and too heavy. At 5'9" she was a lithely muscular blonde, a striking woman but way too tall to be a jockey. Gertrude's summer lessons had been responsible not for the direction but for some of the possibilities in her life.

As Emma dozed uncomfortably in her plane seat she recalled her grandmother with fondness and some irritation. The old lady had been domineering all right. That first summer Emma had wanted to knit blankets for her toy horses. The blankets she needed would be about two inches square. Gertrude had taught her to knit on the first day and then insisted that in return for the knitting lessons, Emma would also knit a sweater, a human sized sweater. She did too, she recalled; but it was a grim smile that passed over her face.

When Emma's parents had moved to Vancouver, Gertrude had become a surrogate parent while Emma studied Veterinary medicine in Guelph. Her grandmother had been incredibly generous, but had expected a lot in return. Clean room, high marks, attention to the arts as well as to horses. Emma had been dragged to the Shaw Festival and to Blyth when she would much rather have been riding. Later she had been hauled off to England and taken to the major steeplechases, had actually enjoyed several months of apprenticeship with a trainer at Newmarket. Her grandmother, knowing that Emma wanted to race, had insisted that she consider being a jump jockey. While she was there Gertrude had also insisted that the young woman inhale what Emma thought of, in a sweeping dismissal, as culture. Cathedrals, galleries, libraries. Gertrude was a force.

Geoff arrived at Gertrude's apartment building first. It was a small building on Wellington Street, not far from the town centre. Gertrude had taken it with an eye to walking to the stores and taking buses when she 'got old.' Within easy walking distance were parks and trails along the lake for the Sinisters, as well as easy access to commuter trains to Toronto. She disliked the huge suburban parking lots surrounded by box stores; she preferred local shops, local craftspeople and merchants even if they cost a bit more. But she had still driven her car, drove to the cottage. Now she would not 'get old.'

Eric arrived just as Geoff was going back to his car, looking for his phone and intending to call his tardy brother. Together they fiddled with the keys, checked the mail box and took the elevator. The two men did not look alike. Geoff's posture was more erect, which gave the impression that he was several inches taller than his brother. His brownish hair was cut close and still managed to curl tightly. There was, unfortunately, not much of it. Eric was rounder and darker with curls hanging almost to his shoulders.

Once inside the apartment Eric went directly to the kitchen and began opening cabinet doors. Geoff stared.

"Don't you remember? On one of these doors, ah, there it is." And in his hand Eric had a list which had been attached to the door nearest the refrigerator.

Locker #79 in the basement. The keys are with other spare keys: top left of black monster.

Outstanding bills usually on the desk under the phone.

I own the cottage and the car outright...no loans or mortgages.

They read on down the page as Gertrude outlined what she owned and where the papers for each item might be found and in what color file folder. There were files for bills and files for investments and files for insurance as well as a file for the dog's veterinary record. She detailed the numbers of her bank accounts and where the passbooks were, the drawer where keys to her safety deposit box and spare keys for her cottage and car were, and the people to contact about her car, her apartment, and her cottage. The names of her lawyer and her doctor, her financial planner, the various publishers of her books, and the dog's veterinarian were all there. She noted the location of her instructions on Power of Attorney and her Living Will, neither of which they'd be needing now. Below all the details of property and care were the phone numbers for each of them – startling to see their names there – and their children, and her one remaining brother. There were also instructions for the finding of her friends. The final line requested the reader to heed the instructions for her burial and her memory party which were printed on the reverse. Eric almost dropped the paper. Then he turned it over.

PARTY

*1. Have my body cremated and keep the ashes out of sight until you
get to the cottage a week or so later. The whole cremation thing is
already paid for and the number to call is on the attached card.*

*2. Rent a hall. Probably the following Friday or Saturday Evening 4
-7 or eight ... what used to be called the cocktail hour.
Allows folks to come after work and still go out in the evening. The
Yacht Club or a Golf Club or somewhere with a nice view if you can
find one available. If not, not. In town here.*

*3. Get a DJ or good dance music...music to which people can dance.
Don't play it too loudly but let dancing be possible. Old-fashioned.
Not gavottes but stuff where people actually have to move together.*

*4. $8,000 for music, hall, hors d'oeuvres, and wine. The sum is speci-
fied in my Will; so get the lawyer to shake it loose, or spend it and
get it back later from my estate. Bargain for the first two items so
there is lots left for the last ones to be good quality. The number for
the caterer is on a card inside the cover of the phone book.*

*5. In my desk you'll find a CD with the longest version of 'Jeremiah
was a Bullfrog' that I could find. Play it several times...whenever the
party slows down. At about 5.30 or 6, when you figure there are the
most folks there, my women's group will sing 'The Rose,' then you
can play the 'Bread and Roses' song from the CD and anyone who
wants to say something in under two minutes may. Whoever can be
the most vicious in enforcing this should be MC of the proceedings.
Melody, might be asked. She's a retired JP and has the experience
required to choke off the long-winded and do it politely. Then put on
'Jeremiah was a Bullfrog' again and get back to eating, drinking
and dancing.*

*6. Later that weekend whoever wants to make the trip can scatter my
ashes over Lake Huron if the weather is good enough, or in my garden if it's pissing down rain or freezing cold.*

*7. Announcement should read:
Gertrude Moseley, mother of Marilla Moseley and Geoff and Eric
McBain, at ...... on..... . There will be no visiting hours. A party
to remember her life will be held at .... on...from 4 - 8 pm on ....
Please come and celebrate.*

Although I know I'm dead and you may do as you please, try to resist the temptation to edit. I've tried several ways and this is the one I want.

*

Holding the paper they moved, without speaking, to the table in the living room where their mother had eaten and written and sewn and entertained. The table had once had a fake wood finish, some sort of veneer over particle board, Sears oriental hardwood, Gertrude called it. The entire surface was now painted. The central pedestal was a textured, bark-like brown with a green leaf or two, the top was a brilliant yellow on which one huge fuchsia-colored hibiscus blossom in the style of Georgia O'Keefe bloomed voluptuously. Gertrude's apartment was female, no other word for it. No man would have lived there. Not fussy in any way, but feminine. The kitchen was the same yellow as the cottage dining room and kitchen. She said she'd wanted to bring a bit of summer home for the long winters. All of the other walls were painted a soft pink, not a pink you'd notice, a pink that warmed the space. The trim and most of the furniture was a riot of color, blue, yellow, green, purple. Whenever she was depressed Gertrude had reached for a paintbrush and colored her world. The hardwood floor tiles were covered with Persian carpets. The only pale object was the muted corner of the couch which had once been covered with pastel flowers but now matched the pale grey of the comforter on Gertrude's bed and for the same reason: the dogs slept there. The cushions also sagged a bit at the front edge. The Sinisters, in addition to being comfort loving, had been oversized for their breed.

The two men made a list of people to contact and items to find. The black monster was, of course, no longer black. It was a huge bow fronted chest of drawers, the only furniture rescued from her marriage – well not rescued exactly; her husband had insisted that she remove the ugly, space-consuming bastard. It had, when Eric and Geoff were small boys, been black but had since undergone several color transmogrifications; however, they had no difficulty recognizing it, in her

30

dining area, beneath its parrot green disguise. Like Gertrude, they still thought of it as black.

They phoned the funeral arrangers listed on the "attached" card and the funeral arrangers said, "Wiarton. No Problem." They'd be pleased to track down the whereabouts of Mrs. Moseley's remains and get back to the gentlemen if there were any difficulties. Geoff phoned a Rotary Club friend, paged him on the golf course – the club house of which they wished to use, indeed – and were guaranteed, for the following Friday evening, a large room with a view across the ninth hole and Burlington to Lake Ontario. Their mother had never played golf, had loathed the idea of hitting and fetching a ball. Dog exercise she called it. But they thought the view would have pleased her. By the time they had reached the caterer and left messages for the lawyer and all of the financial people and found all of the papers which Gertrude had indicated, it was past noon. In the fridge they found enough food for a quick snack. Then Geoff phoned the cottage and asked whether the women could be prevailed upon to remain until the two of them arrived at 4 or 5 p.m.

*

Emma arrived at Pearson Airport first. She had just time to rent a car and to call her Aunt Rowena at work – thus learning that her uncles were already on the way to the cottage – before she hurried to the Arrivals gate and flung herself at her parents as they came through the doors. Despite their pleasure at seeing her, Mar and Mike wore the dazed look of travelers who hadn't found an in-flight movie and a dry sandwich a good substitute for their usual routine.

"Leaving a message at Information is too intimidating. Have you ever noticed that when you need Information most, you can't find it? One really needs Information to find Information. Anyway, I thought I'd talk to you in person instead. I got away amazingly quickly. I've rented a car. Geoff and Eric are at the cottage, still on the way I guess. Someone's saving supper for us there. Here's a luggage trolley." Emma waved the keys at them, realizing that she was babbling but also realizing that none of them wanted to speak about Gertrude just now, just here. "I'll drive. Then you two can snooze if you want." Emma helped them to the car and maneuvered skillfully through the maze of roads leading out of the airport into the countless lanes of chaos leading west along the 401 to Highway 410. There she turned north.

*

Reaching the Huron Shore from points along the Golden Horseshoe entails a drive through some of the lushest farm land in Ontario. Unlike the cottager heading up the superhighways to Muskoka, the person leaving Oakville or Burlington or Stoney Creek and going northwest has options. Southern Ontario's network of Concessions and Sideroads provides a multitude of cross-country choices for people willing to risk the occasional gravel road or single lane bridge. Like Emma, those coming from Toronto usually start up Highway 10. Those coming from further west usually opt for Highway 6 which runs north from Burlington to Owen Sound and then, after a jog, bisects the Bruce Peninsula heading for Tobermory. Highway 6, despite its accidents and bad press is for any number of reasons preferable to Highway 400, the road north to the rocks and lakes of Muskoka. But an even better option cuts away from Highway 6 and angles further westward.

While the trip to Muskoka always begins when the first rock outcrops shoulder toward the road; the trip to Southampton, Sauble Beach, Oliphant and points north begins, for those who live in Oakville and points west, after they pass Guelph. There is nothing wrong with Guelph that synchronizing the stop lights to the speed limit on the Hanlon Expressway wouldn't cure. The Royal City retains qualities of community and culture which are enviable and many of its citizens are wise enough to summer in Sauble and Oliphant; but for vacationers it is only north of Guelph that the journey becomes pure pleasure.

There is no question that the trip begins in spite of Guelph, that Guelph is in the way. There is a question as to how far north of the city the trip begins. South of Guelph there are patches of farm land but there is much that is strip mall and subdivision. Geoff and Eric argue as to whether the journey begins at Guelph or Elora, but Geoff waves his hand at the windows and insists that after turning left onto the Silvercreek Parkway at Eddie Shack Donuts they are immediately driving between the fields approaching Schuett's Corner, with its aptly named Paradise Farm and then into Ponsonby with horses and grain and cattle belly-deep in grass beside the little stream; all this agriculture is well south of Elora. Beyond the turn onto the Elora Road, at the Department of Highways depot, the road runs almost straight to the next turn, three quarters of an hour later, at Clifford. Granted there is a long left and right curve as Alma's main street stretches north, and a long right and left curve through the lights at Teviotdale but the road cannot be said to wind. Beyond Clifford, after a brief twisting through Neustadt, as if to get the hang of it, the road runs ruler straight north-west to Allenford. One tiny twitch mars the straightness between Hanover and Chesley and between Chesley and Allenford. At Chesley a mile long correction requires a left and right turn through Scone. Then, from the huge steer guarding the northern edge of Chesley, the cut in the trees can be seen, beckoning, straight for 30 kilometers, leading the driver to Tara's Yonge Street and then on to Allenford. In Ontario, perhaps all Yonge streets roam northward.

A straight road with a variable horizon provides a constant sense of achievement, of opportunity and closure. Like fiction it opens predictable vistas, shifts the perspective and finally, satisfies. A curving road plays games, hides and breaks promises; like non-fiction it is unpredictable. The deer may run across the road just as you round the turn or a tractor may be backing out of a drive. The lack of curves on the Elora Road and county road 10 makes for ease of driving, speed too, on occasion, but not for boredom. The road is straight, but not flat and the view is always changing. There is no time of year when the drive is not a feast for the eyes. Even in winter, when the drive can be downright exciting, the view is a pleasure.

The last 20 minutes of the trip provide the only twisting road. Between Allenford and the turn at Sauble Speedway a series of curves carries the traveller around Gould Lake, the first smooth expanse of water on the trip. Gould Lake feels like destination. Then turning left at the Speedway the road west heads straight into Lake Huron. As the car tops the last rise there – beyond the archway proclaiming that this is Sauble Beach – the immensity of La Mer Douce takes the breath away. Every time. North from Sauble the road curves more and more tightly as it approaches the shore and follows it north to Oliphant.

Through most of the year the best time for the trip is at sunrise or sunset when the slanting sun lights the trees and fields with clear color. In May when the first, absolute green, the green untouched by the drying days of June, presents field after field, each painted greener than the one before, the trip to the cottage is almost as wonderful as the arrival. The trees provide a range from chartreuse to the dark green of the cedars. Whole fields glow a dandelion yellow. Everywhere there are lilacs, clumps of lilac, and lilac hedges. In one overgrown spot an entire fragrant acre of lilac blooms. Then further north, in under the trees, trillium shine, thousands of trillia; on wetter land marsh marigolds compete with the dandelions for the yellow prize.

The range of creatures is enormous. Feed lots and veal calves and milkers: Jerseys and Limousins and Holsteins are advertised and the fields are busy with calves. There are sheep and goats, pigs and turkeys, rabbits and Muscovy ducks and even ostriches. Once there were bison but now a small statue in front of Bison Auto Sales is the only souvenir of the large beasts which used to pasture in the field at a bend in the road. Signs advertise Shelties and Goldens and Dobermans, guard dogs and field trials and boarding. The traveler loses track of the number of Veterinary clinics. When Emma drives north she tries to count them. She also notices the multitudes of horses. Registered Miniature Horses, ponies, work horses and riding horses, some with young colts, graze in the fields. But some of these horses are more than hobby horses; many of them provide a living for their owners. Signs proclaim that 'HORSE DRAWN VEHICLES USE THIS ROAD' and the occasional Mennonite buggy moves briskly along the shoulder. The paraphernalia of equestrian and hunter jumping, tastefully arranged, nudges the fences along the road more than once and the road passes at least one private sulky track in addition to curving around the barns and stands of the Raceway at Hanover. In May the occasional turtle crosses the road.

The equipment of farming fills several roadside fields with more or less new machinery: red Massey Ferguson, green John Deere, bright paint and dark rust, metal shapes inspired by space fantasies and dark dreams of torture and Rube Goldberg jokes. Then there are auction barns, feed stores and feed manufacturers, fertilizer manufacture and sales, embryo implant stations, experimental plots, and waste disposal.

Streams curl under and around the road, old streams mostly and gentle except when the ice competes with the water in early spring. There is of course the gorge which the Grand has cut at Elora, and there are dams over the Saugeen tributaries at Hanover and Scone where water spilling under the road speaks of power. At Harriston and Rothsay tributaries of the Maitland flow more gently and at Allenford and Tara the Sauble river is domesticated to amble past the houses. Ponds, once muddy depressions, filled with runoff and presided over by muddy cattle bloom here and there in landscaped elegance, decorated by willows and patios and garden furniture. In pond alley, south of Neustadt, four ponds in two kilometers improve on nature – well three of the four do; the fourth pond, mysteriously unfinished, has for several years confronted the equipment which shaped it and neither of them is winning.

For those who want to read, each town announces its heroes and special days. John Diefenbaker and David Winkler at Neustadt, Karl 'Speck' Winkler and Tommy Burns at Hanover, Nellie McClung Academy at Harriston, festivals at Elora and Chesley, a PowWow at Allenford, Fall Fairs at Tara and Hanover. And along the way there are the schools. The Bruce County School Board office at Chesley has the face of today but the softer face of yesterday's brick school houses also lines the road. In most places the old school houses are residences now, and the driver longs to stop and see what ingenuity made the large rooms into livable space and to ask whether children's voices can sometime still be heard on the first Tuesday in September, or on the last school day in June, or singing at the Christmas concert on the first snowy nights of December.

There is a baseball diamond in the school yard at Ponsonby and others visible from the road in Elora – on both sides of the highway, Alma – north and south of town, Teviotdale and Elmwood proclaim the game still healthy in rural Ontario, though it may have died, or be very ill, in the cities. There is even a diamond in the middle of nowhere between Harriston and Clifford, next to the gas station which almost always offers the lowest priced gas of the trip. Once this was a rather rural affair, but concrete islands and Self Serve pumps have moved in.

All of this can be seen on the trip to the cottage, marked out as clearly as blocks in a board game, and with about as many players. Three or four cars may line up at the stop lights which mark the town centres, or where flag persons patrol the summer's road construction, but the nearest thing to a traffic jam occurs on the day in summer when the Volunteer Fire Department collects money at the intersection in Harriston.

*

While Emma was making her way up Highway 10, further to the east, the men enjoyed the trip up Highway 6, reaching Oliphant in late afternoon. When they drove into the cottage yard there appeared to be women everywhere, most of them bending over.

The phone call at noon had discomposed the eight women. Having decided the night before to continue with their weekend, they were rather startled to realize that Gertrude's children might have other plans for them. Their morning had been busy. After an hour spent piecing together the words of "The Rose" and running through it a few times, they had dug a hole between the rue and the rhubarb for More Sinister. It took quite some time. Then they had lowered the garbage bag into the hole, said a few words and sung their song. Jean, when she returned from a long walk to the fen boardwalk with Natasha, had found a rock shaped rather like a dog's head to place beside the rue and the two of them had set it in the dirt loosened by the digging of the hole.

The group had spent what remained of their morning on the item which had been intended as the centre of the agenda for the weekend, well, one of them. They had postponed their discussion of 'sexuality and aging' for the Fall Retreat. They were well practised in postponing that particular topic, might have been postponing it for the entire thirty

36

years; so not discussing it on this particular Saturday was not a hardship. Instead they discussed how their need not to hurt each other's feeling was still, after so many years, causing them to be uncertain whose needs were being met in the group and who was 'going along' as Natasha put it. Authenticity, truth, honesty, consciousness, how could such words be defined and used in an intimate relationship? What secrets must be told and which might be withheld? There was no shortage of situations to cite where people had hurt others by withholding too much, or by telling too much. Often, Natasha suggested, they tested each other's affection by the wielding of information. They continued chewing at the topic as they prepared and ate lunch, and as Margaret washed up.

The discussion had been raging when the phone call truncating their weekend had arrived. However, after some thought the group agreed that Gertrude's children were entitled to be at the cottage, needed to spend some time together; they also agreed that there would be no space for several more people to sleep, at least not comfortably. The original plans for dinner were revised. The women always brought too many vegetables; so there would be plenty. Natasha and Jean wanted another excursion, wanted to escape again to continue catching up on the time they'd been apart; so they would drive to Wiarton right after lunch to purchase splake to augment the vegetarian casseroles which Melody and Sarah had already prepared. With the addition of four pounds of fish there would be enough for an army of extras at dinner. Most of the women also agreed that they'd spend the afternoon in Gertrude's garden, clearing out the winter debris and weeding the ambitious early growth. They'd wanted to organize Gertrude's garden for years. Thus except for Maude, who was having a nap in the bunky, the women were in the yard, weeding and clearing dead stalks from the summer before, when Geoff and Eric drove in.

The men knew the women, had heard their names many times in their mother's conversation, had met individuals at their mother's parties, had seen pictures. The whole group together, however, was intimidating. They became aware that they were 'two young men with eight old ladies,' as Eric put it, just before he opened the car door. The words 'young' and 'old' were clearly relative; the men were both close to sixty. Maude, hearing the noise in the drive erupted from the bunky and hugged Geoff whom she knew best; Natasha hugged Eric. There was a moment of silence and everyone started talking about the garden.

Melody made introductions, reminding the men of which woman was which and then Edwina offered the inevitable tea, coffee, or whatever. This latter word was accompanied by a wave of the hand that took in unspeakable mixed drinks as well as more acceptable beer or wine. Sarah said that an early dinner would be ready shortly, and that there was enough for everyone.

Eric said he'd just unpack and then could they all talk in the dining room. So, in half an hour, the women had cleared the weeds away to the compost, and made themselves tidy while the men had brought in a cooler and shaving kits and a plastic bag or two. Geoff had never got the knack of suitcases. The shaving kits they dropped on the bathroom counter. The plastic bags Geoff dropped on a chair in the small bedroom. Thus unpacked, the men seated themselves at the table and waited.

Silently Eric passed around Gertrude's plans for her memorial; he'd had the foresight to make several copies at the variety store in Hanover while Geoff put more gas in the van. Eric couldn't figure why Geoff stopped at Hanover when the gas between Harriston and Clifford was cheaper but it was Geoff's credit card and the place had a copy machine, which was lucky.

On the bottom of the page Eric had handwritten the details about the Golf Course and the times for the party and the ash scattering.

"Do you know what song she's talking about?" Geoff asked when each woman had access to a copy.

"Oh, yes. We practised it this morning. Do you want to hear it?" Several voices spoke together.

The men glanced at each other and pushed on. "Is it convenient for you to get to the party? Would you like us to organize transport for you?" The fact that the women had managed to find transport for themselves to reach the cottage rather passed by the two men who saw before them several fairly elderly persons who were no doubt blind and deaf as well as senile and had probably had their licenses revoked years before. The women took several moments deciding who would pick up whom and where and at what time. They wanted to take a minimum of cars but have maximum freedom to arrive and leave when they wished.

Then the plans for the ashes were discussed. It was warm enough. Edwina FitzGibbon knew people with boats. Most people had their boats in the water by May 24; so there shouldn't be a problem. They'd need a fairly large boat for all of them and all of the family. It was not clear how many women would come, nor how many of Gertrude's family. Because the party was to be in Burlington on Friday night, people would need to drive up to scatter the ashes on Saturday morning. The scattering might best be at noon on Saturday. Thus most of the details were in place by the time the group had finished eating dinner.

They were just having coffee and feeling that they had, under the circumstances, accomplished a good day's work when Emma drove in. Once again introductions were required. Living on the west coast, Mike and Mar had heard of Gertrude's friends, had seen photographs, but not met most of them. Emma had seen them only rarely since her childhood summers and university years. Mike carried luggage in and Emma stowed it by the beds they'd agreed upon during their drive north; women bustled about getting plates and cutlery and setting up dinner for the latecomers. Mar greeted her brothers and Gertrude's three children held each other tightly sniffing more than a little. Eric, to his horror, did the crying now that he had not done the night before.

It wasn't until she'd been at the cottage for quite a while, until she was getting her dessert, that Emma asked,"Where's More Sin?" It seemed strange, when she finally noticed, that he hadn't been nuzzling her pockets, sniffing her horsy boots, licking her hands or begging for some of her dinner. The person she asked was her uncle Geoff, who was standing nearest to her in the kitchen getting coffee and (naturally) he was not much wiser than she.

"They probably put him in the porch or the little bedroom. Maybe they didn't know how to handle him," he suggested.

"He would have barked," she said and her uncle shrugged. Clearly a dog was not something he was willing to add to his list of chores.

So Emma went looking. After a fruitless tour of the cottage she went into the dining room and wedged her way into a brisk argument over who was bringing what kind of hors d'oeuvres to the memory party.

"Where is More Sinister?" she asked.

Eight faces looked up at her, embarrassed, surprised, she wasn't sure which.

"Oh, my dear," said Jean.

"Oh, my," said Natasha.

"We buried him in the garden this morning. We gave him such a nice ceremony."

"We were practising for your grandmother's party and it came out rather well," Sarah added this as if it explained Edwina's previous statement.

"You what?"

"Well I tripped over him when I went to wake your mother, Emma and so we had the police carry him out to the shed for the night."

"We put him in the far corner between the rue and the monk's hood. It's very pretty back there." Maude added, "We hoped you wouldn't mind us digging part of the garden."

"The truth of it is," said Melody, "that we didn't even think of you. We felt the dog was a problem and we solved it."

"Gertrude would have preferred him to be in the garden and not in some vet's garbage." Jean said this last bit forgetting that Emma was a vet and it left rather a silent moment behind it.

"All that may very well be, but did you kill him just to keep him out of some vet's garbage? And how did you manage it?"

"Oh no, my dear." A whole chorus of "Oh, no" filled the dining room.

"As I said, he was dead when we got here, lying beside your grandmother. That's why I tripped over him."

There was a long silence broken by Melody saying, "It never occurred to me to tell Geoff about the dog when I phoned him. I'm sorry."

Emma began to shed for an old dog, the tears she had been thus far too busy to shed for her grandmother, though she supposed, as she stumbled out of the door and into the yard to look for the grave, that they were tears for both.

When Emma finally returned from the garden it was dark. At dusk she'd replied to calls of goodbye as the women had packed their cars and departed, but otherwise she'd sat quietly on the bench in the garden thinking about her grandmother and wondering why the dog and the woman had died at the same time. That happened in books, of course; creatures died of broken hearts, but she wasn't sure why it would have happened here. More Sinister was a gregarious dog; used to being with Gertrude day and night but still fond of company and happy to be cared for by friends when Gertrude travelled. Not a one person dog. Even dogs with broken hearts, even fictional dogs pined. They didn't just lie down on the spot and die.

When she returned to the house her parents and her uncles were seated around the dining room table, amply supplied with drinks and loudly discussing the terms of Gertrude's will. Though they realized that the copy which had been in the chest of drawers might not be the final word, what was written there was exactly as she had explained her wishes years before when she first made her 'arrangements,' as they are so euphemistically called. They were trying to decipher Gertrude's handwriting and decide whether she had got right the disposition of her pictures, her china and her Persian carpets. Over the years they had all put in requests and now, as if it were some sort of final exam to which they were subjecting their mother, they were applauding and booing the designations in the list and making exchanges in some cases. The bartering became heated and humorous with memory. Then they would recall that she was dead and someone would cry or say how much they would miss her. The memorial service and the party were subjected to the same half humourous, half pathetic scrutiny. After making a substantial dint in the liquor in the kitchen cabinet and becoming quite maudlin, they went to bed. It was late.

CHAPTER III

SUNDAY MORNING, MAY 31

AFTER BREAKFAST THE NEXT MORNING Eric and Geoff decided that it was time for them to get home. They had lives to live and jobs to go to the next day. Their unspoken, perhaps unacknowledged, longing for familiar showers and quiet homes might have been the result of substantial hangovers. They agreed to continue making the legal arrangements with Gertrude's lawyer and accountant and publisher if Mar would take care of the sorting of property. Having made their decision, Geoff and Eric packed up, not an onerous task since neither had brought much more than a toothbrush and fresh underwear. The beer they'd brought had been the first thing to disappear the night before. Mike, Mar and Emma would stay a day or two, tidying Gertrude's personal effects from the cottage, talking to any local officials, making the place ready for the scattering of ashes the following weekend. Then they would proceed to empty and clean Gertrude's apartment. No one thought that it was strange that a daughter should fly several thousand kilometers to clean house, two houses, in fact.

Thus it was not until Sunday afternoon, after eating a hearty brunch of eggs and Sullivan's sausage (one of Wiarton's hidden treasures) with rolls which the women had left for them, that Mar, Mike and Emma began to sort Gertrude's belongings. Mike was assigned to the outbuildings. Mar had the upstairs and Emma began with her grandmother's sunporch bedroom. She unplugged the laptop and put it away in the case. She could look at that later, when she got home maybe. The bed was neatly made. Matching brightly flowered pillows and sheets were tucked in against the wall. The half of the comforter away from the wall was more faded than the rest; the pattern was worn to an indeterminate grey. Stray dog hair, bits of grass and a gritty feeling were testimony to More Sinister's usual sleeping place. The floor beside the bed was gritty also. Gertrude had swept most of the sand from her bed when she'd made it on Friday morning. In memory Emma could see the old dog climbing on and off of the bed, probably being helped by her grandmother, although quite aged and creaky animals, including humans, can be remarkably agile when performing an accustomed action. This is one good reason for maintaining as large a repertoire of accustomed actions as possible. As she swept under the bed and bent to retrieve stray hairpins, she figured women's housekeeping activity had been vastly underrated as a reason for their tendency to outlive men. Hormones were only part of it.

The book was beside Gertrude's pillow. Emma went to clear it out of the way so she could change the sheets. She wasn't sure whether anyone wanted to sleep on the sun porch the next weekend but it was certain that the sheets had to be washed and the few clothes hanging on the back of the easy chair disposed of. As she pulled the sheets towards her the book slid out from beyond the pillow and a pen rolled with it. The cover declared it to be *Bleak House* by Charles Dickens. It was lying open, face down and Emma had closed it and put it on the desk before she realized that in the brief glimpse she'd had inside, she'd not seen print. She flipped it open. It wasn't *Bleak House*, not unless Gertrude had rewritten all of Dickens' book by hand for some reason.

"Mom?" she called out. "Look at this."

"What?" came Mar's distant voice. Then silence. The stubborn conversation of two people, neither of whom wants to move.

Waiting for her mother to put away whatever she was working on and come down the stairs, Emma turned the book over in her hands. The spine had the spine from a *Bleak House* dust jacket carefully glued in place. The front was from the same dust jacket, also carefully glued in place. Why not use the whole dust jacket? Emma wondered. Perhaps it didn't fit. Anyway she began to read. Each page had at the top left the date and day and time, usually early morning, and the place. This journal was almost full and began in late November of 1997. Her grandmother's days were detailed, two pages for each, faithfully. Flipping through, Emma could see not a day missing, though the day on which her grandmother had flown to Kentucky to spend Christmas, was partially written on the plane and partially written later in the day. That entry ended abruptly with "Emma has dinner ready, must go." How odd to read about herself in that way.

As she heard her mother coming across the living room she closed the book, somewhat guiltily and smoothed it between her hands, turning it over this time and noticing that at the bottom of the spine was the number 195 in stick-on numbers neatly placed between the author's name and the publisher's. She started as her mother entered the porch.

"Look. It's a diary. Did you know grandma kept a diary?"

"Well, yes, I suppose I did. She called them journals. I never thought much about it."

"Okay, but why would she have this on the cover?" Emma held the book so that it faced Marilla, "and could she have written – mmm ..." and she looked back at the spine, "a hundred and ninety five of them? If she did where are the rest?"

"A hundred and ninety five!" Marilla was shocked. She looked vaguely about the porch, as if the other one hundred and ninety four might materialize before her. "Well, if she did they must be at the apartment. Are you almost done out here?"

"About fifteen minutes. I'm changing the bed and I've already thrown a load of clothes in a pile for the laundry. Are we taking them into Wiarton or waiting until we're south?"

"South. We'll go in the morning. There'll be far more stuff there and I don't know about you but I've only got a week off work."

"Don't you want to read this?" Emma held the book out and Marilla twitched away from it.

"Not now." Tears welled up but she blew her nose and shook her head.

"Maybe later."

"Do you mind if I read it?" Mar shook her head again and, pressing her lips between her teeth, hurried back upstairs.

They ate leftovers for supper. There was still some of Friday's soup and Saturday's fish and there were rolls and salad. How many rolls did those women need on a weekend? Perhaps Gertrude had bought extra just in case. They were conscious of trying to clear out the fridge, take inventory and leave things tidy for the following weekend when there might be more people to feed, more beds to be made. They did not stay up late. Mike and Mar had had little sleep on Friday night and had talked late on Saturday night; so they walked out the causeway and back and then went to bed in the bunky. Emma was sleeping upstairs in her old room. She took the journal with her.

It was good to be back in her bed. She thought of it as her bed although she was aware that other people slept there. It was the room that she and her grandmother had painted together. Once again she was 9 years old and her grandmother was calling up the stairs, "If you don't turn off that light, you won't be able to get up in the morning and you'll miss your lesson."

Emma opened the journal, wondering what her grandmother's last days had been like, finding it odd to be able to enter her grandmother's rather inscrutable mind on the morning of her death. Had Gertrude any idea that she was writing her final entry?

May 28, 1998, Friday   *Oliphant*   *7:15*

We couldn't see the water until we were almost in it this A.M. The surface near us was as smooth as insincerity and a pale mist lay just above the water. The shoreline was visible but, looking back toward Lonely Island, only part of the causeway along which we'd walked was still there, and the tops of Lonely's trees floated above the mist. The air held itself very still. The high piping of nesting birds and the buzz of an occasional bug was all the sound which broke the stillness, and the sssss of our feet through last year's dune grasses. The new grass is just inches tall yet, tender and easily broken. More trotted ahead of me down the causeway and onto the beach, checking to see what had become of the carp he'd found washed up on the beach 2 weeks before. He will check that spot every morning until some other piece of garbage comes along to intrigue him. Almost human.

Then in the reeds I could hear them – all along in the shallows a distinctive splashing would break the silent surface of the water. Late carp. They seem to come to our beach in two waves. The first fish arrive when the water begins to warm in mid May, usually in still weather. A huge number. Carp spawn in groups never – or I've never seen them – in pairs but in threes or fours or fives. They move into the shallowest water, even some distance up the little streams running across the wetlands, streams which are usually 6 - 8 inches deep in spring. A group will swim about, twisting and circling for as long as I've ever stayed to watch. They swim silently for several minutes and then there will be a slap and splash. I stand and watch for perhaps an hour whenever they are here. In the first wave there may be a hundred pods of fish carrying on in our little bay for three or four days. Then they are gone, leaving a residue of yellow eggs marking the shoreline. Maybe two weeks later another, smaller wave arrives. I assume these carp are different, not merely disappointed.

I throw a stick for More Sin while I stand as close to the water as I can, and watch. I remind myself to tell my friends later today and offer them my Wellies if they want to come and look. It hasn't happened often while they are here. More Sinister won't go into the water anywhere near the fish. They startle him every time they splash and he jumps into his guard dog pose and then backs away. So I throw his stick up into the dunes and watch the fish until I'm hungry.

I cleaned the cottage yesterday, and aired the bunky; everything is ready. Lots of coffee, tea and milk. Lots of toilet paper in each bathroom. I swear they take the stuff home, so much disappears on these weekends. Still it's better they steal it than throw that quantity in the septic tank. Fresh towels are out and I picked three of those really sweet smelling narcissus for the upstairs to take the musty smell of winter away. Later today when the sun comes in that upstairs window I'll open it for a while and let the lake air in.

George called yesterday, from Toronto. Very odd. Said he wanted to meet me. I told him this weekend was inconvenient, out of the question. He has never been a considerate person; his needs always come first. He pushed to find out when I'd have a free moment. When he understood I was expecting a crowd this evening, he insisted that he would come today and he would bring lunch. Says he enjoys cooking, that he cooks all the time for his mother. She must be quite an age. I offered to provide potato and Stilton soup. I'll make extra and there will be plenty both for George and the group. I have no objection to eating it twice. Can't imagine why he wants to meet me after all this time.

I'm meditating on my goals this week – what have I decided? Odd to be so near the end of life and still meditating on goals. I wish I knew what I'd been when I grew up. Our goals are determined by our vision of who we are in the universe. Our vision changes forever and forever as we move, as Tennyson so romantically put it. I hold no brief for Tennyson but he was right about that. Since we make our gods in our image, our view of ourselves in the world is hugely important; we have no other models. So we imagine gods as huge as thunder as sublime as a sunset as determined as a river as innocent as a kitten as faithful as a dog as loving as...what? Human love is so limited, frail, perfect in the moment, turning to ashes over time. How could we imagine the universe as open and loving when we are disregarded by our families, our employers, and our government? Mostly we imagine gods as greedy and spiteful as we are. Difficult to imagine a powerful god, when we are weak – only a vindictive one. How do we surmount our environment and imagine gods as various and full of promise as we could be? As children we are told how to behave and how to think; often we are told how to feel. Children's gods are parental, with all the limits that imposes. As our spirits grow so must our gods. What god does a writer, a painter, an artist have? A creator, absolutely, one who creates endlessly a universe constantly created and destroyed, not the reverse. Too easy for writers, artists to destroy work they haven't made yet, edit it to blank paper, paint it over and over or not at all, look at the clay in dismay and walk away   a creative god doesn't do that. Writes and writes and writes and paints and paints, moulds the clay and lets others judge. So a non-judgemental god? Not one which sits and looks at the tools. Sitting staring at the tools does not hone the craft. Still less does washing dishes and cleaning floors get books written. Who's to say which is more important if we do not make judgements? Any product is better than none. The platypus and rhinoceros as beautiful as the gazelle, as real, as fitted to their environment as most creatures. Bacteria are far more adaptable than humans; who's to say which is some god's superior creature? Create! Write! Imperative mode. Also, today, clean!

Won't have much time for meditating or creating over the next two days – will barely have time to write my journal in the morning before the others are up. Thank goodness, I've just about finished R's last book. The publisher is waiting; so maybe I should tell George about it. My present book is coming along nicely – at last. Only the rewriting and proof reading remain. Then I might garden for a month and read junk before I put myself to the torture of the next one! Or not.

Emma held the book away from her for a few moments. Had her grandmother felt intimations of mortality? Not obviously, not on Friday morning. Emma had meant to start at the beginning and read the journal like a novel but the urge to know about the ending, about her grandmother's last day had drawn her to the final pages and now she was confused. She lay in the familiar bed in the familiar room listening to the whine of the vent fan on the roof and the wind coming in off the lake. Occasional patters on the metal roof, not heavy or prolonged, were hard to distinguish. Was she hearing squirrels or were showers passing overhead?

She reread the entry going quickly through the description of the spawning carp and lingering, puzzling over the final paragraphs. Who were these people? How could she find out? Maybe if she'd started at the beginning of the journal she'd know but she hadn't and she didn't. She didn't know everyone her grandmother knew; that was certain. In a lifetime of social work her grandmother had met and worked with hundreds, thousands of people. She'd kept in touch with one or two colleagues whom Emma knew about and there were clients, foster parents, children too, no longer children, who dropped in to have coffee, to show Gertrude their children and grandchildren, to talk about their triumphs – ask for help with their tragedies. Gertrude shared anecdotes with her family; so Emma knew many such people existed. Perhaps George was one of those. The important thing was that he'd been at lunch the day Gertrude died. He'd been the last person to talk to her, perhaps. And who was R. and what books did she or he write?

Of course there were Gertrude's books. Emma supposed there were people whom Gertrude met in connection with her writing. Perhaps George was a fellow writer. His name was mentioned in that context in the journal. Emma had read some of her grandmother's books, had been given an autographed copy of each and kept them somewhere in her apartment, though she'd be hard pressed to say where. Her apartment was overlaid with tack and medical magazines and dirty laundry; books tended to sift down to the lower strata. Perhaps R. wrote mysteries too. She realized that she'd never heard about other writers, or publishers or that part of Gertrude's life. Did Gertrude have an agent? Her uncles might know. Emma was aware that her mind was beginning to sound like a soap opera trailer – all questions and listen in tomorrow!

The family rarely thought of Gertrude as a writer except when, every three or four years, a new book came out. Gertrude had begun to write late in life, wrote novels, murder mysteries mostly, embellishing her experiences and the places she knew, writing scathingly about the abused and abusers, the courts and government officials of her years of social work. She sometimes used her family, thinly disguised, in her books. For this reason her children were nervous when each book appeared. Gertrude said she did this as a test, a way to ensure that her family read her books even if no one else did.

She said she'd always written. She said that the millions of reports she'd written over a lifetime of child protection were largely fiction. But it was only after she'd retired that she'd begun to enjoy writing about her job – though the journal entry suggested that enjoy might not be the most precise word. She'd said she didn't much care if she became famous or widely read, so long as she had her computer and could write for a few hours each morning she was happy. The journals. Emma thought. Gertrude had never talked about writing those. Emma had assumed Gertrude meant her novels when she said writing. Maybe she'd meant her journals. Perhaps she wrote her stories in her journals. Perhaps there would be information about these George and R. people in the journals. If there really were 195 books, there could be quite a bit of information! Wondering how on earth she'd find answers to her growing number of questions Emma fell asleep.

CHAPTER IV

MONDAY MORNING, JUNE 1, 1998

OVER BREAKFAST THE NEXT MORNING Emma asked her mother what she knew about Gertrude's friends, other than the eight women who had formed a central part of her life for as long as most of them could remember.

"Well, there were the people she worked with," Mar said tentatively, echoing what Emma already knew, "but I only know a couple of them. She stopped seeing most of them after she retired. She said they drained her energy and she'd rather garden and travel and write ... and spend time with us of course."

"Yes, well about the writing, do you know who her agent was, or her publisher or what writing friends she might have had?"

"What's the point, Emma? What difference does it make? She's dead and your mother really doesn't want to deal with an inquisition." Mike often defended Mar, usually in her absence, but perhaps he was considering her to be absent on this occasion. What was more, he was always nervous talking about things which could lead to intimacy or emotion. Dwelling on the details of Gertrude's life seemed likely to open wounds he didn't want Mar to examine, his supply of bandages being rather limited by his own affection for Gertrude.

"The point is that she had invited someone named George to lunch on the day she died. She mentions it in her journal."

"She probably met lots of people. She was a busy person. She had a wide range of interests. Presumably people read her books. What dif-ference does it make?" Mike repeated.

"This is a person who is willing to drive three hours to talk to her. She and her dog are found dead. One or the other of them I can see dying but not both at the same time and not right after lunch with one acquaintance and before supper with others without her calling anyone or writing a note or giving any indication of illness other than the angina she'd lived with for years. Wouldn't it be nice to know if they had lunch together and what she was thinking and feeling just before she died?" Thumping her hand on the journal which she had brought to the table with her she went on, "Here's a mention that her book is almost finished and that R.'s is too. Who is R? Why does she care that R.'s book is almost finished? There are just too many questions and I was hoping that the two of you might be able to help me find some answers. I'm sorry if I sound a bit crazy but as I think about it I start asking more and more questions and I get no answers."

"Emma, calm down. This is real life, not a mystery story," said Mike and began to clear the dishes to the kitchen.

Emma sat, silenced, feeling for a few moments like a child again. Then she checked that there really were no other journals in the cottage, packed her grandmother's final words in her suitcase, tidied her bedroom and started carrying laundry, stuffed into garbage bags, to the car.

They did not get away quickly. After breakfast the cottage had to be vacuumed, the water shut off, blinds closed, the luggage loaded. The three of them arrived at Gertrude's apartment in mid afternoon. They'd stopped at Guelph for lunch, bought groceries for the remainder of the week, and found a bargain on garbage bags while they were at it. Mike had found the garbage bags at his favourite store, Canadian Tire, while the women bought food. The liquor stores they passed along the way provided a trunk full of boxes. Then they had to stop at Geoff's house to pick up the keys to the apartment.

Emma tried again to find out who George and R. might be.

"Sue, did grandma ever mention a person named George or someone whose name begins with R?" Once again she explained that her grandmother had met with George on her final day. Sue was intrigued; she loved gossip and secrets but she couldn't be helpful about George. She did give Emma a list of the women in Gertrude's group, names addresses and phone numbers which she'd used in preparing for Gertrude's 80th birthday and not disposed of just in case it were needed again. Emma asked to borrow it. Sue said she didn't think she'd be needing it again in the circumstances, not after the memory party anyway. It was probably pretty up to date, except for the woman who'd moved out west. Maybe one of the others would know where she was staying. Sue wanted to know what man Gertrude had lunched with. Alone. Not telling anyone. Very interesting. At least Aunt Sue was curious too.

Gertrude's apartment had already gathered the smell of a place where the air is not breathed. As they stood in the hall, looking at Gertrude's plants and holding their groceries and suitcases they decided to continue with their stereotypical jobs: Mar would sort cloth in closets and drawers, Mike would box books and Emma, who was a woman on the one hand and a doctor on the other, would sift through Gertrude's papers. Fortunately the division also reflected their genuine interests. They needed to clear through a large apartment quickly, take loads to the Salvation Army the next morning and assess how much longer they'd need. Mike, who could not leave his business for long, had a return ticket for the next day, Tuesday, and if there were lots of boxes or furniture to be moved it seemed wise to do it while he was still there to help. Some grandsons could be pressed into service later, when the hundred-year-old chaise-longue, or the Persian rugs had to be carried to new homes. Mar wondered who would want the monster which had been a fixture in Gertrude's life for sixty years. But, for now, they carried on. Emma realized she was enjoying the prospect of spending time alone with her mother. She phoned her assistant and arranged the rest of the week. As she went into the study, she asked Mike to shout when he found the journals.

Mar's job was fairly straightforward. Clothes went to the garbage chute, or to the Salvation Army. By 7 in the evening she'd finished clearing most of Gertrude's bedroom, and had driven a load to the donation box at the neighborhood supermarket parking lot. The closets were practically bare. A few handmade, or especially beautiful things she'd put in one closet for the moment. Emma, who was rarely out of riding pants and tailored shirts, was not interested in her grandmother's elegant flowing smocks. However, some of the in-laws might appreciate a beautifully designed cloak or smock as a memento. The jewelry chest was almost empty; Gertrude had given most of her treasures to her granddaughters when they were teenagers. Each had, at the same time, been given a written account of the original owner or the story that went with the piece. Gertrude had never cared much for necklaces or bracelets but she had had tie-pins inherited from her grandfather and she bought huge evening rings as souvenirs when she travelled. All that now remained were two pair of earrings.

Emma headed for the study. Gertrude had four file drawers of papers. One held what Emma thought of as documents: tax receipts, household accounts, investments, insurance, contracts. These she sorted, quickly pulling out the current ones and putting them in a box for her uncles and the lawyer to deal with. One drawer held travel magazines and maps, theatre programs for Shaw and Blyth mostly, and some for Canadian Stage and Theatre Aquarius. There were also photo albums. Gertrude had not taken photos, preferring her journal when she travelled. People were less apt to steal a notebook than a camera, she said, and added that she was also less likely to break a notebook or drop it overboard. Apparently other people had supplied her with visual souvenirs.

The travel brochures and souvenir books Emma bagged for the garbage. The photos she saved for the enjoyment of people who came to the memory party. One drawer held rough drafts of Gertrude's books and articles. Emma labeled these and put them aside, wondering whether they were worth anything and who would be able to tell her. She really would have to find out whether her grandmother had an agent. One drawer held letters and mementos. She noticed a card that she'd sent her grandmother for Christmas when she was quite small. Apparently she'd stuck white cotton batten on a red construction paper Santa and then mounted him on a horse which had been cut from a magazine. Emma tried to recall whether she had purposely mounted Santa on a horse or whether she had simply forgotten to paste antlers on her creation. Two days and she was missing her horses. They asked questions too but their questions didn't seem like tests of affection or loyalty.

She was getting tired so she consigned most of the cards and letters to the garbage without examining them. Then, wearily, she leaned forward and retrieved the whole lot. She began sorting, looking for things which might give a clue as to who George and R. were. She was amazed at the numbers of people who sent admiring cards to her grandmother on every possible sort of anniversary.

Among a pile of postcards, cards from clients and friends, cards ranging through humourous and scenic to artistic, she discovered fifteen from Scotland, most picturing sheep, and saying such things as, "A friend indeed is a friend in need. R," or "Un ami...c'est un ami. R." One later one which pictured Hadrian's wall with not a sheep in sight read, "G. there may be some sheep hiding in the bushes. R." The postcards were bundled together with an elastic band which disintegrated as soon as Emma removed the first card from its grip. The postmarks, where she could make them out, began in 1960 and ended in 1985. Aside from a fixation on sheep and a weird sense of humour, the cards revealed nothing about their sender. That they had been kept revealed something about the receiver but Emma couldn't tell what.

Mike meanwhile began boxing books, working silently and steadily, across the room from his daughter. He liked looking at her, was proud of her beauty and achievements. He knew it had not been easy for her to reach the top of her profession in a man's world. More women were becoming trainers and jockeys and working with large animals now, but when Emma had studied veterinary medicine most women cared for cats and dogs; they had not been welcome out on the farms or in fancy stables. He was sad that her work had apparently cut her off from marriage and children but he was comfortable with her choice. She would have laughed and said he was jealous of any guy she dated but that was only partly true.

Books were like that, he realized, more complicated than they first appeared. It seemed easy at first to put them in a box, but you had to get them to fit and the size and shape became important and then, perhaps. there should be labels on the boxes: history, psychology, feminism. Yes, he'd write on the boxes. He carried the boxes to the living room and stacked them neatly in a corner. He was very meticulous, rearranging the stacks so that the larger boxes were on the bottom, not filling the boxes so full that they couldn't be lifted by the women who might have to clear them out.

Eric arrived at the apartment as they were finishing a late dinner. He'd been in touch with the lawyer, chased down Gertrude's will. Yes, he'd found Gertrude's agent, a woman named Victoria something, since Emma asked. Geoff had been in touch with the accountant or financial planner or whatever these people called themselves. The will remained unchanged since its creation 45 years before when Gertrude had left her husband. After expenses and the money allotted for the party, sums which had been regularly updated, each of the children was to receive one third of the estate and what happened after that was their business. There was the cottage of course. It formed, according to the accountant's best estimate, slightly more than one third of the estate. They would have to decide whether to sell it. Mike and Mar, he supposed, would not be interested in sharing it since they were rarely in Ontario in the summer. Geoff used it most but didn't want to keep it. He'd use the money to buy something else, somewhere else: bush and a pond likely. Eric would pay off his own mortgage and be free for the first time in years. Even thinking about it made him look younger.

There would be a continuing income from Gertrude's books which could be divided at each year-end; the accountant said it was not much but it had been a delightful supplement to Gertrude's pension and allowed her to travel each year. She'd read accounts of her adventures at family gatherings sometimes. Of course, Emma thought, somewhat startled, Gertrude had read from the journals. Bus tours and cargo ships and trains. Gertrude, even in her late seventies, had not sat still for long, usually taking a trip just before and after the cottage season, limiting her time in the apartment to maybe three months in the winter, her knitting and sewing months, she called them. In reality the knitting was usually done on trains and planes and ships and only sewing was done here in the apartment where there was a huge cutting table as well as neatly stored buttons, ribbons, fasteners, threads, whatever a person sewing needed, Emma was sure. Gertrude wrote in the morning and sewed in the evening, if there weren't meetings or social engagements: at least that's what she did when the family was around. Perhaps when she was alone she stayed in bed all day and ate chocolates. Emma smiled at the idea.

What had her uncle said about selling the cottage? Her cottage. She'd always thought of it as hers. She supposed her cousins had too. Sold. Just like that. Her horror had not completely overruled her curiosity, however.

"No other bequests? None?" Then she had to explain R. and George to Eric. She also fetched and read some of the sheep postcards, as if producing an exhibit would confirm the existence of R. when her grandmother's journal would not.

"Emma thinks there is some mystery about these folks," her father said.

Eric looked puzzled.

"I just want to know who they are and why grandma was writing about them on her last morning. Never mind the mystery, Uncle Eric. I do, however, need to speak to Victoria Something about all of grandma's papers. I'd like to talk to her tomorrow. I want to know whether she'll negotiate a sale price for the drafts and notes for Grandma's books, or whether we should. I'm not sure whether we have copies of all the contracts, what their terms are, and how long she's been Grandma's agent. If she's new then we need to know who might have an interest in the earlier books. Unless you'd rather?" If no one in her family could help, she supposed she'd try speaking to the agent, and soon. Emma was amused to note that she'd switched to business language and that her father and uncle were now paying attention. Her uncle asked her to call him in about an hour.

It was about an hour after Eric left that Mike and Mar both made discoveries. The three of them had agreed to go back to work until 10 and then go out for dessert at a neighboring café. Emma had thrown out most of the notes and vet bills and had started to empty the kitchen shelf which Gertrude used for vitamins, her own and More Sinister's, when her mother called from the hall that she'd found more papers for Emma to deal with. "Good Heavens, where, Mom? I checked all the shelves and drawers."

"Well, you didn't check the linen closet did you?"

"You know I didn't. Why would I?"

"Come and see why you would." Mar had begun at the bottom of the cupboard, removing dog food and throwing out a shelf full of the soaps and bath oils and perfumes which were the flotsam and jetsam of Christmases past: gifts which might have been used but hadn't, sunblock which hadn't been finished, ancient mosquito repellent. Mar had bagged up all the towels and sheets which were used regularly. The next shelf held spare blankets and pillows. Then on the top shelf, behind the sheets and pillow cases which did not fit the beds or were a little too stained for company but might be useful for interfacing or dusters, were rather large piles of paper. Emma got a chair so that she could reach to the back of the deep cupboard. She carried the piles into the study and put them on her grandmother's cutting table. It was while she was doing this that Mike announced that he had found Gertrude's journals.

The books filled two long shelves in Gertrude's dining area. There were indeed 194 of them. The early ones were often thin: notebooks or foolscap in folders which were clearly the result of schoolgirl scavenging. For a couple of the early collections of papers Gertrude had found document boxes and they were covered with dust jackets for *A Child's Garden of Verse* and *Grimm's Fairy Tales*. By number 9 the parade of bound books began in earnest, often with commercial diaries, one or two with little locks and keys; well, there may have been keys; the keys were not immediately apparent. They might surface as her mother sorted bureau drawers. If they didn't, the mechanisms could be shifted quite easily with a pin, or ripped off instead, of course, if it came to that. Many of those early books looked like gifts, gilt edged, 200 pages at the most. Then Gertrude had clearly found suppliers of more serious journals. There would be ten, even as many as twenty of these volumes which had been ordered at the same time or bought from the same supplier. These she had covered with more ambitious authors – at least more ambitious in terms of quantity. One whole series was devoted to Agatha Christie. An early section, the years when Gertrude had been working and raising children, was covered by the complete works of Lucy Maude Montgomery, books devoted to women's experience, books in which men are largely invisible. Then there were the books of Margaret Laurence followed by the rest of the Canadian canon, Engel, Munro, Atwood. Atwood's *Surfacing* covered the first part of 1953, at about the time Gertrude was leaving her husband. Emma pulled that journal from the box and with it a few others whose titles were promising. What sort of laughter had accompanied the choosing of appropriate jackets to cover her journals? Sardonic, probably.

Emma wondered whether all the covers had been applied at the same time in a fever of cutting and pasting or whether it had happened gradually as more and more room was required for journals. The numbers varied in size and style; so they had not been put in place at the same time. The early journals had numbers painted with something that looked suspiciously like nail polish. Later ones had stick-on numbers, the ones stores sell for houses, or mail boxes or doors. However, Emma considered, most hardware stores didn't carry more than ten or so of one number. Even if Gertrude had bought them all at the same time she might have had to go to several stores, especially for the 1 which was the most frequently required number.

"There used to be more books," Mar said on looking at the shelves and going to the other rooms to check. "Where did you find books, Mike? There used to be several shelves in the bedroom. And I remember when the lower shelves of the tea carts in the living room were piled with all her gardening and herbal books. Three closets used to be filled with clothes too and wool and cloth everywhere. I wonder when she started clearing things out?"

"These journals and her own books and some reference works are all that I have left to do here. The rest of the books were in the study. I checked before I went out for that last load of boxes. Does anyone want the large Oxford Dictionary, with magnifying glass, by the way?"

"I was just wondering whether you'd packed copies of the L.M. Montgomery, for example, or whether she'd discarded them and kept only the jackets. I remember when she gave me a bunch of kids' books; Emma was about twelve at the time, but I don't recall whether they had their jackets or not. How odd. At some point she started giving away books she didn't think she'd read and using their dust jackets to cover her journals. She was cleaning out her life, or shifting her focus, and none of us noticed."

Below the journals, on the bottom shelf, were Gertrude's own books, as well as some reference works and a large number of scholarly looking works which Emma assumed were also reference works. She asked her Dad to box all of Gertrude's works from these shelves separately and label them to go to Kentucky with her. The reference books could go to the junk dealer as could the furniture no one wanted and the books from the study.

It was midnight when they came back from eating a sickening combination of ice cream, pastry and chocolate, not much improved by the walk which followed. Emma selected journals 145, 155, and 165 from the boxes and set them beside her bed. A sampling at approximately five year intervals might be instructive. She thought of it as a core sample through the centre of the work from which she might detect changes in family, friends, work, attitudes. She deliberately mined only the years of the women's group, hoping to find clues to that group's existence and information for her interviews.

She'd decided as she was eating the last of her chocolate pecan pie that she wanted to talk to her grandmother's friends about that Friday afternoon, and maybe find out about R. and George while she was at it. She opened an empty notebook she'd found in a desk drawer. At the top of every fourth page she wrote one of the names from Sue's list, and with it the appropriate phone number. In the morning she would call and make appointments for Wednesday and Thursday.

Then she began to skim through the journals. The book she'd read the night before was good training for deciphering the others. The writing was more legible in earlier years and Gertrude had used fewer symbols, short forms and cryptic expressions. Most days she began with a weather report; she wrote as she ate breakfast, after she and the dog had already been out for their morning walk. Sometimes she simply reported, cold and rainy, or cloudy and humid. On other occasions the description was lyrical; Emma wondered whether these were practise exercises or paragraphs which might later be used in books. Then Gertrude chronicled the events of the previous day, often quite briefly and dispassionately. Suddenly her grandma would change topic, writing about her past or meditating on a color or place. She might write long lists of fanciful ideas. She might draw designs for clothes. Sometimes she worked out the plots or pages of books she was writing. There were symbols and colored pencil markings in the margins, often beside these passages but in other places too.

It passed through Emma's mind that students or scholars, she shrugged as she amended the terminology, might want to use these parts of the journals; people did research on all sorts of popular writing nowadays. But how could the parts which described the writing, or were first drafts be separated from Gertrude's news of the family or her discussions of her own body or the experiments with hideous food she was cooking for her dog? Emma smiled when she happened on those recipes. She'd forgotten the problems that the first Sinister had had with his skin, had forgotten the smell of mackerel and potato stewing, of brewer's yeast being stirred into warm mush, as her grandmother had prepared meals for the young pup. Would the family want strangers reading all of this? Would they care? The personal was so very personal, vulnerable. She would care. Whose business was it that her young self had insisted on a night light being left on? Battles she'd heard about in the news, battles about authorized and unauthorized biographies began to make more sense to her now. The unwillingness of some families to collude in their own public disrobing took on a personal application.

June 1, 1973 Friday   *Oliphant*   *7:45*
Hot and muggy. Still. Lots of bugs. There is no horizon over the lake, just a pale absence between the islands. The trees on Vimy are a darker shade of pale. Good line that. The water waits for the weekend, girds itself for motorboats and water-skiing and dogs barking. After a cold May, June is promising that shimmering heat that makes schoolrooms and offices intolerable and focuses all eyes on July.
We are late risers today. Last night was group meeting at Natasha's. I drove north, leaving her place at 10 and getting here around 12:30. She is studying astrology and making us her guinea pigs. Tonight she gave us each preliminary findings, based on whatever birth information we had supplied. She was puzzled by mine, she said. I'd written the hospital and received a form giving time and date of my birth. The signs, she said, pointed to my always being in close relationship,

probably with a man. She laughed and suggested I'd been holding out on them; maybe I wasn't really divorced. Scary. How does such non-sense approach so near the truth? Odd that I have never mentioned R. or even the existence of a lover to these people with whom I am in every other way candid. The habit of separating my life into compart-ments must have been deeply formed by the time I began meeting these women. It never even occurs to me to mention a huge and constant part of my life. I wonder what secrets each of the others conceals. I hope Natasha does not persist with her questions.

What would I do if she did?

Yesterday morning I walked Sinister up to Sandy Bay and back looking for orchids. We found a few of the little pink ones, Calypsos and Swamp Pinks as well as quite a few of the Yellow Lady's Slippers, but the Showy Lady's Slippers aren't out yet. It is dry enough this year for us to walk across the fens from the Marina to the next point north. I wore Wellies and could be quite bold about wandering through the long grass. It's not very long yet. Sinister is still puppy-nervous about the water. He runs a bit, kicking up great sparkling arcs, and then stops, looking back over his hind quarters to see where the water which splashes him is coming from. He suspects a conspiracy. I won-der whether he will go in deeper when the children are here. Maybe, if they throw a ball around.

Too buggy to work in the garden except right after breakfast when a bit of breeze came up. I hustled out and pulled some of the grass which has invaded the sorrel.

In between moments spent reading Margaret Laurence's Diviners *I worked out the design for a huge tapestry of daisies, the flowers six or seven inches across – maybe double that – large enough that the cen tral yellow is deeply textured, doodling on a notepad and trying differ-ent overlappings. Want it to be 4' by 8' so that it dominates a wall. Daffodils would be good too...bit phallic, could the phallic be also made into a deep tunnel, mystery in the dark centre of the flower, suck-ing the viewer into the ambiguously male and female night? Continued the planning as I drove south in the late afternoon.*

Yellow. light. sun. life. hope. joy. makes green younger, until there is too much and then the bleached flaxen color of fall. takes the eye from spring to fall from greenish to brilliant summer to beige and all the shades of brown. makes red flash. red without it is blood, with it is fire. red is passion. yellow is life. the St.John's Wort is coming, then the Black-eyed Susans, then the mums. the flowers know the direction of the sun. is the goldenrod really a darker yellow than the buttercup or birdfood trefoil or do we see it through a darker eye, the eye that fears the coming on of winter? lyric poetry is green and yellow. novels are red and blue. epic is too, with lots of black. bananas. lemons. yellow is such a wonderful shape, and stipple textured.

Remembering a scifi story I read not long ago. A man steps off the board walk when time travelling and changes history...of course we accept that the building of the board walk did not change history but authors get away with what they get away with by pointing the finger firmly in another direction...rather like dog training. Anyway, if whatever we do changes the universe in unforeseeable ways, not just us, not just two-legged beings with opposable thumbs but everything on earth, or in the universe makes a difference, has unlimited power to make a difference, but, and here's the joke, what sort of difference? We have, in our Judeo-Xn enclave, been taught that 'all things work together for good'...all things!! For years the justification for disease and pain and unwanted children and the agony of war was that out of evil might come good. People grew from their suffering, might be re-formed by pain. What if the reverse were true. That out of all our good works come poverty and disease and war. Where is the incentive? The best life might be the one which makes as little difference as possible! The contemplative life, the ascetic life, just being.

When the roll is called up yonder who'll be there?

Emma fell asleep still in volume 145, still looking for more clues to the R whom her grandmother had hidden for so long. Emma needed to sleep. They'd set their alarm clocks for 5 am. Mike's plane, intended for business folks who'd get to the west coast in time to do afternoon deals if they were still conscious, left early and the limousine insisted on picking him up two and a half hours before his flight.

CHAPTER V

TUESDAY, JUNE 2

IN THE MORNING, LYING IN BED, listening to her Dad get ready for the limousine, Emma remembered the papers she had removed from the linen cupboard. They would have to be boxed and sent to her place in Kentucky too, she supposed. Where would she put all this junk and when would she look at it when she got back to her real life? She got up hurriedly and, still in her sleep shirt, went to look at the papers. On the top of the pile were spare copies of scholarly articles and notices from conferences and then, forming a vast cliff of paper, the typescripts, bound individually with double strands of heavy crochet cotton, of several books. At first Emma thought that these were earlier drafts of Gertrude's books. The pages, when she flipped through a couple of the bundles, were much annotated. But there were too many bundles. Then Emma briefly wondered whether her grandmother had had a hidden academic persona, which was not impossible given the mystery that seemed to be building around her. The drafts bore no titles and no indication of author but the off-prints of academic articles at the top of the pile were all written by Roger Coventry; some articles even identified him as professor at the local university. The R. from the journal? Maybe. A name certainly might be a help. Emma was quite excited. She went immediately to the phone book. Her farewell to her father was perfunctory. Mar accompanied him down to the lobby. Emma dialed the university. Then she realized that it was a bit early. She went back to sorting dishes and silverware until the secretaries arrived in their offices.

At nine, a cup of coffee by her elbow, Emma dialed the university again. She had had time to get excited and nervous. As soon as the canned voice of the operator came on the line inviting her to enter the number of the party to whom she wished to speak, Emma realized that she didn't know what to ask. She waited through an entire menu, cursing voice mail, and when she got a live voice, she asked for Roger Coventry; she put a 'professor' in front, just in case. No one there by that name.

She hung up and went back to look at the off-prints. The titles were interesting, peculiar but not exactly helpful. There was "Death and Pollution: A study of river burials," "Death in the West: Where the sun goes," "Mining for god: Salt, gold, copper, brass and early civilizations' concepts of god." Well. She took the articles with her to the phone as insurance and dialed the University again. This time she asked for the department of Religion. After Emma had read the titles of several of the articles to the secretary in the department of Religion, she was referred to the Department of Geography. The secretary of the Geography Department had never heard of Roger Coventry. However, Emma was learning as she went and this time she asked to be connected to whatever senior professor might be in his or her office. At last she was connected to someone who recognized the name; this person was also puzzled.

"Professor Coventry died last fall – um – I forget exactly – but he'd been retired for some years. Were you interested in any particular area of study? Perhaps I could recommend someone else?"

"Did he have family in the area? Anyone I could contact?"

The voice on the other end became hesitant. "Hm, well, his wife might still be in the area but I wouldn't know where she's living. Professor Coventry retired, as I said, some years ago and he did not maintain contact with the department. Was there any other way in which I could assist you?" This question was purely rhetorical but Emma was desperate to hold onto the first person who'd had any light, however, dim, to shine on her ignorance.

"Would you be aware of there being anyone at the university with whom he did maintain contact?" She noticed she was sliding into the unknown person's circumlocution, but she didn't care. When with Romans....

"Hm, well, I'm afraid I can't specify anyone just at the moment. Perhaps you'd leave the particulars which would allow us to reach you and if I recall anyone who might be suitable, I'll be able to forward the information to you."

"'Don't call us; we'll call you' in academic dress," thought Emma as she sighed and gave her grandmother's phone number. She wondered whether Roger too had had the up-your-nose accent and tone of the professor on the phone. So much for that. She pulled the phone book from its drawer and began searching for Coventrys. There were three or four in the larger centres and one or two in most of the others covered in the area phone book. She'd save that for later. First perhaps it would be useful to ask the women in her grandmother's group what they knew about Roger or George. She had the journals of course, if she could only find time to read them.

Her father had boxed the journals and labeled them with her name. She wondered how she'd get such a huge lot home. Mike had called her to witness the books and his organization before he boxed them. On a sudden hunch she looked at the other boxes which had been taken from the dining room shelves. Yes, what she had thought were simply reference works on religion and geography and history, the books next to her grandmother's books, were the works of Roger Coventry. She counted twenty-two of them.

Over lunch she got out the final journal again, 195. She gave her mother the 145th to look at, really to keep her busy and to avoid the charge of rudeness. She was being rude. But it was as if Gertrude were being rude too, or purposefully difficult. Emma skimmed most of the final journal again and found only six references to R. other than the one on the last page. No reference to George. Each of the references to R. had to do with editing or typing. Gertrude had the rough drafts.

Emma went to the boxes in which she'd packed Roger's rough drafts and held one of Gertrude' pages and one of Roger's side by side looking carefully at type and paper. Yes, maybe. But it would need an expert to match them for sure. Suddenly she remembered the computer. Behind her suitcase in a corner of the study she found the laptop and plugged it in to the adapers on Gertrude's desk. A few moments to warm up and a few to search and there were Gertrude's files. Sure enough. RC1, RC2, RC3 and so on to RC Bib. Roger Coventry's books, at least the most recently written chapters, were on her grandmother's computer. For one wild moment she returned to her original theory that Gertrude had written academic books under the assumed name of Roger Coventry, but she recalled her conversation with the distant professor at the University. There was a real R.C. and her grandmother had typed his books for him. Why? And how ever had she found the time?

Gertrude had books of her own – the most recent was also on her hard drive, as were her Christmas letters and several articles for magazines. She'd put in brackets at the top of each article the magazine to which she might send it, or was it where she had already sent it? A copy of her funeral instructions and her kitchen door list, updated in May 1997, these Emma also found. But she returned to the books. Gertrude's, filed as Oliph1.doc, Oliph2.doc, etc., a mystery set in Oliphant, was indeed almost finished. Or what appeared to be part of a final chapter was written in any case, if a chapter titled "No Further Entries" could be presumed to be a final chapter.

Emma decided it was time to call Victoria Something. There could be income from this book too and it might be crass but wise to publicize it along with Gertrude's death. Yes, definitely, a phone call. Did Gertrude need the money from typing other folks books? If so why only Roger Coventry? Emma doubted it. She had no idea how much time it would take to type a book, edit and format it but she doubted it was well paid and Gertrude didn't seem likely to have enjoyed the "fiddly, fussy bits" as she'd called the work in one of the references to R. in the journal. I loathe the "fiddly, fussy bits and things like Bibliography above all," to be specific, was what she'd written in an April journal entry.

Emma found the scrap of paper on which she'd scribbled the agent's number before going out to dessert the night before. As she listened to the phone ringing she wondered what her uncle might have told this woman. As it transpired, when Victoria, whose last name ironically enough was Seller, answered and found herself ear to mouth with

Gertrude's granddaughter, all that Eric had told the agent was that Gertrude was dead.

"Oh, I'm so sorry to hear about your grandmother. She's one of my favourite people. So calm, and certain about her work. I was shocked to receive the message on my machine when I came in the morning." So that's the contact her uncles were having with the people for whom Emma had so many questions. "What can I do for you?"

Emma asked whether her uncle's message had included an invitation to the memory party if Victoria would care to come, and then moved on to Gertrude's final book. Did Victoria know there was a book almost finished?

Yes.

What would happen to it?

Victoria agreed that publishing the book as soon as possible, in conjunction with a restrained campaign describing it as the last of Gertrude Moseley's works, might very well boost sales of the final book and of some of the previous ones.

"By the way," said Emma as casually as possible, "there is a quantity of paper here, journals and drafts and so forth. Who might be interested in buying those? And all of Roger Coventry's drafts and papers are here also."

"You have to understand that while I enjoyed working with Gertrude, and while she had a dedicated following, Moseley is hardly a household word nor of great academic interest. I'm not sure that the papers and journals would be of interest to many people."

Emma sensed a drop in temperature. Victoria clearly did not want to work too hard, or perhaps, to be fair, she did not want to work at something out of her area of expertise. "There are 195 journals. Just the quantity would seem to be worth something!" Emma protested.

"One – hundred – and – ninety – five? You see you'd need an editor or a researcher to deal with all that. You might find that one of her readers would be qualified. If I learn of anyone I'll suggest the interested parties contact you. Who will have all the material? You might mention the journals in the obituary you give to the newspapers. If you haven't done that already I could prepare a draft and send it out to the larger papers." Emma, ignoring – forgetting in the heat of the moment and rationalizing later when she realized what she had done – her grandmother's instructions, gave Victoria Seller the details of Gertrude's life and death and asked that the literary details be filled in appropriately.

Emma said she was taking the journals to Kentucky and realized that whereas she'd been thinking in terms of boxes in the basement she was now committed to having the materials accessible to researchers. An incongruous vision of her living room fitted up like the reading room of the British Library, complete with dome and balconies, floated in the air between her and the phone. "Then you have no contract which continues after Gertrude's death? The book she's just finishing and all of her other materials are no longer of interest to you, is that correct?" She could be chilly too.

"The book she is just finishing is one I've agreed to see through publication. I'll take a disk of that if you have one. When that is done I've no further contractual obligation to Gertrude Moseley; that is correct. Her publishers – I can give you a list of those involved – will still be under obligation to the estate, or vice versa. You could find the publishers by looking at the books but it will be easier if I just print off a list of names and addresses."

"You didn't say anything about Roger Coventry's books. I have one of those almost finished on her computer also."

"I've never heard of Roger Coventry." Victoria said rather shortly and their conversation languished into farewells with a commitment to meet at the party on Friday. Emma made a mental note to get her uncles to do more than leave a message for Victoria. She wanted a lawyer to check the contract for the Oliphant book before she handed over the disk.

While she was at the phone she turned again to the Coventry listings. If R.C. had a completed book on Gertrude's computer what publisher was waiting to receive it? She picked up the receiver and sat there a while passing it thoughtfully from hand to hand until the recorded message came on asking her to hang up, "Please, hang up now!" She did. She sat and stared at the phone. Then she started dialing. She dialed only the R. Coventrys. There were six. At least a third of Coventrys were R. Coventry, she noticed. Surely a failure of imagination on the part of the clan: Roger, Robert, Ralph or Rafe, she supposed, or Rose of course, and Ruth. The first two calls, both in the largest municipality listed, reached rather puzzled persons who did not know of a Roger Coventry who'd been a professor at the University. Two had answering machines. Damn. She left messages anyway. She'd decided to play ignorant of his death and see what happened. She flipped through to the next town. A person answered; he said he'd had calls for Roger before and it was very inconvenient and he wished this Coventry fellow weren't so well known, or would identify himself more clearly in the phone book so other folks weren't always being disturbed. This call suggested to Emma that she might have found the correct municipality to call and as there were only two R. Coventrys listed for that town the other might be the one she was seeking. She circled the remaining Coventry and then sat and stared at the phone a while. Suddenly nervous again, she put the phone down and went and pulled all of Roger's and Gertrude's books out of the boxes.

Mar, coming in from delivering another load of clothes to the Salvation Army was not pleased. "Emma, we're packing, not unpacking. What are you thinking of!"

"I want to know who Roger Coventry is, why his books are in grandma's computer and in her cupboards and on her shelves. Did you ever read her dedications? Who bothers, right? Look!" Emma handed Gertrude's books to her mother one at a time open at the dedications. Each one ended in the same way. Some of them were entirely and exactly the same. Probably were cut and pasted from one book to the next.

For my family who love me, my friends who encourage me, and for my first reader who waits patiently for me to finish.

Mar read. This was from the most recently published book and the one before was the same. Some of the earlier books acknowledged the help of various libraries or police or specified a family member or friend who'd provided information but always they ended with the same sentence. They had read the sentence, if they had bothered to read the business at the front. They'd seen reference to "a first reader" and none of them had ever noticed, or asked who it might be, had assumed that it was one of them, for she sometimes read sections out to them as a book progressed.

Then Emma pushed several of Roger Coventry's books toward her mother. Beginning with about the fifth book, the last line of each Preface read,

I reserve special thanks for my editor and first reader who deciphers my inscrutable writing, inspires the text and always welcomes the next act.

"So what, Emma? Maybe he needed an editor; everyone has a reader. These are not surprising, or in any way different from any other Prefaces or Dedications. Please, pack this stuff out of the way and help me carry boxes down to the car."

Nonetheless as Emma balanced boxes, poked elevator buttons with her elbow, juggled her way through the security doors and loaded the car her mind went around in the same circles it had been following since the moment the women had told her the dog was dead. She sensed she'd run the route long enough to wear ruts in her brain. Given that there was something curious about Gertrude's death, given that she felt something was missing, she had to come to grips with her suspicions. Who did the evidence point to?

Emma realized that she'd been thinking of R. and George for two days. She'd now put a name to R. but was no closer to finding out much about him and she'd overlooked George and the eight women. She'd not given a thought to those sweet elderly women who'd hurried the dog into his grave and reminded Geoff that his mother wanted to be cremated. They had no way of knowing about Gertrude's instructions – or did they? So that was another question for her list. What list she wondered. Why was she making a list of questions? But her mind continued with its questions as she labelled and lifted and balanced.

She went over what she could recall hearing about the afternoon of her grandmother's death. The four women who had arrived together at 5 p.m. had the best alibis. They'd presumably been together since around 3 and, according to Natasha, Gertrude had been alive just before that, speaking to her about what wine to pick up on her way from the airport. Of course Natasha might be lying. She'd certainly made sure everyone knew what time it was when she'd spoken to Gertrude, and she had not arrived at the cottage until after the body had been found. Which left Maude and Edwina and Jean as being just as likely candidates as the elusive George to have seen Gertrude that afternoon, to have killed her.

Emma was alarmed at having thought the words and then surprised by her alarm. She'd been curious; that was natural. She'd felt something was suspicious about Gertrude's death but until this moment she had been incapable of suggesting that her grandmother had been murdered. For a while Emma considered her reluctance to consider murder. Her love for her grandmother? Her unwillingness to believe anyone hated or feared her grandmother that much? If her grandmother had been murdered there might be other suspects, there might be other victims. A crazy person on the loose. Her aunts and uncles? Her parents. Her mind was running now. Furious and jealous and suffering yet another bruise from the slamming of the security door on her elbow, she realized that her grief was a huge wave pushing her anger before it. She was sobbing quite loudly when she turned the key in the apartment door and shoved a load of pictures from the couch so that she could sit down. Mar stood in the hall for a moment watching her daughter. Grief slams as unexpectedly and as painfully as a heavy door. Sharp corners hit vulnerable bones.

After a long silence broken only by eye wiping and nose blowing Mar said, "Is your search for information about Gertrude's past your way of dealing with her death?"

Emma had to admit that this was so, but after another silence she added, "You know how we felt about the way she sometimes made us look in her books. Then she'd smile that calm smile and say, 'It's fiction, my dear. Why would you think that person is you?' Others may have thought they recognized themselves too. Maybe people less balanced than we are – if we are. She had secrets, maybe large secrets about which we know nothing. I am almost convinced that someone killed her." The words were out. She'd said them. And she felt relieved. "Yes, grief is part of my motivation. But I think someone killed her. That's the other part of my motivation. Now I want to know who and why."

Once the words had been spoken they finally became real to Emma. The realization had been pushing its way forward all afternoon and now it was in the open. She'd been avoiding her own discomfort.

"It isn't just that grandma is dead. It's that I don't believe the death was natural. Everyone else is acting as if it were to be expected. Too bad and all that, but she was an old lady and she's dead; let's get on with it." Emma wondered whether many elderly people were murdered and dismissed, but before she wandered off into another escape from the subject she brought herself sharply back.

"I think she was murdered, Mom. Not in a mystery book. In real life. She was well when she spoke to those women earlier in the day. There was no sign that she'd been in pain and struggled to get to the phone or even tried to get her medication out of the bathroom. She might have lain down for her afternoon nap and died peacefully. We know grandma loved her afternoon nap, but she had company for lunch and she expected company for dinner. I'm not sure whether that was an occasion for a nap. Perhaps it was. But I keep coming back to the dog. Why would the dog die at the same time?"

"I don't know, Emma."

"It was a rhetorical question, Mom!"

"No, it wasn't, Emma. Your grandmother taught you better than that. A rhetorical question is one to which the expected answer is clear and probably implied in the question. You don't know the answer to your question; therefore it's not rhetorical!"

"Oh, Mom!" Emma groaned.

And then a heartbeat later gasped. "But I could find the answer to my question. I could find out how the dog died." She was almost shout ing by the time she finished her sentence. "I have the dog's body. I wonder where I could get the equipment. I'll call around. See who I might know in this part of the country. I could do an autopsy on the dog. Send the results to the local police, insist that they act. How much more do we have to do here? When can we go north? I have to see some of the women but they live around Kitchener and Waterloo and I could drive up to the cottage and back tomorrow morning, get a sample of blood and tissue analyzed in the labs at Guelph while I'm at it. Do you want to come with me?"

"Of course not, Emma. You're crazy. You're overreacting. We still have the kitchen and bathroom to clear out and the whole place to clean."

Marilla paused and then added, "but if you think going up there will make you feel better, then, you'd better go. I'll maybe get one of your aunts to help me finish up here. Which reminds me, we're due at Sue's for supper in half an hour. I'll beat you to the shower."

It wasn't hard for Marilla to beat her daughter to the shower. Emma stood for some time still hearing the echo of the word 'murder' repeating in her ears, in her head, against the walls of her grandmother's apartment.

Dinner was ready when they arrived and conversation turned away from death and funerals. The shift occurred naturally as Marilla and Sue considered what furnishings from Gertrude's apartment might be appropriate for each of Emma's cousins. It seemed unlikely that Marilla, Eric and Geoff would want anything but souvenirs. Their children, however, might make use of much of the furniture and linen and kitchen equipment. They agreed to get as many people as possible together at the apartment on Thursday night to carry off the things they wanted. That would leave only the orphaned, unloved, unneeded furnishings for the Salvation Army to take away. How awful to be a chair or plate or table cloth that no one wanted! Such details occupied most of the meal and Emma had been tuned out for some time when she realized that her aunt and uncle were staring at her. She replayed their conversation in her mind and she heard again, this time in her mother's voice, the word 'murder.'

"Well," she knew that she sounded defensive and hated it, "I can't think of any other way to explain the dog's dying at the same time as grandma."

Geoff looked thoughtful. He hadn't said much during the meal and now he excused himself and went out to the patio to smoke. The women took their coffee to the TV room and Emma cleared the table and piled the dishes by the sink before going to join her uncle outside. He'd almost finished his cigarette.

She stood in silence. It was hard to tell what her uncles were thinking. She wasn't used to thinking about her uncles thinking, she realized. Children accept adult presence. They don't expect adult complexity until they are themselves adult. Then it sometimes comes as a shock.

"If you are right, Emma, if you are right, there is also a murderer." He looked at her thoughtfully. "Let the police deal with it."

"They already have. And they haven't. It's not good enough." There was another long silence. Finally, as her uncle blew the third smoke ring and killed his cigarette in the pot of pink impatiens, she sighed, "I'll call them. Okay?"

They stood there and watched the daffodils moving slightly in the evening breeze.

July 13, 1990, Friday   *Oliphant   6:30 AM*

Hot. The garden is lush. It rains almost every weekend. The marguerites are in full control of both the back and front lawns. I let them flourish in June, only mowing what I hope is an artistic curve around them. They cover about 1/4 of the yard and are absolutely beautiful and absolutely a gift of nature. the bladder campion grows in a wild corner by the lilacs and it is interspersed with spurge. Later there will be Bouncing Bet there to the north, beyond the drive, but this is the time of the daisies. This year a mullien has volunteered and with perfect design sense rises like a spire in the centre of the white ballerinas. We walked this morning way out on the beach. The water is so low that I could walk from the east of Lonely Island to Rutherford's point and scarcely get my knees wet. People take lawn chairs and sit out where boats anchor in other years. Very odd. The up side is that the water comes barely to the rocks in front of my cottage and I don't need to wear beach shoes to reach the sand when I swim.

Odd. Odd is something unexpected. Nothing in itself. If I expect rain and the sun shines, that's odd. If I usually walk on rocks and now have sand, no bruised toes or scraped shins, that's odd. If a parent expects compliance and gets independence that's odd and we do not like the odd. Odd challenges us even when it is pleasant and it so rarely is.

I digress.

My trips to Oliphant rarely involve digressions. The road stretches infinitely north. The promise of digression is there. Signs point to parks and wool shops and butchers of pork, but I do not digress. I load the car with my suitcase, computer and groceries, put the dog on a lead, gather up my purse and keys and shut the apartment door. A short trip down in the elevator and a moment of effort to transfer the stuff to the front seat of the car and we are off. Three hours later we step out at the back porch and are in a green world. If I could teleport I would.

My life has been a straight line: birth, school, marriage, children, career. I don't like superhighways but I stay on paved roads. I love the possibilities of side roads, of shady trees and sheltering hedges, the occasional glimpse of a stream, and I can't help wondering whether somewhere there was an adventure, a different career, another lover to change my life. R. is my only digression onto a winding gravel road.

Anna is visiting this week. She arrived on Wednesday afternoon and will leave tomorrow. Hard to believe the number of years she's been visiting me here, a few days each summer. She reads her erotica to me and we wriggle and giggle still, thank heavens, and I edit the odd word. She's made bundles at it over the years. She tells everyone that she made enough to allow her to quit teaching – which is partly true I suppose. There was also the problem of school board members discovering what she did in her spare time. Strictly speaking there was nothing illegal about it but they didn't like the idea that the principal of one of their elementary schools was writing smut – their word. Moral turpitude used to be the word in the Education Act. Strictly speaking, the writing of smut might be grounds for dismissal. I wonder how they found out. I didn't tell them – though I certainly threatened to a few years ago, well quite a while ago now. I wonder whether I wrote about it then – maybe not – though it's possible that I make this same entry every summer when she visits.

I remember how my heart beat when she told me about meeting R. Odd that they would meet. It was quite accidental or serendipitous really – nothing to do with me – she and R. also went for coffee after his visit to her school. I say 'also' because he and I began our relationship after he'd come to talk to a group of us, Social Workers doing some upgrading, learning about cultural differences, and we went for coffee after the meeting. He wasn't really an expert on the topic, but he was on the University's rota of speakers and came as close as anyone else on the list to being able to entertain us with the idea of where our clients might have come from. When Anna met him she was doing research for her erotica, she said, and that was why she went out for a drink with him a couple of times after work; she had then, and has now no idea that he is mine. I do not believe he told her and I certainly never did – but I did suggest, and point out the consequences to her marriage if she persisted, that he was not a suitable lover for her. I wonder whether she remembers him too when she visits me.

CHAPTER VI

WEDNESDAY, JUNE 3

ON WEDNESDAY MORNING, before leaving for Oliphant, Emma
made several phone calls, one of them to the OPP in Wiarton, whom
she urged to reconsider her grandmother's death. She wasn't sure what
response she got from the constable who took her call. Perhaps, like
her parents, the woman on the phone regarded her as hysterical. She
regretted phoning and hoped that she would have time to stop in Wiarton before she started home from the cottage, but she had other chores
on her list. The first chore took her to the Veterinary Clinic of a one-
time classmate in Guelph. Then she headed up the road to Oliphant,
trying once again to count the number of Veterinary clinics she passed
and once again losing track as she gazed at the lushness of the mead-
ows beside the meandering North Saugeen and passed the clinic on the
north edge of Chesley.

Approaching Oliphant she wished she'd been more determined to
bring her mother. The dog would be heavy and awkward with no trol-
leys or hydraulic lifts. She also realized that a witness might be a good
idea. She had no doubt about her mother's ability to help lift heavy
burdens. They'd been moving furniture for three days.

Then she realized that she needed an impartial person, preferably
with muscles – doesn't everyone! Her mother would not have been a
completely disinterested witness. So just before reaching her destination, she stopped at the bustling garage and shop which advertised itself all year round as the Oliphant SkiDoo agency and had just put up
a banner advertising SeaDoos too. She offered to rent a workman for

an hour maybe a bit more – unskilled labour – $50. Conversation stopped. Sudden silence hung in the huge garage which a moment before had been loud with business.

The dark space, heavy with metallic sounds, redolent of oil and male sweat might have been a smithy 85 years earlier. Sparks lit the dark. Machinery and parts hung from the ceiling and walls. A new season was about to begin. Boats were being readied for the water. Repairs which people had postponed in the fall were now urgent. A young chap, hanging about waiting for repair or replacement of a frost plug which had blown in the winter, grinned at the men in the shop and offered to take her money. As they got into the car she explained what she needed. Did he look relieved or disappointed?

She warned him, as they drove north swooping around the shore past several very old cottages, one the neat little log structure with flamingos, boarded up more summers than it was open, and begging for a family to play croquet on its wide front lawn, that the job would not be pleasant. As far as she knew the dog had been placed in one or two layers of plastic garbage bag. But the dog was large and, depending on the state of rigor when the constable was removing him from the living room floor, might not have fit neatly into a bag so that one end could be tied tightly. In addition a certain amount of dragging and heaving was likely to have ripped the garbage bags. She had brought with her a heavy gauge of plastic on which to place the bags; she didn't plan to open the bags at the site, but she felt it only fair to warn the young man that the smell, despite the cool June weather might be rather strong. He swallowed, as she explained how they'd move the bags onto the heavy sheet and then slide it onto the zip-up body bag before lifting it into the trunk of her rental car, keeping it in the one position as much as possible. She hoped the car rental folks could find enough air freshener to rejuvenate their trunk; they at least didn't have to drive to Guelph with the body in the car with them.

As she was describing the worst case to prepare her assistant, she had visions of having to resuscitate him and lift him from the rue and carry him to the car. Then memories of Sinisters past rose and she found herself describing Gertrude's dogs.

"She got the first pup when she retired, as soon as possible after. She'd planned to get a Bull Mastiff. Done all the research, determined that Bull Mastiffs had the formidable size, and low energy requirements to suit her perfectly. She was aging and she lived alone; she wanted a protector and an incentive to get out of her apartment and exercise but she was aware that sometimes the dog would not get to run far or fast. Then, suddenly, just as she was expecting the owners of the mother to tell her to come and look at the pups, a call came to tell her that the bitch had miscarried, not a common occurrence but it was a first litter and may have been too big – too many pups struggling *in utero* for sustenance. Anyway, Gertrude looked in the paper that night and there were blue Dobermans advertized. Gertrude had never heard of Blue Dobes but, intrigued, she called. Of course, once she went and saw the pups it was all over. So much for research. She walked out with the largest of the litter, a placid, cheerful little guy who grew into a placid, cheerful huge guy who was big enough to match her criteria but needed about five times the exercise. She'd planned all along to call him Sinister, left hand. She said there were already lots of dogs named Dexter, right hand, and the canine world needed some balance."

Emma lapsed into silence as she remembered Gertrude talking about her dogs. Her shadow side, her left side she said Sinister was, and as he matured he became very much her shadow side. He gave her power to walk the streets at night, to enjoy the dark and mystery and the quiet of the streets after a long day. Sinister's height and strength encouraged her to walk tall and he introduced her to strangers. He gave her freedom.

Emma remembered the first Sin best because he'd been her constant companion during her summers with her grandma. He'd often had to play the role of horse, being led and bossed about, though Gertrude was firm about no riding. He'd also bitten her more than once. Her finger automatically traced the tiny scar by her ear. Placid or not he was capable of violence. Emma's first surgical stitches had been sewn in the Wiarton emergency room, on her – not by her. Perhaps Sin had been jealous, perhaps not. He'd loved all the grandchildren but sometimes treated them as litter mates and he had a short temper with puppies if they wrestled too roughly or prodded too deeply or confined him. So long as the children were willing to pet him and lead him about and drop food to him at the table he was a happy dog, even in old age, for by then the grandchildren, being pretty much the product of the same decade as he, were reaching the age which best appreciates dogs. That age of child also least appreciates unusual or healthy food, especially liver, spinach, and anything exotic or mixed. Sin lay quietly under the table benefiting and adoring. When he died Gertrude thought seriously about severing her ties to pets. At over 70 the effort of training a pup and dealing with its energy was a far from engaging prospect.

After a year of confinement, however, her need for companionship and exercise, her passion for evening walks, her delight in the lives of strangers who stopped to talk to the dog, became overwhelming; she'd even missed the responsibility and social excuse, the need to return to wherever the dog was at regular intervals, to feed and relieve him. She'd called Emma several times asking her to be on the lookout for mature Dobes which needed rescue. And one night, when Emma was almost finished her Vet training, a female Doberman and five surviving pups had been brought into the emergency clinic from a puppy mill. She chose very carefully for her grandmother, observing the pups over several days as they gained strength and energy.

More Sinister would need to be even more placid than his predecessor but he especially needed to be intelligent enough to learn without exhausting his mistress. As before, the largest of the litter, also blue, was the most suitable dog. More Sinister was not so tall as the 33" Sinister but, regardless of his difficult beginnings, he was still over the standard for the breed by about 2". Gertrude liked the size, not for its imposing presence, though that was good too, but because it allowed her to rest her hand on the dog's shoulder without stooping and Gertrude was not a short woman. Thus she could train and control him without folding herself in half and she could use the dog for support sometimes, especially on icy streets. Emma remembered the stately stride of the huge dogs at the age of two or three. In memory she saw them loping like young deer across the low foliage of the fens, ears forward, eyes alert for frogs hopping out of the way, tail straight up, every muscle oiled and trigger ready. They had the beauty of a horse a moment before it takes a jump. The Sinisters had always reminded her of her horses because of their huge chests and muscled hind quarters.

"This guy will weigh just over 100 pounds." Emma had begun to speak aloud again, realizing that the young man needed to know how heavy the load was going to be if he were to lift effectively.

As she was talking they swung onto the causeway, hitting a few pot-holes hard before slowing to accommodate the road. Then they were in the yard. She retrieved a pad of paper from her purse and asked the young man to write his name address, phone number, the time and date and place and any other circumstances of the occasion that would help to explain what he remembered about this job. She also wrote a similar account. Then she left the papers and pen handy on the front seat. She reasoned that after they'd dug up the body the young man might not have much stomach for writing out an affidavit.

Emma fumbled a few moments with keys and then opened the shed where there were shovels, rakes and garden gloves. Armed with these and pushing the garden cart they headed for the gate. Inside the fence, the marker still stood where Jean had put it, but no marker was really required. The ground rose at least three inches and the chips which Gertrude had used to cover paths had been carelessly redistributed. Now Emma and her assistant scraped the chips to one side and then raked very gently to find exactly where the body was. It was not deep. The bags, there were two, end for end and maybe more underneath, she didn't check, were fairly intact. There was only a faint odour; per-haps pin-holes pocked the bottom where the plastic had been shifted into place. They spread the heavy plastic sheet between the hole and the body bag, donned plastic gloves and then garden gloves, poised themselves to heave the body upwards and sideways, and felt gently for a part of the body to grip firmly. One heave and they had the bags onto the plastic.

"Done." He smiled up at her. They were head to head and bent al-most double still.

"Well almost. That's the tricky part I suppose. Here. Get a good handful of your end of the plastic and lift it onto the bag. Now these flaps have to be folded over and zipped and sealed to prove that the load you put in the body bag is the load which has the autopsy this afternoon." They did this in silence and then, each taking an end of the bag, smoothly lifted and slid it into Gertrude's favourite wheelbarrow, a large-wheeled affair from Lee Valley Tools which had most often been used to carry children, towels, chairs, buckets and shovels to the beach. Emma smiled fondly at the cart as the young man maneuvered it slowly to the car and they heaved the load into the trunk. The smell would, after all, be tolerable on the drive south. Emma went back and filled the hole; mindful of the guests on the weekend she spread the chips evenly over the path, even tramped a little back and forth before storing the equipment in the shed and locking up. While she'd been away the young man had completed his affidavit and she took some time to write a few notes also before sealing both of their papers in an envelope given to her by the same colleague who'd provided the body bag. She hoped she'd been scrupulous enough about the evidence.

Emma looked up at her assistant as she licked the envelope. She'd been impressed by his helpfulness and told him so. Then she drove him back to McKenzie's SeaDoo. His boat was still unfinished.

He was about to say something, had drawn in his breath, when she stopped him. "Perhaps we should get someone, the boss comes to mind, to witness your signature. He could use the envelope.'

Her passenger swung out of the car and made his way to the back of the shop where an elderly man was supervising the installation of a new cleat. They talked; the older man nodded, glanced toward Emma and signed. The men lounging by the door watched, smiling, as Emma paid the young man and said good-bye. She drove south, past Evergreen Campground first, then turned south at the Women's Institute corner. It wasn't Saturday, and in any case it was too early in the year for the weekly flea market on the grounds of the Women's Institute.

✳

She saw it in her mind's eye: the wood-crafted bird houses, and children's toys, the pickles, jams, canned beans and carrots, the bread and sticky buns, the tables piled with second hand books, the junk and the fresh produce all in predictable places around the edges of the lot. Up

83

and down the road were cars parked, and in a huge lot across the road. Where did all the people come from week after week? Maybe once a summer someone in the family would venture inside the Women's' Institute building, usually a small person needing a toilet, and there find more of the same: food and crafts, fudge and beads, cleaning products, a coffee bar, and kids screaming. Emma was lost in her memories almost to Allenford. She realized that she had not gone to Wiarton. Then she began to plan what orders she'd write for the person doing the autopsy.

When she'd looked in the phone book on her grandmother's desk for veterinarians who might have been students at Guelph with her ten years before, she'd been lucky. The second woman she called offered her help and office to Emma any evening but she then went on to tell Emma of a classmate who was now teaching at the Veterinary College. He was surprisingly easy to reach. When Emma explained her needs to him, he had been most helpful and pointed out that it was likely better if she did not perform the examination herself. If she could get the body to him by 3 in the afternoon he'd have some students look at it and then he'd take a look at their work. She could get a preliminary report later that evening, though the blood tests and so forth might take a little longer. Would that do her? She was much obliged. She'd drop the body off, drive out to interview a couple of the women and come back in time to talk to him and his students as they finished up.

She looked at her watch. She was going to be cutting it pretty fine. So she pushed the speed limit a bit on the Silvercreek Parkway, changed lanes a few times on the Hanlon and eased into the left turn lane at College Avenue a minute or two before 3. She got lost a few times and then, after she'd found the right building and a lane to take her around the building to the service bay, she had to beg help from a couple of sturdy looking students. They heaved the body onto a cart she'd found in the corridor when she was scouting around to be sure that she was in the right place. They also helped her wheel the cart to the appropriate lab. Having turned the dog over to her colleague and cautioned him about the seal and witnesses, she set a time for her return and set off to interview Natasha who'd booked a hotel room in Guelph.

Natasha was a dark, voluptuous woman. She'd maintained her black hair and fortunately her skin had survived the years well enough to let her get away with it, allowing her, even in her late 70s to wear brilliant colors and startling patterns. She also cultivated a trace of Russian accent, though it was unclear whether this was her own or borrowed from her parents who had been part of the exodus of Central Europeans searching for land and peace before the first World War. The accent was subtle but authoritative, as were the brilliant flowing clothes and the dark flashing eyes. Having buried two husbands she had certainly still the animal magnetism to encourage a third, had she wanted one.

Today Natasha had chosen a flowing purple robe with an embroidered surcoat in gold and orange. Bangles and chains gave the impression that she was carrying most of her wealth on her person. Emma wondered what she'd worn going through airport security. Natasha met Emma in the hotel lounge where a tea pot and scones were arranged on a coffee table. Emma considered crossing her palm with silver but restrained herself. Instead, having missed lunch, she gobbled a couple of scones. They talked about Natasha's most recent book and how exhausting tours were and that led naturally to her flight from Vancouver. Emma mentioned that her parent's flight had been early and she'd scarcely had time to rent the car before they arrived. Emma did not indicate which flight her parents had been on. Natasha was certain that her plane had arrived right on time, though her reasons for being certain were unclear. They talked a while about Vancouver too, Natasha with the enthusiasm of a new arrival, Emma as an escapee from Lotos land.

And then Emma asked whether the police had contacted Natasha since the Friday evening.

"No. Vy vould they? They had my statement." The accent thickened.

Could she recall what she'd told the police?

The dark eyebrows lifted a fraction.

Emma found herself talking too fast, asking too much too quickly but she couldn't stop herself. What flight had she told the police she'd taken? Where had she been when she'd phoned Gertrude? Had she been able to see a clock? Natasha said her flight was due at 2:30 and she'd picked up her baggage and filled in the forms to rent the car before she'd called Gertrude; so it must have been 3:00 mustn't it?

"Did you hear anyone in the background or did Gertrude say anything that might have led to think she was not alone?"

"No. Vat makes you think she was not alone?"
Emma hesitated a moment and then decided on discretion. "I don't know but there might have been a local person drop by. That would give another witness to grandmother's activity before she died. When did you change your watch to local time?" Emma asked, indicating a rather large and decorative watch which hung around Natasha's neck on a heavy chain.

"Oh, never! I travel constantly, you know, and I would ruin it by changing it so often. I've become very good at figuring the local time. My astrology requires conversions of time every time I construct a chart. I must know exactly the time of births and deaths and the events people consult me about to determine the stars, you know. I am quite accustomed to it."

"So what time do you estimate you arrived at Oliphant?"

"Ooooo. It must have been about after 6. I stopped for coffee and the washroom in Flesherton."

What was going on when you arrived at the cottage?"
Emma was considering how fast Natasha must have driven to arrive so soon after the others and also trying to recall whether her parents had taken the first flight out of Vancouver in the morning. Something about Natasha's times did not quite fit.

"Let me visualize it." Natasha appeared to be preparing for a séance; she furrowed her brow dramatically and placed her hands in an attitude of supplication. "Maude was carrying her box of books into the bunky. She stopped to put them down and we hugged. Jean was sitting in her car. She said she was just waiting for her taped book to finish. Maude called out to tell the others we'd arrived. We were still standing by her car window breathing in the air of cottage country, when several voices called out for us to come in. We hurried over to the door and there were the four of them all standing in the kitchen looking as if they'd seen visions from the spirit world. I'd never seen Anna look so frightened. That was what shocked me, I think. Anna and Melody and Sarah just don't get frightened. I don't recall who, Melody maybe, said Gertrude was dead. Then there I was crying and I don't remember what happened in what order after that."

"Did you go into the living room?"

"I don't think so. I stood at the door. The place was not good. I didn't want to go in. Even at bedtime I hurried to my room without looking where she'd been."

"Why did you stay?"

"Well, the policeman wanted to speak to each of us and when we'd answered his questions supper was ready and I was very tired. I didn't sleep well. I had nightmares."

"Who moved the dog?"

"I don't know. The police maybe. They were the only ones who could have aren't they? It's not likely the doctor did. He didn't stay long. It would have needed more than one."

"Oh?"

"Well, it took three women to get him into the cart in the morning. So he must have been heavy." So the women had used the cart also. Emma longed to ask more pointed questions but Natasha became evasive whenever the questions required specific answers. So she changed the topic completely.

"Did Gertrude ever speak of men named Roger or George? Were there any men with whom she spent a good deal of time?" Natasha's eyes widened. Instead of waiting to see what Natasha might say Emma pushed on, realizing even as she did it that it was a mistake.

"You did a horoscope for Gertrude many years ago. Did you do another more recently?"

"I don't know these men. Gertrude had family and, when she worked, colleagues, and when she started to write there were people who sold her books. But relationships, never. I would have known."

"But when you read her chart years ago you said that it was most unlikely that she would be without an intimate friendship with a man, living with a partner. Do you recall telling her that? Then isn't it likely that she had a lover?" Saying the words, suggesting that her grandmother should do such a thing, shocked Emma. What was happening that she kept saying words that she'd no idea she was going to say? Natasha looked surprised.

"How do you know about my reading? What I say to my clients is confidential."

"In her journals Gertrude wrote about all sorts of things. In the very first reading you gave her you suggested that it was unlikely that she'd live alone. Don't you remember?"

"That was twenty, thirty years ago. How would I remember?" Natasha shrugged and waved her hands dismissively.

"Would you say the same thing of her if she were alive today? Would your reading of her horoscope lead you to that conclusion?"

"Of course. The stars do not change their minds."

"I just meant that you have more experience and information now."

"I had enough then! It is possible that her family and her friends filled the requirements of the stars. I don't think so. Maybe it was the dogs. I never thought to work on their birth signs." Natasha looked as if she were seriously considering this.

"They were Cancers – both of them. Don't ask me why she would have told me that or why I would have remembered it. Perhaps you told her something about Cancers." Emma could see that Natasha was not going to tell her anything about Roger or George. She would need to find a better way to ask about the men.

"Cancers are very nurturing. It is a good thing that the dogs were Cancers." Then with a distinct change of tone, "Do you think it is proper that you read her journals?" Natasha asked.

"Why not?"

"Perhaps they should be destroyed unread."

"Good heavens. Why?" Emma was truly shocked by the suggestion.

"They are personal and you have not her personal permission to read them."

How had it happened that Natasha was on the offensive? Emma shook her head gently.

"There are 195 of them. She left them on the shelves of her apartment. It is hard to imagine that she did not expect them to be found and read. Destruction would be a fairly large undertaking in any event."

"We could have a bonfire at the cottage after we scatter the ashes. Think about it. How wonderful; her spirit drifting in ashes to the corners of the world."

"It doesn't even bear imagining. The journals are a gold mine of information about life in this century. They also could bring back all sorts of memories for me and I suppose for the rest of her family and friends."

"You are making a mistake, Emma."
The interview lasted only a few more moments and they parted without Natasha ever rising from the table. Emma did not offer to pay for her scones.

*

After she left Natasha at 5 o'clock, Emma still had a couple of hours to kill before returning to the lab. She took out Sue's list and checked Anna's address. As she'd thought, Anna lived just south of Elora. The phone in the lobby of the hotel was right by the exit. Emma called to assure Anna that she was still coming if it were convenient.

Had Emma had dinner? No. Emma had just barely finished tea. Well come along and have part of dinner anyway. Anna was just getting it ready. So Emma took the Victoria Street route to Marden and crossed over Highway 6, reaching Anna's half an hour later. She made note of the times, if only to consider when a driver from Guelph would have passed Elora. She would have to do the same thing from Kitchener. Perhaps when she went north on Saturday she'd go through Kitchener and time the drive north from there.

Anna's kitchen was warm. Anna may have been getting dinner together but she was also making orange marmalade and the sweet fog filled the room. Emma rested her hands and her notebook on the gently uneven surface of the table which centred the kitchen. The casserole would be ready in a few moments. In the meanwhile Anna poured coffee for both of them and then sat opposite. Emma reflected that the amount of coffee and tea which might be required to float her through all the interviews she had planned could leave her hopelessly caffeine addicted or insomniac. Did detectives claim from Workers' Compensation for bladder failure? At least the caffeine would help her to stay awake at night and get her through more journals. Natasha, it seemed, was afraid of what they might say.

"I'm trying to make sense of my grandmother's death, Anna. It would really help me if you could tell me what you remember about Friday. Not just what happened after you reached Oliphant but what happened on the drive up and before." Emma felt less nervous beginning her second interview.

"Let me see. Margaret, Melody, Sarah and I talked about going together to the retreat at...the meeting a month before the weekend meeting...we called them retreats. Is that starting early enough for you?" Emma couldn't tell whether Anna was being serious or mocking her. The voice was sweet and the eyes candid but there was a small twitch at the corner of the lips. Emma nodded.

"The three of them live over in Kitchener-Waterloo; so it was a bit awkward about who'd drive and where we'd leave our cars. They thought coming here was out of their way. It's not really, well no further out of the way than leaving the cars at Maude's in Arthur, which is what we finally agreed to do. We've done that several times before but usually because we're picking her up. This time she wasn't going to be home. She had an appointment of some sort, which is why she came up a bit later. But we left our cars, well Sarah's car, in Maude's drive. I don't know why we renegotiate this every time we drive up, every spring for thirty years, but we always do. It used to be because one of us would need to leave a car for a partner, or was going to be late from work. Now it's because some of us see better to drive at night or get better mileage, or have more comfortable car seats. We'd each phoned the other three or four times over the previous week. During those calls we'd also worked out who was bringing what food. Actually, Margaret doesn't bring food and I was sharing Saturday lunch with Edwina, but Melody and Sarah, who were bringing Saturday supper, wanted to be sure I'd have space in my trunk for their coolers as well as for their sleeping bags."

"Did Gertrude know who was driving with whom?"

"Gertrude? No, Gertrude didn't know much about our plans. She prepared Friday night soup and we did the rest. People were expected when they got there, any time after lunch on Friday, really. Once in a while someone would call Gertrude to see whether she had a rice cooker or a food processor for a special recipe. If she didn't, people would bring their own, or change the menu. I suppose she knew then what was on the menu. As it happened I did phone Gertrude that Friday morning to ask whether she had a crêpe pan. I thought asparagus crêpes would be nice for lunch. She laughed the way she always did when we asked about a piece of equipment she didn't have, and said, as she always did, 'Anna, this is a cottage, not a gourmet restaurant.'"

"She did hate gadgets to clutter up the kitchen. That's for sure. She and my dad used to have battles, mostly in fun I guess, about his love for kitchen gadgets. He gave her a battery operated pepper grinder with a light on the bottom once. I think it was a joke but maybe not. By the way, what time did you call?"

"About 11.30. I'd already bought the asparagus and made the batter and was starting to pack my cooler and bag. So I threw in my crêpe pan. We could have used the big fry pan, but the crêpe pan is dependable. Anyway. I had lunch and then packed my car around 1.30 and left here around 2. It's about half an hour to Maude's. I waited there for the others. They were later than they'd said. I expected them by 2.30 but it was closer to 3. I sat in Maude's garden and smoked. I knew it would be a long drive with no cigarettes."

"Did they say why they were late?"

"Margaret." This was said as if no further explanation were required. "When we got to the cottage everything looked just the same as usual. Gertrude's little car was tucked in next to the house. The glass door was open, but the screen was shut. That meant that it was a bit cool in the house. It might have been warm enough to have the door open at noon, but by 5 it was a bit chilly. I remember that. The fire in the dining room was cold, which suggested that if it had been lit at all on Friday it must have been early in the morning. I guess it was a warm day up there. We had all worn our winter jackets to drive up and bring in groceries and look around the garden; so it wasn't until after the excitement was over and we sat down that someone realized it was chilly and tried to stir up the fire. Melody set a new fire and got it going in the dining room while someone else was getting supper.

"So, what did we do first? We unloaded our stuff and carried it in. There was hot coffee in the thermos, ready, and I poured a cup and went out to look at the garden. It's restful looking at gardens, don't you think? Seeing what has survived the winter, and is, like us, still here. I'm sorry; that was thoughtless. Gertrude's lovage and beebalm and feverfew and lemon balm had been in the same places for thirty years. They had fresh green leaves and new life, as they'd had every year since she'd planted them. I chewed a leaf of lemon balm. Most of the garden is edible you know, except for the monk's hood and night-shade. They're edible too, I suppose, in their way." Anna broke off and looked into space a while. "Then I sat on the bench by the back door and finished my cigarette before going in. I figured I'd driven up; I didn't need to rush in and help put food away." She paused again. "I don't even want to talk about the next part."

"What exactly did you see when you went into the living room?"

"There were coffee cups on the coffee table and Gertrude was asleep on the couch. I thought she was asleep. I really did. She was lying there with a book beside her on the table, her glasses on the book, the bright beads of the glasses chain spread out. I reached down to take her hand, her elbow really, and she was cold. I stepped sideways very quickly and that's when I nearly fell over the dog. He wasn't over on his side, you know, he was lying with his head on his paws. He was stretched along the floor beside the couch!"

"You mean he was in a formal down position?" Emma found herself demonstrating, more or less, the curled haunches and head straight above front paws. She smiled rather apologetically as she straightened her legs, thanking her stars that she hadn't actually gone down on the floor to make her point.

"Yes." Anna smiled too.

"That must have made it quite awkward to put him into the bags later."

"I don't know. Melody asked the policemen to do that and they did. There were two garbage bags, end for end required."

"Yes, I noticed." Emma could have bitten her tongue. It had not been her intention to tell anyone about her exhumation of the dog. She tried, belatedly, to think what explanation she could give.

"You noticed?"

"Yes, I tidied the path for Saturday's guests." This was true so far as it went and perhaps Anna would not push it. Thank heavens she hadn't said that she'd noticed it that very morning!

"Who cleared the coffee cups away?"

"Pardon?"

"You said that there were coffee cups on the table in the living room."

"Margaret, I suppose. She was on dish duty."

"Did any other women go into the living room. Might someone else have cleared away?"

"Anyone might go into the living room. People going to the bathroom must cross one corner of that room. You know that. And we are of an age where we use a bathroom pretty frequently."

"Well, then. What happened after you tripped over the dog?"

"I must have cried out because next thing I recall I was in the middle of the kitchen and Melody and Margaret and Sarah had their arms around me. And then there was a greeting from the back yard and we knew that others had arrived. After that it all got rather noisy and busy, you know?"

"Did you and Edwina serve anything other than asparagus crêpes for lunch the next day?"

"There was a salad and a sticky cake and fruit for dessert. Edwina likes sweet stuff and she brought that. I used some herbs from the garden, chives and lovage mostly – a bit of thyme – in the white sauce for the crêpes. The parsley wasn't tall enough. Lovage is better in any case, stronger, a bit bitter. People could choose to have the sweets and starches or eat the fruits and vegetables as they pleased."

"When you went to bed had all the cups been cleared from the living room?"

"Oh, yes. I think so. Margaret is a demon, you know. Gertrude used to say she didn't need to do spring cleaning, because Margaret would do it for her."

"Did Gertrude ever mention Roger Coventry?"

"I don't think so. It's not a name I recall. She did have many male colleagues, however." Anna found Emma's leaps in conversation unsettling.

"I think it was a more intimate relationship than that," Emma persisted. "She had known him for many years. And Gertrude was aware that you also knew Roger. She wrote about it in her journal. When you phoned earlier that day, about the crêpe pan did she say anything about lunching with anyone?"

Anna was silent for several seconds. While trying to make sense of what Emma was asking she tried diversion. "On Friday? No. I'm sure not. I'd have remembered. Not just anyone was invited up there, you know. It was a kind of sanctuary. She kept it pretty quiet and devoted most weekdays to her writing. Sorry I can't be of more help. I wasn't aware that she kept her journals."

"Oh, yes. There are a very large number. Well, thanks for the dinner. I've got a clearer picture of how the weekend began. Thanks for that too."

To herself Emma thought that the events of Friday afternoon were becoming clearer with each interview. The timing was becoming frustratingly clear. Maude was unaccounted for at three o'clock; Anna said she was alone in Maude's yard. Margaret was late and thus it might be that Melody and Sarah were also unable to furnish an alibi for the crucial time before they came together for the drive to Oliphant. Any one of them might, until Emma found a way of checking their stories, have been driving south from Oliphant between 1 o'clock and 3. It was pretty clear that something odd had happened but that discovering what it was would be much more complicated than she had thought when she began.

Anna could see Emma getting into her car as she put the dinner plates into the sink. She gave the marmalade a final thoughtful stir and turned on the gas under the canner to sterilize the jars. Then she went to the phone and began to call the women in the group.

Leaving Elora Emma drove, rather too quickly, back to the Veterinary College labs where she spent a fruitless quarter of an hour searching for her classmate. Eventually in a far corner she ran him to ground, just washing his hands and clearing instruments away.

The report was brief. The dog was amazingly healthy for a twelve year old Doberman, especially an over-sized one. A bit of arthritis, tooth decay, cataracts beginning but no serious problems that they could see. The students had enjoyed the forensics lesson but had been disappointed at finding no obvious cause of natural death. Perhaps Gertrude's homemade food deserved some research. The students had been more excited by finding that the dog had just eaten at least two biscuity doughy things. One was still almost entire. Greedy creature had swallowed it whole. That and the rest of the stomach contents had been sent for analysis too. The other biscuit was better dispersed. Since it wasn't likely the dog had chewed it any more thoroughly, it had probably been eaten some time earlier. Emma thanked her colleague and got a number to call for the results of more specific chemical analysis of tissue and fluids. She'd have to wait until Friday morning, at the earliest, for the results. She walked slowly down the corridor. She was not much wiser, except that she did not recall that they'd been served biscuits at the cottage, only a multitude of rolls. No, but there had been a couple of raisin scones which had been left from the women's breakfast. She and her parents had eaten most of the leftovers. Could the vet be more certain? She turned and went back to find him. No raisins. The biscuit which was entire showed low levels of gluten, just the granular composition of a quick bread; it might have had cheese in it. She chewed on this thought as she drove south to Gertrude's apartment.

CHAPTER VII

WEDNESDAY EVENING

SHE FOUND THE PLACE EMPTY when she returned, still mulling over the health of the dog and impatient for the results of blood and tissue analysis. She sat, not deliberately but because it was the chair nearest the door, sat beside the phone and in a moment found herself fumbling with the phone book and then dialing the number for the last Coventry.

A man answered. She was a bit startled, expecting a wife, a widow, she supposed.

"Hello," he said for a second time, brusquely, as though shifting hands preparing to hang up and swearing, inwardly at least, at wrong numbers who don't have the guts to apologize.

"Might I speak to Roger Coventry?"

"He's dead." Emma didn't know what she'd expected when she finally reached the Coventry home but this wasn't it.

"Oh, I'm so sorry." What could she say next? "Might I ask, to whom I'm speaking?" It sounded pedantic and lame but it was the best she could manage and she was terribly afraid that he'd just hang up.

"George Coventry, if it's any of your business and who are you?" Oh, my, Emma thought and then realized she'd spoken the words aloud.

"Who's speaking?" he repeated.

"My name is Emma, Emma ...." Had she known she'd be speaking to George she might have planned some strategy. Did she want to tell him Gertrude was dead or would she ignore that topic and wait to see whether he assumed Gertrude was dead or knew she was and then gave himself away by knowing that information. Knowing would help Emma but if she were to do that what could she say to explain her call?

"I've been looking at some of Roger Coventry's books and come across some early drafts as well as an unpublished copy of his most recent book and I expected that he would be interested in having them?" There. That was pretty vague. Downright confusing. Of course he'd ask for clarification but she'd bought a second or two. What did she really want from him? She wanted to know whether he'd visited her grandmother on the previous Friday and whether her grandmother was dead or alive when he left the cottage. If Gertrude had been dead, he could hardly be expected to say so, and he might not be very forth-coming if she told him he was the last person to speak to a living, breathing Gertrude; so her best strategy with him was to pretend her grandmother was still alive and see what he did.

She also wanted to meet with him. For this purpose the papers and disks provided an excuse. But where? When? Alone? She was pretty nervous about that. What if he'd read the death notice? Had it been in the paper yet? He could hardly have missed it! If he'd killed her grand-mother, of course, he'd hardly need the paper to tell him. If he hadn't, he might not have noticed the obituary. Not everyone read the Hatched, Matched and Dispatched. He might only read it to make sure Gertrude was dead.

"I didn't catch the last name. Emma who? did you say?"
Emma gave George her father's last name. It was fair enough although she didn't usually use it. In her family the women had begun to retain their own names in a rather arbitrary way. Looking for a name that was not too hard to pronounce or spell and sticking with it for a few gener-ations. Emma and Marilla both went by Moseley, which wasn't as-sured of correct spelling but was easy enough to pronounce.

George was horrified. Here he was trying to get rid of all his father's stuff and this woman was offering him more. Where on earth had she found it and why hadn't she left it there?

"I've taken most of his papers to the University Library. You might just as well do the same."

"There's quite a bit. First drafts of most of his books, including the latest, I think, and several articles. They all have his notes in the margins. You might find material of a personal nature there too; I haven't looked at all of it. I'd rather give it to Professor Coventry's family than just leave it with the library." She hoped the "personal nature" might get his attention.

"Yes, well. I'm rather busy."

"How about 5 p.m. Friday. I have to be at Pine Woods Golf Club for a dinner but we could meet ahead and I'd buy you a drink. I'll show you the size of the collection. You might want to clear space in your trunk." She gave him directions and hung up quickly. He hadn't asked how she'd got the material and she hadn't told him. She'd suddenly realized that Gertrude's party would be going on then and there would be lots of company. The address was one he would not be able to trace to her or her grandmother, although her grandmother's name might be in the lobby of the club when he arrived. Would he stay or leave? She felt inspired until she considered lugging the load of books and papers down to the trunk of the car.

George hung up feeling puzzled and then angry. The woman had not given him any answers. It was as if she were blackmailing him. "Personal nature." Did she have any "personal" material and what might that be? Well he'd find out Friday and that would be that. At least the golf club was on his way home and he wouldn't have to stay long if she had a party to go to. Who else had his Dad been playing with. Why hadn't these drafts been in his study?

*

George's father had died in October, 1997, at the age of 81. He hadn't seemed 81. Well, to George he had, but most people had trouble believing that the smooth faced, slightly rounded little man was more than 70. He still walked miles every day and worked in his garden and wrote and wrote and wrote. He'd written 22 books, none of which George had read. But he'd died just the same. In California. His car had been struck by a truck going the wrong way, on the freeway.

He'd been in California to install tapestries for George's mother. She couldn't just pack the things up and send them off. No. She'd insisted in supervising. The show had been a great success but, once the tapestries were hung, George's father had gone off to some fancy library to check the research on his newest book. George wouldn't have thought his father's death would matter so much but it did. The results were disastrous.

By the terms of his father's will George inherited his father's estate, on condition that he move in with and care for his mother. First he'd had to go to California and cope with the paper work. And he had to collect his mother, who'd accompanied her husband to California but, finding libraries totally boring, she'd been safe with friends at the time. George had to get her home, and his father's body too. Then he'd had to decide who would care for his mother and what would be done with his father's estate and there had been the funeral, a big university thing. That's when the flowers had appeared, totally out of place among the soulless formal arrangements. There was a sprig of rosemary, a sprig of rue and one single red rose tied in a red ribbon; there was also a card on which was written a poem by Rupert Brooke, "Dust". Well, that was appropriate anyway. The bouquet had obviously not come from a florist.

He'd thought at first it was from one of his father's colleagues, or perhaps a student who was particularly fond of his father. It was hard for his 55 year-old brain to imagine anyone being particularly fond of his father, but students had often sent postcards from far flown parts of the world with messages saying in what way the scene reminded them of one of his father's lectures; so he supposed it was possible. His father had written books on the connections between history, geography and religion for fifty years, was finishing one on mountains or earthquakes when he died, and there were readers, and researchers all over the world who sent letters about that stuff too. George had never paid much attention to his father's students.

After the funeral, when the rather unctuous young man from the funeral home asked what was to be done with the flowers, George did not send the single rose with its herbal companions to the old folks' home, nor did he leave it on the grave with the other more grandiose floral tributes.

He looked up Rupert Brooke a week or so later, when he was boxing up books in his father's study. Not long after his father had retired all of the books which he had gathered over a long career were moved from his university office to newly constructed shelving in the room which he called his study. The small room had become, as a result, almost as narrow as library stacks and Roger's desk, in front of the window at the far end was not unlike the impersonal desks found in library carrels. In fact his father had probably found the desk in a university storeroom and offered to clear it away. He had been an inveterate collector of second hand books, left over art and garage sale furniture. The walls were covered, even behind the shelves, with antique maps. None of the furniture matched. Under one side of the desk a single drawer contained hanging files. On the desk was a computer, an old radio and a plant. George had been mystified by all the history books. How many people could write about the same events he wondered? By the time he got through with the geography books he was irritated. The books of maps were huge. A special shelf had been built for them and a box for all the rolled ones. What was the question? There was a map of the world, maybe with topographical features, and that was the end of it he figured. The miscellaneous shelves were more interesting but exasperating in their own way. What was his father thinking of with a twenty volume set of medical books, published in 1897? There was a two volume dictionary from the 18th century. George thought Webster had created the first dictionary. This was not by Webster.

George hadn't intended to look up Rupert Brooke. But when he came to the *Oxford Companion to English Literature* it occurred to him to see if the fellow was in there. He was. Wrote, among other things some war poetry, apparently.

Then there were a couple of theses. Well, his students might have given him those. The titles were dreary enough. Except that one of the theses was about women and World War I poetry. That was curious. It was by someone called Gertrude Moseley. Never heard of her. But he noticed, when he opened it that she'd written a dedication to his dad on the front page. The index had references to Rupert Brooke. So the guy wrote poetry about World War I. How did that hook up with the poem which had accompanied the single rose? That poem did not appear to be a war poem.

The first day George got most of the History and Geography books packed up and made a start on the others. He figured he'd clear out the shelves and use the room for his own bed and computer if he had to stay here with his mother. He was tired of making up the couch in the living room each night and having no place to put his papers. When he'd cleaned up after dinner and tucked his mother into bed and looked over his day's transactions he was exhausted. So it wasn't until the next weekend that he got back at it.

He was methodical. He'd started on the left side of his father's desk and worked along that wall, then along the stacks in the centre of the room, where most of the miscellaneous books were, and then from the door back to the desk. He had some difficulty deciding what to do with the dusty globes and astrolabes and other odd bits of surveying equipment which were on the top shelves but decided that the whole mess could be delivered to the university and they could deal with it. He hoped they'd give him a substantial tax write off for the donation.

A whole series of University Calendars were at the very end of the shelving, next to the desk. They began just after the Second World War when his father had arrived at the university, when the university, to judge by the pictures, was a pretty poor affair with only six or seven buildings surrounded by gardens and conservation land.

For a few moments George became interested in following the growth of the university, opening calendars at random and checking out the new buildings as they appeared. Then, out of one calendar fell three pictures.

One picture showed his father, perhaps sixty years old, though with his dad it was hard to tell. Behind him was water – nothing but water. Another showed a woman in the same setting as had been in the previous picture. The third picture was of the two of them, his dad and that woman, together. The three pictures had been taken at the same time; the individual photos were clear, his father smiling rather stiffly at the camera and the woman looking past the camera into the distance.

The picture of the two of them together was not so well focused; the woman's left arm was partially out of the frame. George wondered about this for a moment or so and decided that perhaps the camera had been on a tripod or rest of some sort, and the woman, for it must have been she, had misjudged how much room she would require when she ran back to get herself into the picture. In all three pictures a large grey dog with large floppy ears grinned goofily at his father. George could not figure what kind of dog it was but it was easy for whoever was holding it to rest a hand on its shoulder without bending. George put the pictures back in the calendar but placed that volume on top of the thesis about women poets, and the copy of each of his father's books which had been next to the desk on the left side.

That week George had most of the shelving removed from his father's study. At the same time he had the bed, desk, chair, computer and stereo equipment from his Toronto apartment moved in. Anything else from his apartment had been sold on consignment as had all of his father's clothing, and his father's meagre personal possessions. All that remained to sort were the files from the desk. On a dark November Sunday he'd begun to sort. There were several notebooks full of quotations. One was labelled Commonplace Book and the others were, George noticed, school notebooks which had his own name on the front and Arithmetic or Spelling in a childish scrawl, above which were the words Commonplace and a date. The quotations filled what must have been the empty pages he had left at the end of the year. Had he thrown the notebooks out? Likely not; more likely his father had cleaned his room and saved the unused paper. There was a file for each of his father's books, saving and recording his correspondence with his publishers. George made a note to contact these firms and redirect any income. One file had contracts, not all current: the house, several cars, his agreement with the university and details of his pension. One held bills. There was not much that was intimate, or even personal, even George could see that. In a folder at the bottom of the pile of paid bills was an envelope. It contained 253 dollars in cash and several Canadian Savings Bonds. One had just matured and the others matured regularly over the next ten years. The most recent had been purchased only a few days before his father's death. Two or three thousand a year his father had put away in this drawer. It wasn't an enormous sum but George whistled a little when he thought that he'd intended just to throw all the files out without looking at them. He put them in his brief case. They'd need to be cashed in and put to better use as soon as possible.

It had taken George a long time to figure it out, and an even longer time to get angry. He'd been using his father's room – he always thought of it as his father's room – for a couple of months; so likely it was February.

He'd been angry for a long time of course, but not about this, because he didn't know about this. For years he'd been angry at his mother for not loving him, for being caught up in HER painting and HER physical disability. He'd been angry at his father for not being there, for working long hours all seven days of the week and then spending the time when he was at home caring for his wife. George had thought that his father's absence had to do with his mother being ill and with working. So it took him a long time to connect his father's long hours away to his own anger and to wonder how his father's absence was connected to the person who'd sent those flowers. The anger grew steadily even before he made any connection consciously.

George's mother had always been ill. Maybe that was not true but it seemed true. Perhaps when he'd been small she'd been tall and strong and laughed a lot. He couldn't remember. When he was rational about it he could remember the weeks after the accident.

Accidents. Long ago his mother. Now his father. His grandmother had looked after him when he was little. His father hadn't been there, had been at the hospital, he supposed, looking back on it. Then his father had turned carpenter; he'd been absent then too. George remembered those months because his father wouldn't let him help. George would have liked to hammer and hold boards. His father worked like a demon. Bought books and tools and sat for hours with drawings, when he was at home.

His father had become a very good carpenter, adjusting all of the benches and equipment in his mother's studio so that she could still work. She made huge silk hangings and she hooked, sewed and embroidered tapestries which sold for very large sums of money. They also took a very long time to make. His mother did most of the work from scratch. She said she hated leaving the spiders to spin the silk and the sheep to grow the wool because she thought maybe she could do it better. However, she had to make do with their raw materials and from then on it was her creation. So in the studio there were dye vats and wash kettles and huge frames and looms. There were also pulleys and swings so that his mother could hitch herself out of her wheelchair and move herself up and down the wall to work on the frames or back and forth from the dye vats to the wash kettles or hang suspended over the ironing board. His father had been very ingenious.

His mother had for a long time refused to be seen, didn't even want him, her own son to see her. Still goes into hiding for long periods of time. Then she'll go out somewhere crowded. Says the crowd gives her anonymity. The trip to California had been hell. She'd only gone because she had a sister there with whom she could stay and because the exhibition was very prestigious and wouldn't include her if she wouldn't come to supervise the setting up at the gallery.

Mostly George's father took care of exhibitions and sales and accounts as well as looking after the household details and carrying on his own teaching and research. George had never stopped to think about his father's life until his father was dead. Then he had to take over the visits to customs to pick up imported dyes or cloth. He had to shop for items his mother found in catalogues. He had to go to the library and find the pictures of plants and animals and landscapes which she needed to stimulate her visual imagination and produce it accurately. Sometimes she even sent him out with a camera when a client wanted a part of a garden, or a part of a house or a pet included in a wall hanging.

He had to take her work to the galleries where she usually showed and he had to put up with all the admirers who phoned and wanted to see the artist. When she was in pain or depressed she wouldn't even answer the phone. Then George hated his father for spoiling his mother, for letting her think she could be such a tyrant. Now that she was almost 80, she wasn't likely to change much was she? He wasn't as good at woodwork as his father; so fixing frames and helping with blocking those big chunks of canvas was a real pain. What had she ever done for him?

It hadn't been his fault that she was on the way to pick him up at the baby sitter's house when her car had been hit by a truck. It hadn't been his fault that his three year old brother had been in the front seat without any sort of restraint and had flown through the windshield and splattered over the road. It hadn't been his fault that her spine bounced off the ceiling of the car as it rolled. Those days they didn't have kids' seats, or seat belts even, not on most cars anyway. He'd seen a picture of the accident in a newspaper clipping. His mother had given it to him the year he graduated from university, a kind of coming of age gift. Odd that his Dad had been killed in much the same way that his mother had been injured so many years before.

So, now she knew who George was. Well, she had a niche for him, at least. Emma sat and looked at the phone. Clearly she would have to read the journals more thoroughly to find how Roger and George fit into her grandmother's life. Dipping into the journals at bedtime had proven interesting, intriguing, sometimes inspiring but a more methodical approach was going to be needed. And she was going to have to see all the women. Someone must know about Roger. Well, Anna clearly knew him, but did she know about the relationship between Gertrude and Roger? When had Gertrude first met him? She might have been less discreet in earlier journals, might have described him when they first met. Emma went back to the boxes on the living room floor and pulled out a pile of journals which stretched back over 40 years. She was glad that her mother was out. Before she allowed herself to begin reading she set to work on the chores her mother had left for her.

Sue brought Mar home late. By that time Emma had carried the bags which her mother had labelled GARBAGE down the hall to the chute and listened to the satisfactory 'thunk' each made, hitting bottom, after a moment of falling silence. She had also taken to the Salvation Army depot another load of clothes, dishes, candles and stationery, all the bits and pieces which accumulate around a life, bits and pieces which, despite Gertrude's obvious purifying of her surroundings, still remained, stubbornly necessary and unpurified. What remained when Emma went to bed were objects which might be useful or interesting to the other members of the family. And the dirt. Behind pictures and furniture, under carpets and beds, no matter how careful we are, we leave behind our dirt.

Emma had also made rough plans. She had been in bed reading for about an hour when she heard her mother come in. They said good-night but were too preoccupied to talk long. Emma resumed her bed-time reading and was asleep just after midnight.

October 15, 1977, Friday   *Oliphant   9:00*

Almost closing time. The end of this week likely.
We are late this morning because women's group was last night and I drove up from Anna's after the meeting. Got here about 1. Couldn't sleep. Went for a long walk in the autumn evening. Mixture of depression caused by the shortening days and exhilaration from the meeting and the drive. After ten years the group still excites me. We teach and learn so much together.
Tonight it was toys. I remember paper dolls. When the children were small I think they (paper dolls) were in their heyday – during the war and just after. I'd had one lovely lady when I was small. I think she came with one or two dresses or maybe just a coat, or cloak. Yes, an evening gown and a cloak which went over. I remember making other dresses for her, not easy because her original dress was quite fussy and covering it was not easy. I think I eventually trimmed some of the ruffles a bit, so that I could make my creations without having to have ruffles always in the same places, especially on day dresses. The ones I bought for Mar were much nicer. We had small children dolls first, I think, and I remember once buying two books, one for her and one for me. I played family with her for hours, being 8 again and happy, no critical mother around. My critical husband was off at war and me half hoping he wouldn't come back but he did. Then when she was 10

there were movie star cutouts. Hedy Lamarr and Zazzoo Pitts and all with bathing suits on. How wonderful! Any dress fitted easily over that. They came each with a grotesque feathered or sequined gown for one of those production numbers where a staircase dominated the set and statuesque women lined the edges while the leading dancers tapped their way up and down doing impossible steps, the women wearing impossible heels and smiling impossible smiles. Mar had no interest in making her own clothes for the dolls and even then I think she preferred playing with the families of child dolls – rather than the fancy movie stars. She made beds and houses for them and took them through full days of activity. I kept the paper dolls for years after the children left home. Well, not past tense. I went down to the storage room yesterday and rummaged around and found them to take to the group last night. I didn't have my own to take. My mother cleared everything out when I left to go to university. But last night I took Mar's cutouts, and told of my own lost lady with the lovely dresses which I'd fashioned for her.

Funny how much I remember when I'm driving and how much gets into my journal and then into my books. I think the group suspect me of writing down everything they say. Several of us keep notes after meetings. When we first started we had a group journal but some of the women were very uncomfortable, fearing that their lives would be frozen in someone else's print. So Maude and I and sometimes Anna and Natasha wrote our reflections and kept them privately. Ironically I suppose this meant there were four or more sets of minutes, not just one. But the reflections are so personal that they bear little resemblance to the real meeting. Of course that might be the problem.

We had a bit of crying last night when people told of lost toys, toys that parents, or brothers and sisters had destroyed. We also laughed over the toys we'd wished for. I wanted a kaleidoscope. Melody, one of those perfect dolls with the china head. Natasha envied her brother his bike. Edwina remembered candy – well, sweets she called them. Someone in the family was very ill with the flu, the one at the end of the war and all Edwina could think about was that her brother, or sister, was getting sweets to build him back up. She said that childish envy was her reason for still loving sweets, even though they were bad for her. I asked how she felt about eggs. Nasty of me really. She said, "I beg your pardon?" I said I thought they'd been short of eggs too and that he'd likely been prescribed lots of custard. She looked at me, said yes, she'd forgotten all about that and that she hated custard. So much for that rationalization. Edwina is into gadgets these days. She's about to get her first wheelchair; the nerves in her feet and legs are deteriorating badly and she wants a chair that will have a motor and save her the trouble of pushing. They are very expensive...and heavy. How we shall get her to meetings is a problem we shall face in a few years. Perhaps by then we shall all be living in Seniors' Homes and it won't matter. We'll just wheel down the hall and meet in the lounge.

CHAPTER VIII

THURSDAY, JUNE 4

ON THURSDAY MORNING the women held their regular group meeting. Emma was not aware of the meeting or she might have organized her interview schedule differently. She hadn't really considered that the women would communicate with each other, would share her questions and their answers and try to figure out what she was up to. They were definitely of the opinion, after Natasha's and Anna's interviews, that she was up to something.

They met at Sarah's house, arriving around 10, hugging, making tea or pouring coffee and getting settled. A bowl of fruit and some chewy cookies were on the counter next to the teapot. Not long after Margaret, the youngest of them, had retired, ten years before, someone suggested that instead of driving after dark and slipping and sliding on the ice in winter they might now meet during the day. The idea was warmly welcomed. They met at 10, and ate at 12.30 or 1; usually they parted by 2. The food was rigidly prescribed, to prevent the great cooks in the group from spending the whole meeting in the kitchen. Soup and salad. No dessert. Cookies or coffee cake sometimes stole into the opening moments of the meeting, as had happened on this occasion. Melody voiced their concerns about Emma's activity.

"So, what is Emma up to? Is she trying to learn more about her grandmother in order to deal with her grief or is there something more sinister about her inquiries? You sounded worried when you called yesterday, Anna."

"She asked whether Gertrude had mentioned a luncheon guest? It seemed unlikely that she would have a visitor to lunch on the Friday of our weekend, unless there were some special reason. Did Gertrude mention anyone when she was talking to you, Natasha, or say anything about making lunch for company when she was talking to you, Maude? What time did you phone?"

Maude thought for a moment or so. "I was talking to her around 11. Funny, no one else has asked me about that. How did you know Anna?"

"I was talking to her not long after, about a crêpe pan; so, if she were having company to lunch, the person was likely there from noon to 3, though he might already have been there when you called. What was your impression Natasha?"

"Why is my call the only one people care about? How could I tell whether she had company when I called? I called from the airport. I couldn't hear a thing, hardly could hear her voice. I asked about what time people were arriving and what I was supposed to bring. She said between 5 and 6 and bring lots of white wine. Everything else was under control. What I want to know is why Emma is asking about these men, Roger and George, and where she got names to ask about."

"Why do you think it was a man she had lunch with Anna? You did say 'he,' didn't you?" Melody broke in.

Anna ignored the question. "She's been reading Gertrude's journals. She says there are quite a few journals. Did you know there were quite a few?"

"I remember Gertrude talking about a journal, back when she first retired and started writing. I think she used to make some notes...hmmm...way back, about our meetings too. I didn't think she'd been any more faithful about it than the average person. A few weeks or months at most, on and off, journals for most people are a matter of would rather than should, desire and not deed, fantasy really. I've never managed more than four days consecutively," said Sarah.

"Emma asked me about an incident I'd – " Anna paused, unsure whether she wanted to get into the details of the incident now, when she'd been unwilling to years before – knowing that if she weren't careful the group would extract the information that she knew who Roger was and discover the secret of her long ago non-affair with Roger and the facts of her speedy retirement – information which she'd provided in a carefully laundered version at that time – "told Gertrude about in confidence years ago. I thought perhaps a warning to the rest of you was in order. She may ask about things you'd rather had been kept confidential."

"Who else has she seen?" asked Melody.

"I was first, I think," said Natasha, "and she didn't ask anything particularly difficult. She was inquiring about this George and Roger though. She was either acting pretty well or she really didn't know who they are when she talked to me. Who are they?"

"Wait a minute. What is surprising about a granddaughter trying to learn about her grandmother while our memories are still clear? I think it's an excellent idea. I wish I'd been able to talk to my grandparents and their friends, found out more about them while people still remembered. Wish I'd known people to ask, had friends of my grandparents so accessible." This was Margaret.

Anna took a deep breath and replied. "I agree, Margaret, but it didn't feel like that. She wasn't interested in her grandmother much but in the day she died. Who'd been there, when, and who'd cleaned the dishes out of the living room, for example. It felt like an interrogation, as if she were looking for something."

"Who took the dishes out of the living room? Margaret did of course. Why wouldn't she?" Edwina looked surprised.

"Well," continued Anna, "if I were asking that question I'd be looking for something in the cups or on the plate. It seems to me that Emma suspects something was odd about Gertrude's death and thinks that we might know what it is."

There was a long silence. Most of the women did not look up or meet each other's eyes. It might be that they had entertained similar thoughts and dismissed them, or it might be reticence, or simply a need to consider what question, comment or answer was possible next. Anna saved them, eventually by dropping a bigger bomb.

"She'd examined the dog."

"What?" several voices asked at once.

"She said she was tidying the path for Saturday, but she'd been tidying below the surface far enough to find that More Sinister was wrapped in two bags end for end."

"Wow! Anna. You got a lot more information from her than I did. All I found out was that she was looking for Roger and George." Natasha repeated and pouted a bit.

"Who are Roger and George anyway?" Asked Jean.

"No idea." Anna paused for a while. She felt as if she were a fox who had forgotten how to mislead hounds.

"That's not true." She continued at last. "Emma suggested that Gertrude had had a relationship, an affair, if you want, with this Roger over many years. Emma didn't ask me about anyone named George, but she did say Gertrude expected someone to arrive for lunch. It's incredible but Emma has found all sorts of information in the journals."

"What?" the voices had interrupted again.

"Well. Figure it out. She's asking whether anyone was there when we called Gertrude. She's checking dishes. She's asking about someone named George. Sounds like she thinks he was there before us. So do you remember what dishes were in the living room, Margaret?"

"Only cups. The policemen both had coffee and the young one had more than one cup; I mean I think he used more than one cup. But I don't recall any others."

"Does she suspect these men, whoever they are, of..." Jean couldn't say it, though clearly she could think it.

"Maybe she suspects one of us," said Melody, "or all of us."

"I think that only happens in Agatha Christie, Melody," said Edwina.

"You know that wasn't why we all said 'what?' Anna." Glancing around the group, Margaret swooped in on Anna's diversion. "It was the word 'affair' that caught our attention."

"Roger had nothing to do with it in any case. He's dead," said Anna. Heads turned. "He was a professor of geography but mainly interested in the interrelationship of geography and ritual. He was invited to come to my school, oh, a long time ago now, maybe two years before I retired, to talk about Central America or Mexican rituals, or religions, something like that, when the whole school was doing one of those theme things on Mexico. Anyway, I noticed in the paper last fall that he'd been killed in a car accident. His son, I think, was George. Not always a good relationship between them as I recall, but what the son's connection is to Gertrude I have no idea. I didn't give Emma any of this information. I wanted to see what your picture of the situation was first."

"The point is, what do we say to Emma when she comes to call?" said Sarah.

"You may not wish to have her call." It was difficult to tell where Anna had put the emphasis in this sentence. Sarah looked surprised.

"Won't that look funny? As if there is something to hide?"

"I imagine we do have things to hide. But she may know them anyway if she reads the journals."

"That will take time."

"Yes. So, in a way, the busier we keep her the less time she'll have to read the journals."

"Oh. Sarah, you are the devious one," said Edwina. "But it is a good strategy. Are there things we don't want to tell her?"

"I imagine each of us has secrets that we don't share. We've also said things in the group or in private to each other that we might not wish to have Emma misinterpret." Melody looked thoughtful as she said this. "I don't think we could list them and say we won't talk about this or that. If we focus on the events of Friday we should be alright. The truth but not necessarily the whole truth, you know?"

"I don't think I'm much good at lying," said Maude. "Besides why would I be lying? and what would I be lying about?"

"I think you might be pretty good about not telling everything you know, though," said Sarah. Maude looked surprised.

"I don't always know the things you people think I know, if you follow what I mean. Sometimes you amaze me with what you read into actions and non-actions. I just want to deal with surfaces. I like surfaces; they're beautiful. I like things I can touch and taste."

Conversation veered off to a discussion of Maude's latest photo exhibit and then it was time for lunch. Melody's appeared to be the last word on how to deal with Emma. It was not, however, the last thought they had about her. The women respected Anna's intuition. If her intuition was that Emma was looking for something, then there might be something to look for.

The women were afraid – perhaps that is too strong a word – nervous. Gertrude having an affair that she did not tell them about was unsettling. Gertrude's death was even more unsettling. Each of them was slowly concluding that if Gertrude had been killed there had to be a killer. Where an hour ago each had assumed that Gertrude had died peacefully in her sleep, the ideal death, the one each of them hoped for, each now entertained the idea that Gertrude's death had been willed. They had operated for thirty years in honest, though not complete, openness. There had been parts of their lives which it had not seemed germane to share. Gertrude's concealment of her affair with Roger was probably an extreme example of this. But by and large – pain and joy – struggles with aging parents, rebellious children and, later, grandchildren had all been shared. If nine people see each other for three hours every two weeks there is opportunity, necessity even, to prioritize – to choose the problem which is uppermost or the joy which is most apparent. The ongoing struggle with finances or health or housecleaning may not be raised unless the problem is acute. Gertrude had clearly never considered her relationship with Roger important enough to talk about – not even his death. That was a bit puzzling. They thought back to the previous fall when Anna said Roger had died and they tried to remember. They remembered that Gertrude had missed some meetings at about that time.

Who might have killed their friend? Their trust in their world was profoundly shaken.

*

Emma woke on Thursday morning with a sense of time running out. She'd talked to only two people, the memory party was the next day and she had to go back to work on Sunday evening. As they ate she shared with her mother a brief synopsis of the previous day's activities, including the biscuit in the dog's stomach contents.

"Did you see any biscuits, Mom?"

"Rolls, lots and lots of rolls, sure it wasn't a dinner roll or a croissant or a bagel or an onion bun or a cheese roll?"

"Nope, the vet said tea biscuit."

"Well, they're quick and easy and Mom always made excellent ones. Perhaps she ate them all. I've known her to make up one cup of flour and eat the whole thing. She said she'd get a craving for hot biscuits sometimes. Or she and her company ate them all, or she gave one to the dog."

"It's a solution. The last biscuit flipped to the dog or perhaps slipping off the plate as Gertrude took it back to the kitchen after lunch." Emma was thoughtful for a moment. "No, Mom, never. It wasn't in character. Gertrude was too conserving of food for that. Aunt Sue might, you might, but you know grandma wouldn't. She'd been through two wars and a depression, she used to tell us, and she didn't waste food. Besides it wasn't just one; there were also the remains of an earlier biscuit in the dog's stomach."

After breakfast Emma called and could contact not one of the women. She got several answering machines but could make no appointments.

Alone in the apartment after taking her mother to Sue's, Emma was realizing that some organization would help her to remember what questions to ask and to see how each person's Friday had fitted into the general pattern of Gertrude's day. After working for two hours, clearing and packing, she pulled out her notebook and jotted down a list of questions to which she wanted answers and a chronology which would help her to see each person's activities on the Friday. She formed it into a chart.

Emma realized that she'd also need to make a chart for each family member. She hoped she could fill that chart based on casual conversations over the next couple of days. Interviews in a more formal sense would be resented. She could see that. She'd also like to have the same information from George or anyone else who knew Gertrude. She might be able to interview several people, without their noticing, of course, at the memory party. She wrote Sue and Geoff and Rowena and Eric and Marilla and Mike at the top of six sheets and considered her cousins.

She noticed there had been an obvious absence of cousins from the proceedings so far. Of Gertrude's eight grandchildren she was the only one who was on the scene. She added that question to her form. Her brother Dan was ostensibly in the mountains of B.C. somewhere, climbing and surveying and taking geological samples. She knew her Mom had left him a message but had no idea whether he'd received it. For that matter she couldn't be sure he was actually in B.C. Sue and Geoff's three sons, in their late twenties, where were they? They hadn't been at dinner the other night, not even Zack, the youngest, who lived in the same city.

Leyland was a zoologist living in Toronto, working at the R.O.M. Christian was at the height of a pro football career, if such things have heights in Canada, and he had an apartment in Winnipeg for the football season but should have been in town or available in May. Zack was still at school, finishing a degree or several of them, in Philosophy. They were as available as she was. Where were they? Gertrude was their grandmother too. She'd held and played and holidayed with them as well as with her! Been there for their first weeks as well as for hers.

Where was Ailric? Where were his twin sisters? Maybe they should be interviewed also.

Were absent people more or less likely to be guilty than those who were present? What had her cousins to gain from Gertrude's death? The will did not mention them. Did they know that? Gertrude's estate was not large. Did they know that? She had been equally generous and demanding of all of them. Was there one who was particularly angry about something, or jealous? One who was defending his or her parents against Gertrude? Looking at her cousins and her aunts and uncles in this new light was terrifying. Take your family and turn it upside down. For each kind action consider an equal and opposite obligation and the boiling frustration that results. Who could have been so angry or frustrated or needed so little money so much?

Her mood at that moment matched that of the women meeting several miles away. It might have been a phase of the moon, of course, painting the landscape with distrust. To stop the whirling questions, the rising anxiety, Emma got out her grandmother's computer, looked for the manual and finished organizing the forms into which she also typed what answers she'd accumulated. Then she printed pages, and collated them in an order which made sense to her. Calmer now, she picked up three journals and curled herself into a corner of the couch with the phone beside her. Every half hour, not content with having left messages on their machines, she re-dialed her grandmother's friends.

As she read she added notes to her neatly organized forms and expanded her chronological chart. She had listed the titles of Gertrude's books and their dates of publication and the titles and dates of Roger's books. This formed a sort of framework. Then she began to consider the journals. She had learned to decipher her grandmother's writing with some ease, even the abbreviations which were a mixture of medieval scribe and techno nerd. While Gertrude used X as a standard abbreviation for Christ in X^{mas} or X^{er} , she also used, in more recent journals @, a very scribbled @, for most occurrences of the letters 'at' whether in a word or standing alone. @ack, for example, was likely the word attack with one 't' hung out to dry. @ent^{n} was attention. Once she'd figured it out and practised a while, she found it actually made reading faster. She'd also learned to skim for names. People were the problem, or the solution to her problem, she believed and so she looked for names. There were entire entries without a name in sight. But after visits from friends, usually in the summer while she was at the cottage, or on Fridays, after group night, there would be more names. There was often a two-page summary of the group's conversation on the morning following a meeting. Once Emma had discovered this pattern she could skim more quickly. She was almost finished subjecting the third journal to her summary treatment when she began paying more attention to marginalia. Almost at once she noticed a star in the margin beside a Friday entry. There had been other symbols from time to time. Red pencil brackets in the margins, asterisks and circles above the dates, stars and underscoring. But this star was easy to explain. It marked the statement, "Edwina spent some time discussing her affairs." Emma wrote this ambiguous statement beside Edwina's name in her notebook and cross-indexed it on her list of dates. Later there was a star beside a meeting where Melody had mentioned dealing with a particularly difficult case in court that week. Emma wondered whether it would be possible to check this with the newspaper of the time. Of course. If necessary. One or two of the women came regularly to lunch or tea, or spent weekends and once in a while there was a star in the margin beside such an occasion. All of these she noted.

Recalling an earlier thought, Emma pulled the volume covered by Attwood's *Surfacing* from her pile. 1953. Winter. Suddenly there were little hearts, at the top of the page, over the date. At first once a week and then more often. She'd seen the symbols in other journals. Did it always mark a day when Gertrude and Roger met? It was so hokey she had trouble associating it with her grandmother. But suddenly, as she flipped backward through the journal, there it was.

It was a dark and stormy night. Well a dark and stormy afternoon. I met R. in the parking lot of the U. This is the 3rd time we've met this way. The 6th time we've ever laid eyes on each other. To notice. Odd to think how many times we might have passed on the street or in a supermarket and never noticed. The first time was in the cafeteria, two months ago. I was grabbing a sandwich before my evening course and so, I guess, was he. We talked about what he taught, of course. The University is in one of its outreach phases...trying to keep busy after the vets all leave, I imagine, and he was interested in talking to night students about the reasons we take courses, or so he said. More specifically, when he found I was a social worker he wanted to know how our values and the values of the clients who are arriving from all over Europe intersect. - as he put it. I am in charge of an upgrading group at work. We figured a deal could be arranged...so many of his values for so much of our experience would equal a credit. It will have to be worked out with the Extension Department but in the meantime ... We started the visits last week. He came to the office after work and four of us brought our notes about clients. We can't talk specific cases but he's asked for some statistics which I think we can provide. Then he told us about other cultures and gave us hints about how religious affiliations might help us to determine likely behaviours...even if the people came from the same villages they might react differently. We set a whole meeting for dealing with prison camp survivors. After the meeting he and I went out and discovered that it was snowing...snowing a lot. His car wouldn't move; the tires were useless, or his driving was. I drove him home. We talked all the way. VW s are very good in the snow. They also have very poor heaters. The windows fog. This is a good thing sometimes.

The hearts began appearing at regular intervals. At first Emma ignored the evidence, thought, how nice for grandma to have a companion. Then she was shocked. If Roger had been a friend, a person with whom she discussed sociology, why would she have hidden him for 45 years? The answer was pretty obvious. And all these years she'd imagined her grandmother living a celibate, perhaps a frigid life. Or had she thought of it at all? – assumed. She skimmed through the following journals to see how long the hearts continued. They continued.

Then Emma felt ashamed, that she was a voyeur, that she was looking for stars and hearts instead of savouring her grandmother's experiences, learning about her world. Later, she told herself, when I have time. Right now I have a problem to solve. She noticed her reluctance to think about finding a murderer. She always considered that she had a problem to solve, like a diagnosis. It was the way she met each new horse and owner who entered her clinic. What is the problem here and how can I help the horse or owner to solve it? She expected that she'd learned the habit from her grandmother, it was more a social work technique than a medical one. She'd never noticed that until now.

She opened a journal that was almost thirty years old. There was a star beside the following entry:

October 15, 1969, Friday.   *Oliphant*   *8:00*

Up late this morning. such luxury being retired. drove north right after group last night so as not to miss a single hour of this wonderful weather. Season of mists and mellow fruitfulness, indeed. Golden light refracted through the mist rising from stream and lake as the water and air perform their yearly dance of heat exchange. Leaves rot in September's rain. Not the tree leaves yet – the leaves of tender plants killed by the first frosts are the first to begin the migration back to the earth.

Maude talks of the sunrise and sunset hours and the light they cast for her camera lens. I try to open my own camera lenses and swallow the hills and pastures as I drive south to the meeting yesterday afternoon. Avison's poem "Snow" plays in my head. "Nobody stuffs the world in at your eyes./ The optic heart must venture." You must go and will the world in. Open to the widest stop and let flares frame the world. Fall is apocalyptic. I remember all those harvest altars of my youth. Huge wheels of bread and pies among the pumpkins and tomatoes, all round and full shapes. I think of Caravaggio's Bacchus among the rotting fruit. Such a fine line between ripe and rotten. Sometimes the line is only in the attitude.

Sarah tells us last night that she has been contemplating an affair. As if she invented the idea. She's met this wonderful man at the Kitchener market on several Saturdays. He sits and has coffee while his wife who is in a wheel chair slowly goes about the market. Sarah likes this time on her own in a busy place. He likes to sit and read or write in the café. He's not getting much reading or writing done lately, I guess. She thinks she could turn this into something more interesting. He's such a gentle man and so devoted to his wife but she can tell that he might be interested. She uses the word interest quite a few times – I think it means fuck or screw, also euphemisms of course in their way, in their day. I hear through a fine red mist. She's talking about R. What the hell is he up to laying traps in the Kitchener market! What are the odds that he accidentally runs into members of my women's group?

The plumbing is mundane, awkward or ridiculous. Sober considera-tion of the act can only end in hysterical laughter or total disgust. Nei-ther is conducive to passion. Romance, fantasy, hormones, altered states and bad eyesight are absolutely necessary. I wonder that the human race confronted with mirrors and reality, confronted with the necessity to describe the plumbing, has survived as long as it has. No wonder parents are reluctant to spend time describing such peculiar flesh. The female ends and the male ends inserted here and twisted there are not only mundane but irrelevant. They are not why we per-severe.

We persevere because we want to go home. Because we want to escape beyond ourselves. Because we want to be lost and found simultaneously. Because we want to inhabit our bodies in a world of sensation. Because we want to inhabit our minds and our emotions and leave our bodies behind. We concentrate on tiny areas of skin and make them expand to enclose us. We perceive ourselves and the universe through both ends of a telescope simultaneously. We spiral in and in and into a tiny centre of sensation, focusing and concentrating until the nerve at the centre explodes and pulses and sweeps us away for a nano-second or a lifetime. Until the blackness at our centre explodes and pulses with the scarlet and gold of a spiral sunset whirling around us. Until we forget for a nano-second how ridiculously lonely we are. How ridiculous we are. Until we forget.

My kaleidoscope. A gift from my brother. I was just considering taking it to group last night. It sits on my desk; a beautiful egg crafted in hardwood and brass, not like the paper and mirror ones I longed for in my childhood. What we see when we look in is indescribable, beauty perhaps, but not necessarily. Intriguing and various and symmetric and asymmetric and indescribable. In a moment changed illusive and allusive too. We try to grasp the images as they pass and attach themselves to metaphor. Oh see the apples! A cathedral window! A crystal! And gone, even to our own recollection ephemeral. The going is addictive, needing to be renewed. In itself only a pile of trash and mirrors, like us, like the atom and cell of us. A pile of trash posturing in mirrors, the mirrors of our friend's eyes, our eyes, the world's eyes, but dust nonetheless, dust with immortal longings.

*

It had been a trip into a foreign land. George had never gone west of the 400 highway on his way north – maybe a school trip to Midland – he didn't think so, but the name was familiar, Martyr's shrine and stuff. History. His friends had skied at Collingwood or thereabouts, or along in Horseshoe Valley – but he'd gone to Quebec, usually, for skiing. He'd gone to Muskoka to canoe. He was amused by the view of sheep

121

and cattle. He'd forgotten that the QEW used to have horse farms along it, white fences and long legged creatures, open green space when he was in university and taking the bus to Toronto. Yes. Well, there was still space like this. How refreshing! There wasn't much traffic on a Friday morning. The towns were busy. People crossed the street as if they were in the suburbs, not on a serious highway to somewhere. Hunh! Even in the suburbs the cars were more determined than they were here. People paused to lean out a window and chat, or let other people cross. A different atmosphere painted the main streets and buildings. He was feeling quite relaxed by the time he reached Oliphant.

He swung off Bruce 21 onto gravel road. There was a wide cleared area on both sides of the road but a fairly large ditch, wet, yellow flowers in some parts, but mostly debris, a piece of rusting heavy equipment off at the side of the road, no dwelling after he passed the deserted campground and shuttered flea market at the turn. After a mile of fairly smooth gravel he came to a T-junction and turned north onto smooth pavement again. Now there were dwellings on both sides of the road. All manner of reflectors and garbage boxes, and signposts decorated the roadside, identifying driveways and personalities about which he knew nothing. The road curved sharply several times. At the curves a clear view of the lake glittering in a chill May morning spread before him – as far as Michigan. He came to a drive marked by two globe lights. He was so occupied wondering why anyone would need two lights at the end of a drive in the middle of nowhere that he almost missed the road to his left, a gravel road winding west with lake on both sides. He backed up twenty feet, checked the small sign post which pointed to Lonely Island and turned west across flat fen. He realized he was on a causeway. Great chunks of stone spread on both sides of him. He guessed the rocks had not been there long. They didn't look like part of the landscape. Suddenly the road ducked into the gloom of trees and branched right. He hesitated, unsure which fork to take, then remembered that in her directions Gertrude had said it didn't matter.

He looked closely at each sign and driveway searching. How would he know the place. He'd forgotten to ask her that on the phone. He referred to Gertrude always by the pronoun in his mind. HER and SHE. Mind you he didn't use names for his mother and father either. Thought of them in relation to himself not as persons on their own. If he'd been at all introspective he might have realized that this was part of his animosity towards Gertrude. SHE had somehow had a relationship with HIS father. He didn't know what the nature of that relationship was but the poem from Rupert Brooke hinted at feelings which George found deeply repugnant.

He was surprised at the size of the houses he spied at the ends of lanes as he circled the island. Glimpses of two and three car garages alternated with spacious lawns and manicured shoreline. This was not a tourist cabin area. He became a little nervous. She might have servants or guards for heaven's sake!

Shortly after 2 in the afternoon Margaret's call came in, followed immediately by Sarah's, and then by each of the others. Emma made an appointment to see Sarah and Margaret that afternoon. Three others she would see Friday morning. Edwina she couldn't see until Friday evening at the memory party. That would be the women taken care of. She hoped she'd be able to get them to talk about each other. Give her an idea who was reliable. She got into her car and drove northwest.

Sarah lived in a suburb of single floor or side split bungalows with neat lawns and mature trees. She met Emma at the door wearing brightly colored palazzo pants and a fitted black leotard which displayed her trim waist and full breasts. There was a small plate of cookies on the tiled counter in the kitchen and as she offered Emma coffee or tea she explained that the group had, despite their rules on desserts, eaten most of the cookies earlier in the day. Emma filled a coffee cup from the glass pot in the corner and sat cradling it in her hands. She had learned during the phone calls that the women had all been here, eating these cookies, drinking this coffee. If she turned the high stool beside the kitchen counter sideways, Emma could sit facing the sheltered patio where she could see the chairs still arranged as they had been just over an hour earlier when all of her grandmother's friends sat there. What now? Use the line of questioning which she'd already taken. Probably Anna had shared it with the others and they would be expecting her questions. They might have practised the answers. Maybe she'd be a bit less direct and see what happened.

"I'm trying to build a picture of my grandmother's last day, Sarah. What can you tell me about your memories of that day?" This sounded like a Social Worker's question. Well that was okay too.

"Melody and I were bringing Saturday dinner; so I went over there after breakfast. I got ready in a kind of leisurely way – packing and putting stuff ready for Kent to manage while I was gone, and wandering around with my toast and tea. There didn't seem to be a rush. We were to meet Anna at 2:30 in Arthur which meant we didn't need to leave here until 1 or 1:15. After Kent had helped me put my clothes and sleeping bag in the car, oh, and the cooler, I went to the LCBO and the grocery store. I found some Raspberry Basil Salsa and got some chips and sour cream to go with it and some Tzatzsiki as well as vegetables and fruit and stuff for two casseroles. Maude is vegetarian; so I'd decided to do two casseroles, one without meat. The heat from the oven warms the cottage for the night, if it gets cold, and Gertrude used to appreciate using things that would function more than one way, you know?" Her eyes wide open and appealing met Emma's. "Is that the sort of stuff you wanted to know?"

Emma could see where this was going. It might take Sarah almost as long to tell about that Friday as it had taken her to live it. On the other hand the details were useful, some of them, and might be the sort of thing that would reveal who was telling the truth and who was not; so she let Sarah continue her lengthy trip around the grocery store and the bakery and her entire visit at Melody's as they cleaned the potatoes and carrots and salad greens before packing them. Gertrude was amazingly edgy if the pump ran for very long and the washing of vegetables was much easier under running water. What's more if it were practically ready they'd not have to go to the kitchen when they could be talking with the group on Saturday afternoon. Emma recalled that the food had been very good though she'd arrived too late to see the miracle of the clean vegetables going directly from the cooler to the oven.

"But you served fish!" she interjected.

"Only after we'd been told there would be more diners."

"Then you were ready to leave at 1 o'clock?" She said, hoping to skip past the preparation of dessert.

"Well, I got to Melody's around 11 and we put the casseroles together as I was saying, parts of them anyway. After we'd washed the vegetables we sautéed the onion and celery and put them into a container. We didn't mix any of the ingredients just put them together in a bag ready to go. Then we washed the fruit and cut it up and added some liqueur. We thought it would be pretty exotic by the next day. We had made a lovely pound cake the week before and frozen it, the fruit and the cake and some more booze with custard and a layer of passion fruit jam." Sarah caught herself reliving a dream of trifle and returned with a start to the mundane. "Melody and I had soup and a delightful pâté on crackers for lunch."

"We also explored her bedroom and discussed her plans for renovating. We wondered if the curtains could be stenciled to match the wallpaper trim she was putting around the mirrors and doors. Floating patterns on the sheers, you know, and wondered if the stencils should be all over or random or along the hems.

"We'd loaded the car around 1 and were waiting for Margaret by this time; so we just talked and looked at wallpaper samples and the time flew by. We weren't aware of how late Margaret was until we were in the car. I looked at the clock as I turned the ignition.

"I said something like – my gosh, it's 2 o'clock and Margaret apologized. She said she'd been sweeping up her driveway and a neighbor had come along – wanted to collect for some charity and because she hadn't finished – she still had a pile of top soil that she was putting on her side garden in a little heap there in the drive and didn't want to leave in case it rained and the soil turned to mud – she was a captive of the persistent collector.

"But there really is no rule about what time we get to Gertrude's. It wasn't a disaster except that Anna might have worried about us. She didn't look worried when we arrived. She was sitting on a lawn chair in the sun. She was in the process of lighting a cigarette, and having a bit of trouble with the light breeze, when we got there. It's always breezy at Maude's."

"Did she say how long she'd been there?"

"We didn't ask – just worked together putting sleeping bags and coolers into the trunk of Anna's car, wishing again that Maude were there with her van. In fact it was getting so late that someone, Melody maybe, suggested we wait for her. But we weren't sure how long her appointment was. She'd been rather uncertain when she talked to Anna about what time she'd be back."

"What does Anna do with her cigarette butts when she smokes outdoors?"

Sarah looked thunderstruck. "I've no idea. In all these years I've never noticed."

"I'm looking out at your patio and I don't see any butts on the stones." Emma realized that she'd crossed a line here, but she'd spoken aloud while mentally she was trying to figure a way to get out and look around the patio without calling much more attention to her interest.

"Does she smoke in her car?" This was clearly a diversion.

"Never. That's why she'd been out on the lawn while she waited for us."

"Go on. Was anything about the drive or your arrival at the cottage unusual?"

"Nooo. We were a bit quiet at the start. I figured that was because Margaret's mind was still back in her driveway and Anna was a bit cross about having to wait. However, it's a two-hour drive; so we talked about all sorts of things, you know? We likely started with Melody's decorating dilemmas and went from there. When we got to the cottage it was such a warm spring afternoon, so long as you stayed in the sun, that we weren't in the least hurry to go inside. It seemed that we all wanted to get the last hour of warmth. It was a bit odd that Gertrude didn't come out into the yard to greet us, or that More Sinister didn't bark, but the back door was open and I just figured she'd gone for a walk to enjoy the afternoon too. Had maybe gone out to meet us at the road and we'd missed her on the way in."

"What door was open?"

"The back sliding door. The screen was closed but the door was open."

"That's strange." Emma recalled that Anna had also mentioned the door. "Grandmother would usually have had that door closed by about three in the afternoon, earlier in May, because the sun was on the front of the house and she wanted it to heat the house before evening. If any door were open it would be the door to the screened porch, provided there were no breeze.

"We learned that at the age of two or three. She made sure all of us understood the laws of door opening and closing. Sometimes at a family party someone will shout, 'Shut the door,' and we all fall about laughing, my cousins and my aunts and uncles too. It's not the least bit funny unless carved into your brain is a memory of grandma shouting it ten times a day when you were a kid."

"Right," Sarah agreed. "The door might be opened when we were cooking. Otherwise she would slide across the room, materialize from wherever she had been, and quite firmly shut it behind the offender."

"You mean she didn't shout at you? How unfair the world is to kids!"

"As I say, I thought, when I saw the door open that Gertrude was close by. So if we unloaded quickly and settled in before she got back she'd be surprised. We got busy. We took our stuff up the stairs to the bedroom and went to the bathroom. We walked right through the corner of the living room but the light wasn't on. The couch is in the shadow; the window is right behind it and the porch overhang makes that room a bit gloomy anyway. Maybe we were concentrating on getting our luggage up the stairs."

"Hard to imagine that no one noticed her. Who did go upstairs?'

"We'd sorted food from the coolers and put most of the groceries away first, I remember, just dropping our personal luggage, Melody's and mine and Anna's, by the living room door. Sooo when I was about to drag my sleeping bag and suitcase upstairs, I remember stepping over the pile and then picking up my stuff and I guess that's why I never looked at the couch. I'd have been concentrating on getting over the pile, holding onto the door frame, and then on lifting those awkward bundles around the corner. Upstairs I took a moment to catch my breath. I looked out over the lake, and opened the window a bit. The bedroom was stuffy from the afternoon sun and rather heavy with the perfume of the narcissus your grandmother had brought in from the garden. When I came down for the second load I was still facing the luggage and not the living room. I guess I was the only one to go up stairs right then." Sarah was so lost in her effort to try to reconstruct the event that it was a few seconds before she registered Emma's next question.

"Oh. I'd taken all the stuff upstairs, mine and Melody's; I'd been to the bathroom, and I was in the kitchen pouring a glass of water. The drive up is very dehydrating don't you think? Melody and I were surveying the tidy kitchen – she'd done most of the food storage while I carried things up stairs – and feeling good about having everything out of the way so quickly. I'd even heaved Anna's sleeping bag and clothes bag onto the couch by the living room door. I was tired. We were congratulating each other as if it had been a contest when Anna came through the kitchen and went into the living room. Then she screamed. Well, yelled. We went to the door – part way across the room maybe. Gertrude looked quite peaceful – had had her afternoon tea and fallen asleep after putting her book on the table."

"How do you know she'd had afternoon tea?" Emma hoped she'd used a casual enough tone and that the women had not come to a group decision about the events of the previous Friday.

"There were cups – well, not cups exactly, one cup and saucer and the glass mug your grandmother used for tea – as well as a plate on the table."

"Sarah, are you really clear about that?" Emma couldn't help herself. She could see any fictional detectives she'd read, admittedly she hadn't read many, shrugging their shoulders and turning away in disgust at such lack of finesse. "Gertrude usually had tea in a glass mug; so that's not unusual but the cup and saucer suggests she had company." Emma threw a triumphant look at the unseen audience as if to say – see, I didn't mention the plate!

"Yes, I see what you mean." Sarah did. She'd just visualized the scene for the first time since she'd lived it and she did see. Margaret had mentioned two cups. Sarah had not seen two cups and there had definitely been a plate in the middle of the coffee table but the plate had been empty – absolutely – she thought. "Not a crumb on it," she told Emma and added, "The dog might have cleaned the plate. Probably did. The coffee table was no challenge for him."

"The question is," Emma proceeded confidentially, feeling Sarah's curiosity urging her on, "who removed those things from the living room, Sarah? And why?"

"Probably Margaret. It was her task for the weekend." Sarah was back on the alert.

"Who else could have? Who else went into the living room after Anna had discovered that grandma was dead?"

"Well, no one went in for a while. We talked to the others as they arrived. We talked in the kitchen and went into the dining room to sit. We waited for the police. But people did go to the bathroom from time to time; so no one really kept that room sealed off."

"Tell me about burying the dog."

"Well, the police had moved the poor thing to a corner. I told Melody and she asked the young constable to put him in the back shed. I gave him some bags to put More in. I bring garbage bags and take the recycle stuff home after our weekends. The young man was a bit surprised but I guess he could see that we might not want a dead dog in the living room for the weekend, and he wanted to be helpful to a bunch of little old ladies. Clearly there was no one else there to do it."

"What happened in the morning?"

"What do you mean? We got up and tried to have breakfast and a normal morning."

"No, I meant about burying the dog."

"Oh. Well, we were talking about the song for Gertrude's party, seems a bit odd to call it that, but while we were practising someone suggested we could do a full rehearsal by burying the dog."

"Did everybody go out to the garden and sing?"

"Mmmm. Anna and Melody dug the hole and they got Margaret and me to help with the lifting. Jean and Natasha weren't there. They went into Wiarton for splake – or maybe that was later. I'm not sure. Maude was there; she still sings well. The rest of us warble a little."

Emma shifted subject again. She hoped it would seem as if she were disorganized, without a plan. Heck, she was without a plan but she was also visualizing the list of questions in her notebook.

"It seems that Gertrude had an affair with a man named Roger Coventry. She apparently had this affair for many years. Now, I can understand her not wanting her family to know, maybe, though we thought she was pretty honest and open, but I'm sure she must have shared her experience with her women's group."

"You'd think so. As you say, she was very honest and open, hated secrets. But I have to tell you that when Natasha and Anna told us this morning that you had asked them this question we were amazed. She never gave us a hint of a man in her life. She travelled with several different women friends, went to movies and theatre with women friends and told us about her adventures and her struggles but not a hint of a man in her life. Not a hint."

"Odd. Wonder why she was so secretive?"

"Well, clearly he was married, but even then she might have given us a false name. Things being as they are, her relationship can't have been smooth and easy for all those years. There must have been some bad times."

"Like when he died last year?"

"At least then, yes." Sarah sounded aggrieved.

"Or when you were meeting with him occasionally?" Emma smiled and raised her eyebrows, hoping to look conspiratorial and non-threatening while watching closely for Sarah's reaction. Some emotion flickered in Sarah's eyes. She struggled for control.

"We never discussed it."

"Did you know when you were meeting Roger that Gertrude and he had been lovers for hmm... fifteen or sixteen years?"

"We never discussed it."

"You never discussed it with Roger or you never discussed it with Gertrude?"

"Go and find out from your journals. I don't want to talk about it. And I don't really want to talk to you if you continue to ask about a time which has nothing to do with the present events."

"Yes, of course...Anna and Natasha will also have told you that Gertrude expected someone named George for lunch on the day she died."

"Yes, and I can see why what was on the table in the living room might be important if you thought that Gertrude had not died of natural causes.   She did look very peaceful, though." Sarah sounded uncertain. The room was quiet enough that Emma could hear the clock ticking.

"Your garden is quite lovely for so early in the year. The sheltering wall of the patio must help bring the plants near the house along quickly." Emma would have liked to ask if Sarah knew who George was, but sensed that she might be outstaying her welcome and she desperately wanted to get out to the garden before she was asked to leave. All she knew about plants or gardens she had learned a long time before, in the summers spent at Gertrude's elbow, usually under compulsion, weeding and harvesting herbs in the shimmering summer air. Gardening was associated in her mind with the tickle of sweat or bugs and the drone of bees and the whirrr of humming bird wings. Braiding and tying the lavender, sorting the grass from the oregano, rubbing the thyme between her fingers had been wonderful. Working in the garden had not. Sarah's garden was much neater than Gertrude's. Using decorative cement blocks Sarah had built a curved wall about six feet tall and fifteen feet out from the house. Flower pots and sculpture broke the surface of the cement.

Sarah gave in gracefully and escorted Emma to the sliding doors. In the afternoon, without the morning sun, the patio was a bit chilly but Emma stayed a long time, first giving a quick look at the hyacinths budding along the borders in front of the shrubs. Then, pausing for some time to exclaim over the terra-cotta wall plaques and the statues discreetly overseeing the primroses and bright green of the young feverfew and lemon balm, she managed to find the spot where Anna had sat, strategically next to a raised pot of tiny perennial geranium. The remains of her cigarettes were neatly tucked into the pot, under the rim. Emma could see four white-filtered butts. For three hours of meeting. Though there might have been more if Anna had chosen another chair at lunch. No. Once having found a good ash tray, Emma thought, Anna was likely to have returned to the same place for lunch.

Rejecting Sarah's half-hearted offer of another cup of coffee Emma thanked her for her time and left. On her drive to meet Margaret she reflected that it would have been better to go out at once to Maude's before Sarah could call and warn her that Emma was now on a search for cigarette butts!

*

Margaret had agreed to make time for Emma if Emma were willing to accompany her on her daily walk. Usually, she gave Emma to understand, the walk was a morning event but when group met the walk took place in the afternoon. Margaret had given precise instructions, using both directional information and landmarks, for finding the paths along the Elora Gorge where she usually walked on Thursday afternoons. She'd got into the habit of schedules and though they never quite ran on time she still clung to the notion that if the schedule were adhered to her life would be perfect. She wanted perfection.

Emma waited about half an hour in the appointed parking lot. She knew that Margaret had not arrived on time and begun walking without her, both because she herself had arrived a few moments early and because the lot was empty of cars. So she waited and made notes. Clouds were scudding in from the west and Emma hoped it would rain tomorrow and clear off for Saturday. Rain on Friday evening would be fine, would spoil the view from the Golf Club windows but would not be so dreary as going to the cottage and spreading Gertrude's ashes in the rain. Little clumps and rivulets of ashes. Not aesthetic. Then they'd have to squeeze heaven knows how many people into the cottage instead of letting them fend for themselves in the garden. How would they get folks to leave? She worked herself into such a state that she got out of the car and paced up and down the lot looking down the road every few moments as if enough searching or wishing would bring Margaret into view. At last the car spun into the lot, spitting the gravel sideways as Margaret turned hard into a parking spot by the entrance and reversed into the space opposite, ready for a quick getaway.

132

The interview with Margaret was not significantly different from that at Sarah's, except that Emma had to concentrate on her footing. She was also aware that although she could, almost literally lift a horse, her cardiovascular system was dangerously out of shape while the older woman's was amazing. Emma's line of questioning had worked well enough with Sarah that she was not disposed to try another just yet. Besides that would have required more attention than she was able to spare from the brisk pace set by her companion. Margaret told, with remarkable recall for detail, the story of her gardening and the topsoil in her drive and her conversation with the canvasser for some worthy cause. Her story telling powers were well developed and very diverting. She was also observant; she was able to tell Emma exactly where Anna had been sitting in Maude's garden.

She also assured Emma that she had scarcely had time to get into the cottage before Anna's call had brought them all crowding into the living room doorway to see Gertrude lying on the couch. Her activity in the communal unloading had been on the fresh air side of the kitchen door, lifting coolers and bags through to the waiting hands of Sarah and Melody. Because she slept in the bunky, Margaret had used the toilet there and had taken some time removing her sleeping bag and effects from the trunk of Anna's car to the bunky and arranging them to suit her needs. She'd also cleaned the sink and toilet.

She did confirm that Anna had not gone in to the cottage either, had been on the outside team and then sat smoking on the bench. Oh, yes, Margaret had noticed that Anna often used part of her cigarette pack as an ashtray when she smoked, and then before closing her cigarette pack she emptied the ashes and butt into the small herb garden between the back door and the bunky. Anna usually used the edge of her package, or any other object which was handy, a plate or cup, as a sort of trowel, burying the butts shallowly under the edge of the woolly thyme.

When called into the living room Margaret had arrived last. Sarah and Melody were in front of her, part way across the room. Anna was nearest to Gertrude, standing over her sort of. Margaret had been able to see nothing and didn't wish to; when the others turned to leave she, Margaret, had backed out in front of them. She'd noticed dishes on the table but she was not clear about what they were. There were three women in the way. Later she'd only collected the two cups, well two mugs actually, when she did the supper dishes. She was sure that it was mugs which she had collected for washing. She hadn't at any time noticed the dog.

"And you wouldn't have noticed extra cups or plates left from lunch when you did the dinner dishes? Perhaps someone else had put them in the sink and you'd have needed to clear them out of the way before beginning to fill the sink?"

Margaret gave this some thought. "I usually start washing dishes and cleaning up while the cooks are putting the dessert out. That way the dishes are more than half done and dry by the time I want to finish up. But on Friday night we'd run out of cups before supper. People had eaten cookies while waiting for the interviews to finish. We were late eating and ate in stages because the police were interviewing us. The police had coffee or tea too. I don't think anyone else did, the doctor or ambulance attendants I mean. But people used quite a few extra cups and plates. So, no, I couldn't tell you about any extras. They were all extras as far as I was concerned and I was a bit upset at being handed an extra pile of cups. Of course it got worse the next day when all of you arrived."

"We weren't much help with dishes were we?" Emma considered apologizing and thought better of it. She let the complaint lie in the air and eventually Margaret continued.

"The advantage to being in the kitchen was that I could hear the doctor and the policeman, the sergeant, talking. I hadn't known that Gertrude took medication for angina. That was another thing she hadn't mentioned to us. She turned out to have quite a few little secrets hidden away."

"Quite a few?"

"Well, a lover for forty five years. I'd say that was quite a secret. Wouldn't you? Of course she'd already known him for fifteen years before we started meeting so he might have slipped her mind. And then another one with whom she has lunches in the country. Angina pales into insignificance."

"You'd never heard of either man?"

"I should say not and I'm green with envy!"

"How old is your son now?"

"Who told you about – oh, yes, he's not that much older than you is he? I'd forgotten that Gertrude's grandchildren were about the age of my child. I brought him up here once when you were both teenagers didn't I?"

"Yes. He didn't care much for horses as I recall."

"He actually works in the same place as one of your cousins, Leyland. I don't know whether they know each other or not. I've told Jeff to speak to Leyland but you know how men sometimes are about doing the introduction thing if they have no business excuse. Especially at their mother's suggestion."

They had by this time returned to the parking lot and were standing between their cars. Margaret looked as fresh as she had on starting out. Emma felt rather damp of forehead and body. She wanted to get to the shower before going to dinner with her cousins.

"I'm seeing Lee at supper tonight. I'll ask." This sounded like a good exit line and Emma opened her car door. "Did you help bury the dog?" She asked as she turned bending but watching Margaret still.

"Sort of. I'd just done the breakfast dishes when Sarah came in and said they'd need some extra hands to move the dog. I helped lift him out of the cart into the hole. The police had, luckily, dumped him in the cart in the shed. Melody remarked on it. Said she figured it was an accident but we could be grateful anyway. He wasn't very heavy – well, he was – but it was how awkward he was and we didn't want the bags slipping off. Odd that we might have been happy petting him the day before and now we were really unwilling to touch his soft ears or nose – repelled by the idea. I went and got some duct tape to secure the bags before we lifted him out of the cart. As a person who does dishes I get to snoop in most of the cupboards. So I knew where the duct tape was."

"But you'd never been in the cupboard in the bathroom to see the angina medication?" Emma felt distinctly catty but couldn't resist it.

"I don't use that bathroom," Margaret replied with remarkable restraint.

"I'd best hurry if I'm to get to tonight's family gathering, Margaret. I expect I'll see you tomorrow evening. Until then, thanks for the exercise." Emma took her leave, swung south on the back roads to the Hanlon and then onto the 401. She was becoming quite proficient in finding her way between suburban Oakville and the maturer towns of Guelph and Kitchener, Cambridge and Owen Sound.

CHAPTER IX

THURSDAY EVENING, JUNE 4

THE PHONE WAS RINGING as Emma got off the elevator. She jogged across the lobby and scrambled to get the key into the lock and push the apartment door open.

"How did you make out with the dog?" It was a male voice. Emma froze.

"I'm the guy helped you load him, remember? David. David Weston."

"Oh, oh, yes. I got him to Guelph in time. Thanks again for your help. How on earth did you find me?"

"I cheated. I looked at the affidavit when you were getting out of the car."

"But I didn't put this phone number on that."

"No, you put your work number on the affidavit. As if anyone was going to call you in Kentucky! But what did they find out about the dog?"

"The guy in Guelph assured me that the dog was dead." Emma was nervous. Where was this leading? "There was no obvious cause of death."

"And that's all?"

"Look," Emma drew a deep breath. "I thank you for your help but I don't think I want to discuss it further, really. Besides, I'm late for dinner."

"Hey, I just wanted to help. Not every day people dig up dogs. Has to be something interesting going on. I thought we could have coffee and talk about it, that's all."

"I'm not going to be in Wiarton until Saturday and then only for a few hours. I'm sorry."

"Oh, I'm not in Wiarton. My family cottage is up there and I was cleaning out the garden and getting the boat ready for summer. I'm in Mississauga and I could be in your part of the country in half an hour."

"I've got a long list of people I need to talk to and a pile of reading to do. There is a funeral Friday and scattering the ashes on Saturday. I just don't have time and, I'm late for dinner already." She hung up the phone without waiting for David to say another word. Rude, she thought. He was rude. Pushy.

*

Dinner was being served by the time Emma had showered, tucked a clean shirt into her dress jeans, and made her way across town to her aunt and uncle's house. As she slid into Sue and Geoff's front hall, she congratulated herself on missing the preparations for supper, even as she realized that she might have missed a good deal of gossipy chatter, the chatter that reveals far more than her formal interviewing could.

Her four male cousins, all of whom were in attendance, all of whom were in their twenties, took up a great deal of space. They too had avoided dinner preparation but were doing well loading their plates at the buffet which lined the kitchen counter. Young men occupy space. They exude hormones and impressions. The mating game, the survival of the species is stamped upon them whether they will or no. She was reminded of young stallions galloping up and down their enclosures posturing for the mares in adjacent pens.

In their way Eric's daughters also took up space. Each had a child under a year old and each had provided instant decoration for Sue's house with an apparently infinite supply of brightly colored bags: one for food, one for clothes, one for diapers. There were, in addition, the two car seats, scattered toys and a round bouncy chair; the latter,

138

looking rather like a circus roundabout, completely occupied the space in the living room usually allotted to pedestrian traffic. Emma had the sense that in her thirties, unaccompanied by a man or children, she had begun to shrink.

Christian had not shrunk. Her cousin was huge, even without the football uniform and protective gear. He would have no difficulty holding a horse still, or reaching in to turn a calf. Emma tried to imagine him operating. He'd be very good with some procedures, but the thought of him doing a hysterectomy on a gerbil made her giggle. His fingers, the fingers of his right hand, the one holding his plate curled up around the edges looking like escaping Polish sausages. His plate was only moderately filled, Emma noticed as she passed him on the way to the food line. When she commented upon it she received his most thoughtful answer, along with a huge smile. "I've learned that I can eat faster if the plate's not so full that stuff is in danger of falling off. If I eat fast enough I can be on my third helping by the time the rest of the crowd comes back for seconds." He'd also found a chair very close to the food supply.

"Hey," he said as she continued past him. "Hey, it's been a long time."

She paused again. "Yes, I expected to see you last weekend with your folks up at the cottage. You haven't started spring training already, have you?"

"We have, actually, but there's a bit of a long weekend before the season rolls. Mom and Dad didn't even tell me grandma was dead until Tuesday. I was away on the weekend visiting a chum who has place in Haliburton. We left early on Friday, to miss the traffic, and didn't get back until late Monday. I hear you and your Mom got stuck with most of the work. That's too bad. Is there anything I can do now?" Disarming. Christian had always been disarming. Hard to tell how innocent it was.

"Mm, well, you'll see what still has to be moved or carried when we get to the apartment in a while. I, for one, will be glad of your help carrying stuff. I'm beginning to think that heaving horses around is easier than heaving books and boxes. Where are you staying until the season starts?"

"Oh, Mom and Dad put me up here when I'm not in Winnipeg. I'm out most of the time walking or jogging or rock climbing. Trying to stay in shape, you know? But I'm off to Winnipeg tomorrow. I'll miss grandma's memorial do and all that."

"How does Zack feel about having you invade his space?"

"There's lots of room. He still has his bedroom. I use the basement. Dad's old weight lifting stuff is down there. I use it if I can't bother going out to the gym. Lee gets more upset about my being here but he hardly ever leaves his cupboards and bones downtown anyway." Smiling, Emma moved on, grabbing a plate and sighing over the familiar food. It was like coming home to see the counter piled high with kielbasa, summer sausage, cabbage rolls, sauerkraut and perogies.

Zack was waiting for her, not obviously, but keeping an eye on her, waiting for her to settle and then unobtrusively he materialized on the chair beside her, his plate nearly empty. His smile was more tentative than Christian's, more touching. Emma could remember his being held for hours by Gertrude as her Aunt Sue bustled about caring for the older boys and cooking for all the aunts, uncles, parents, in-laws and cousins who filled her house. Gertrude cared for the youngest, whoever it was, kept the baby out of harm's way, stroked and babbled and entertained and comforted. What could Lee and Christian and Zack recall of their turns in such affection. Emma, being the oldest, had seen it, seen the fire in it. Although she could not recall the time when she was held in that warmth she had relived it with each cousin, and her brother. At first she'd been jealous, then, in her teens, she'd learned to bask in the reflection, learned that if they were loved that way she had been too. When the babies edged past toddling, at about three, Gertrude lost interest, waited until they 'became human again,' as she put it. Entering the power struggles of four and five year olds did not interest her but she was one of those rare people who loved adolescents, loved watching the struggle for adulthood, especially when it took place in someone else's children. 'You can share power with a teenager,' she'd say. 'Five year olds don't want to share; they just want to know how far they can push.' Could the boys themselves remember back to the early warmth of her love? Zack could, clearly, but there had been sizeable gap between him and Eric's twins; so he'd been warmed for several years.

Emma looked at Alice holding baby Bruce and thought that the baby cycle had begun again. Who would hold these babies?

Zack followed her gaze. "Too bad grandma had to wait so long for the next generation. She sure loved us. I imagine she was counting on you Em."

"Since when did you get so sexist? You could have married several years ago instead of hanging about in dusty libraries."

"Yeah. Well, I wasn't in the library this week. I'm doing my dissertation on the history of settlers in the Bruce, you know. Checking out all our ancestors. Been rechecking data in the local libraries and talking to the old timers up in the peninsula."

"You been here a while, Zack?" she asked indicating the room with a wave of her hand.

"Got here about 6. You have to get to the food early if you want to keep Chris from eating it all." He raised his voice slightly and nodded towards his brother across the room. "I hear now you've been here all week. I figured you'd not be here until today or tomorrow. Thought the horses needed you."

"Mom needed me. Then, as it turned out, grandma needed me."

His eyebrows went up. Only slightly. Zack could talk with his eyes. He was fifteen years younger than she and she'd felt closer to him than to her own brother in some ways. She supposed it was because she'd held him and looked after him when he was a baby. He'd been born in June and come to the cottage for most of that summer. Her brother, Dan, and Zack's brother Lee, who were the same age had spent that summer in the woods somewhere, collecting bugs and bug bites.

"Not like grandma to die that way was it?" he said now, a perogie poised.

Emma was startled. "Explain, Zack."

"Not alone. She was tough. You'd think she'd have held on 'til her group arrived that afternoon. Or phoned one of us – any of us. Midday. She could have reached Mom or even called us at work. She knew I was up there."

"Up there?"

"I told you. My dissertation is on the history of the Bruce, Oliphant and the western shore especially. I've been staying with a friend who lives in Owen Sound. I went over to the cottage on Tuesday to see what it was like without her. Empty. I wished you'd been there."

"I was. The next day."

"Mom says you've been driving around seeing grandma's friends. Have they been interesting?"

"Yes, to both questions."

"Mom says you've got some idea about grandma's death being not so natural as it might seem." Finally he'd got to it. She wondered how many others in the room wanted to ask her about her curiosity, and how many just thought she was silly.

"Yes, again."

"Are you being melodramatic?"

"I think not."

"We, Lee and Chris and I, each still spent time with her most summers. I loved that place. Lee never got tired of roaming through the bush, looking for varieties of snake and lizard. You'd think he'd have seen them all a million times already, had personal names for them. They probably recognize him! 'Look out! Here comes the guy who picks us up and measures us and counts the number of chains we have on our backs. God, he's got rough hands!' Always looking for the rattlers. I remember one summer he was up about four different times, maybe six weeks altogether, combing the woods. He finally found one living under the pump house, within inches of the back door.

"Chris used to swim. I'd row and he'd swim for miles. It seemed like miles. Maybe it was. Out to the islands and back. I just read. Went up in the tree house or down on the beach or out in the rowboat and read, even when I was keeping Chris company out on the lake. Grandma let us be us. After the dishes were done and our beds were made she did anyway."

"Will you still go?"

"Depends who gets the cottage doesn't it. I don't think so. I think my trip this week was to say good-bye. I expect it will be sold and the money shared around. I could use it to pay off my student loans."

"Would someone murder to pay off their student loans, Zack?"
Emma asked.

"Ho! Back!" Holding his hand as if to ward off a charging horse,
Zack abruptly stood and headed towards the dessert table without asking her why she'd gone north on Wednesday. She picked up some coffee and began to circulate.

Leyland did not eat any more than he had as a kid. Even in adoles-
cence he'd been a frugal eater, 'living on air' Gertrude had said, insub-
stantial like the creatures of the fire, the lizards and snakes which he
studied, the elusive creatures of the forest, spirits who are visible at the
edge of the eye and gone when you turn your head. Emma mentioned
Margaret's son to Leyland when she got an opportunity. Jeff, as it
turned out was Lee's immediate superior. They knew each other well.
Or, as well as that relationship allows.

"Did you know that his mom was in grandma's group, Lee? Did he
ever mention that he and I had spent a week or so together when we
were kids? Chaperoned of course; we were about 11 at the time. At
the cottage." She felt the last was a bit unnecessary as soon as she'd
said it. Where else?

"Nope. We talk about skeletons mostly."

"And have the skeletons kept you busy this week? Dad would have
liked to see you before he flew home, I'm sure."

"Mom said not to come. Everyone was too busy here. I would have
booked a day off otherwise and come home."

"That's too bad. I could have used your help." Emma debated
whether to make her cousin her ally even at this late date. Another set
of eyes and ears, eyes and ears used to investigation, would maybe be
helpful. She realized she was a bit reluctant to trust him. "Do you always work a regular nine to five day at the Museum, Lee, or is your
time more flexible?"

"Most days I'm in to work by 8. I sometimes get away early in the
afternoon. Occasionally I'm called to look at bones or specimens that
some small museum has and wants to label correctly. The museum
lends me out. In fact just last week I spent most of my time in London,
looking at some bones which had been donated to the Biology Department. Snakes and lizards. Bit of a drive from Toronto each day; so I

stayed over on Wednesday and Thursday night. Western is attractive. Ever been there?" Emma sighed and said that she had, when she was an undergraduate, visited for a football weekend maybe.

"Don't believe the part about leaving early in the afternoon, Emma. Lee works to midnight half the time. He probably stayed over in London and never left the lab at Western the whole three days. He needs the overtime to pay for the fancy car he has out there." Christian was passing with his third plate of food.

"Christian's full of it. He knows the museum doesn't pay overtime. I just enjoy my work which is more than you can say for someone who hits people for a living." Leyland's bitterness was a habit. He and Christian had been rivals since Cain killed Abel.

"Don't get angry with Christian. Maybe he was giving you an alibi." Emma smiled hoping her statement would sound like a joke.

"You're kidding. Christian would be more likely to nominate me than alibi me. Why do I need an alibi, by the way?"

"Because you could have murdered Grandma." This came out rather loudly in the crowded space, partly because it coincided with a lull in the conversation around the room. Everyone froze looking at her. Leyland put his plate down and walked out. She heard his car door slam and the engine of his sporty BMW rev as he pulled out of the drive.

"Not very subtle, Emma," said Christian, when general conversation had begun again.

"No. Also bad timing."

"Do you really think she was murdered?"

"Pretty sure."

"And one of us did it?"

"Could have, yes."

Christian went back to his chair and attacked his dinner.

She moved on to talk to Roswit. Her uncle Eric and aunt Rowena had gone in for early Celtic and Saxon names: Ailric, Roswit and Bronwen. Roswit was juggling an infant in one hand and her dinner fork in the other.

"Quite a handful, Roswit. Want some help? I've finished eating. I can hold the drooler, here." Emma reached out and skillfully sat wee Bruce on her hip.

"Gee, thanks. I'm starving. Missed lunch today and then I'm sitting here with a plateful of food I can't eat. Parenthood is torture."

"How come you missed lunch?" It was the only possible next line if she did not want to embark on the horrors of parenthood. Emma felt no desire to hear about Roswit's views on parenthood.

"Been working in Kitchener all week, well the last two weeks, setting up the books for a small firm. But my babysitter's kids have chicken pox; so I've had to take Bruce with me each day. If I feed him at lunch I don't have time to go out and get anything from a coffee shop or restaurant. Today I forgot to put my own lunch in the baby bag. Brucie here...he got lunch but Mommie didn't." This last was addressed clearly to the baby and Brucie gurgled in appreciation, though possibly not in sympathy.

"Didn't know you were back to work. Must be quite a handful."

"Jack is unemployed. Someone has to bring in the food for Brucie...don't they sweetheart. Lucky Bronwen, she works in a day care in the school a couple of blocks from where she lives, she has a job and help looking after little Alice. Not fair is it Brucie. My it's nice to eat someone else's cooking, though. You'd really like this sausage, pumpkin; just wait, soon, soon." Emma was beginning to feel a bit absent. She asked the questions and Bruce got the answers. Well, so far her interviews were certainly increasing the possibilities. Another family member on the road and needing money. Just what she needed.

Still carrying the baby Emma wandered off, ostensibly in search of coffee but actually hoping to find that Bronwen had been chained to her place of employment for the entire previous week. Bronwen had Alice in the huge bouncy chair and was coping rather well with her dinner. Indeed she was also coping well with her job and was very grateful that she didn't have to drive all over the country to get business, 'consulting' as her sister did. Her emphasis on the 'consulting' made it clear that she did not think much of her sister's livelihood. Sybling rivalry is not absent in identical twins, Emma observed. She did not know these cousins well. They were young enough that she had not spent time with them in summers at her grandmother's cottage, had seen them only on occasions like this, crowded and noisy family gatherings to celebrate weddings or funerals. Usually they had had a handsome young man or two in tow. Not tonight.

"I didn't know that both you and Ros were back at work." Emma hoped Bruce would not miraculously develop speech to tell his aunt that this gambit had been used already.

"Oh, they held my job at the day care for me. I took only the regulation maternity leave. I love my job and there's room for Alice there; so it's perfect."

"You're in full time?"

"No, I work Monday, Wednesday and Friday one week and Tuesday, Thursday the next. Half time. It helps to pay for the new house. Jimmy is doing okay but every little bit helps. He's got another year to go before they put him on commission. Then we can afford another baby maybe. Hey, you can put Bruce in the chair now, I'm done eating." She put her plate on the table beside her and swinging Alice up into the crook of her arm began to nurse her.

"So, you're off work tomorrow. That'll be nice; you and Alice will be rested for grandma's party."

"No, worst luck. I may have to get there late, I'll be working 'til 5.30. I've asked to get off a bit early but that will depend on other folks' schedules too. So I'll see you when I see you tomorrow."

A few moments later, dinner over, the babies were scooped into the embraces of their eager great aunts while everyone else adjourned to Gertrude's apartment. Geoff drove his company van, cleared of its rear seats and its usual machinery. He'd volunteered it to carry furniture and boxes to appropriate destinations after the choosing had been done. The ceremony took less than an hour. Each person circled the apartment armed with tape and labels, putting the latter onto anything he or she wanted. At the end of half an hour any items with more than one label were allotted by giving a single choice to each person in turn, starting with the oldest and working down. Fifteen minutes took care of the second part of the process and all of them expressed their satisfaction both with the process and the result.

Emma had followed Ailric around as he chose some antique china and some modern pottery. He knew his mother admired the latter, watched her linger over the piles of table wares, and he planned to give her the pieces he'd chosen for her birthday and Christmas gifts over the next couple of years. Ailric was rather shy and very frugal. Rowena had already chosen some of Gertrude's cut glass to decorate her home but Ailric knew that she would not have taken all the things which appealed to her.

Emma approached as he placed his name on four lilac glazed bowls. As a warm up question Emma asked him how his sisters were doing. He gave her a casual and shortened version of what she already knew, although he did not seem to know that his brother-in-law was out of work. Emma wondered whether Roswit had told her parents, and, for that matter, why she had confided in a cousin she scarcely knew. Perhaps she needed to tell someone a bit about her worries and Emma was enough like a stranger on a bus, the person whom you will never see again, that she could be told.

Ailric was on holiday. He was new man in the electronics firm where he'd begun work the year before and his holidays were not in prime time. He said it didn't matter. He had no kids or family with whom he wanted to coordinate time off. He'd used the time to paint his apartment and tidy his computer files. He told her about his job at some length as he considered whether to put his name on four place settings of Crown Derby's *Brittany* which already had Roswit's name on them.

"So, how long will it take you to pay off your student loans?" Emma asked, as a continuation of her conversation with Zack.

"Oh, I've already done that." Ailric's smile presented a confusing mixture of both his parents and was so triumphant that Emma had to turn away.

"Wow. Lucky guy. How?"

He proceeded to tell her in some detail of his summer jobs and his frugality and his dislike of borrowing if it could be avoided and of his repayment scheme. He'd been able to live at home for his first year at work because his sisters had both gone to college in two-year programs and married young, leaving a space in the house which his parents were happy to have him fill. All in all he was, as she had said, a lucky guy.

"When did you last see Grandma?"

"Probably around Easter, before she began moving up to the cottage for the summer. I hardly ever get up there anymore. Haven't got a car. Don't need one yet. So I only go when the parents go and, given Mom's allergies, that's not very often."

When Emma asked why he hadn't been by earlier in the week to help out with the packing and cleaning he looked so startled that she knew it had not occurred to his father or mother to suggest it. He apologized as he hugged her goodbye and wished her good luck if he didn't get time to talk to her the next day or so. She asked whether he'd be coming to the ceremony in Oliphant and he looked dubious. Once again she was not sure how much information he'd received.

By 9.30 the young men had loaded the van and driven off into the night. Emma looked around the now almost empty apartment and sighed. For the next three nights she and her mother would be camping out amid the rejects.

No one had questioned the pile of boxes in one corner labelled 'Emma.' She had left them open so that her cousins could see that she was taking books and papers. Odd that no one had asked about them. But maybe it was of a piece with their not being around this week. Gertrude was gone. There was nothing further to be done about it. Grandmothers come and go through many children's lives. If they live with their children, or become surrogate parents the emotional ties are fierce. But, in a world of small, even claustrophobic nuclear units, grandparents are ephemeral. Now you see them now you don't.

Emma had driven to the apartment with her uncle, leaving the rental car for her mother. So she was alone. The message machine was blinking. David Weston had called again and apologized for intruding on her grief. He'd left his number and said she was welcome to call. Emma realized that she'd like to talk to him, like to talk to anyone outside the circle of family and friends.

She undressed slowly, wearily, and stretched out with her notes of the day's interviews. She filled in what she'd heard from her cousins. She realized that she had hoped that all of her relatives would tell how involved they had been in the previous week; she'd hoped they would say, "Oh, on Friday I was in the office from 6 a.m. 'til midnight," or, "I got back from the jungles of Central America only last Saturday." She'd also hoped that they would immediately volunteer six references to prove that they had been miles from Oliphant at the time in question. In her saner moments she realized that if they had said any of those things she would have been even more suspicious of them.

As she finished her note making she smiled. The situation was comic. It revealed the difference between life and fiction. In reality each person had ample opportunity to be in Oliphant on the previous Friday. In a novel no one would believe such coincidence. In a novel the detective would have a means of checking each story. The stories were likely all true; Chris had been in Haliburton, Lee in London, Roswit in Kitchener and so on. It was just that she couldn't be sure.

She sighed and picked up a journal, opening it at random.

August 31, 1973, Friday   *Oliphant   7:15 am*

I'm up early. Sin and I play on the beach. The air is so warm that I've thrown on only a sheer Indian cotton dress; the water is so warm that although I intend only to wander along the beach in the shallows I soon find myself in up to my waist. The cloth clings to me as T-shirts do in photos of movie stars. I fantasize. Sin runs clownishly in circles around me kicking spray high in the air. Water drips from my hair and nose. He barks and I laugh. We disturb the blue heron who usually stands watchfully at the mouth of the creek. Today he decides that we are dangerous, or that we are destroying his prospects for breakfast and he flaps laboriously across the causeway to the tall grass on the other side.

They, we, well not we, not I anyway, talked about relationships last night. Three of us are, and have been for years unattached in the conventional sense, although we ran the gamut of marriage and childbearing before achieving our detachment. Three are still on their first relationship and three have had more than one marriage. I do not talk about R. Once again. How very odd that after all this time no one knows about us, R. and me. What would I do without him? There is a side – a time – a whole shelf of my being that no one knows about. It's rather like Bluebeard's castle with a hidden room into which even my closest friends and my most loved family have never set foot. In there R. and I take off our suits and our armour and lounge about in metaphorical silks and harem clothes. We eat grapes and listen to the music of the lascivious lute. We don't really. We talk about our fears and our loves and our imagination and our creative work. We touch and comfort each other and no one beyond the doors knows. Not knowing, of course, means not knowing us. We have made ourselves into other people – people who look like us but are not. People who walk around out there in the world, who eat and sleep and hold babies and listen to the lives of others but do not share a whole life in return. Is that odd? Does everyone else have walled chambers, unshared secrets, whole lives which are closed to the world? I feel sometimes profoundly split, living out the other *in my head, acting, no matter which side of the door I'm on. So the unreality of one half infects the other. My whole life is unreal, to me anyway, though I suppose my friends think they see the whole thing, think they know me, think they can piece together the jigsaw of my life despite the fact that they are missing one quarter of the pieces, the pieces which show me as lover and partner, as girl still, as woman still, as full crone not desiccated, bitter old woman. Or bitter in unexpected ways, perhaps. Bitter about secrecy. Bitter about never being declarative about our relationship, never wearing into coupledom where friends join the two names, see the two faces together, build a whole Noah's Ark. Another illusion stranded on Ararat.*

Maude is here for the weekend. Came up after the meeting last night. The gentians are out. Maude comes for the fringed gentians. They are early. Does that mean there will be an early winter? Hard to believe when it is still so warm, though now that I think about it I recall that two weeks ago I was lamenting the coming on of Orion and the cold blue skies. And the Grass of Parnassus. My favourite. Maude has created a picture for me, well for herself but I have appropriated it, order it 100 prints at a time for cards, made it my signature. Wonder why it appeals so. Such a tiny thing with so much detail. Thousands of them paint a meadow white; the fringed gentians and the Grass of Parnassus; the goldenrod and the purple asters. The fen paints itself blue and white. The edges and hedges are purple and gold. No bugs disturb us. We shall go for a long walk this afternoon, north to Sandy Bay, along beside the fen, taking the flower book with us and identifying sneeze weed and nutrush. It's too bad really that there isn't a way through the fen, a board walk or some such thing on which one could walk and view and not damage the plants. It's really too far to wear wellies, otherwise we could wade north through the wetlands searching for tiny lobelia. Maude's photos can make the miniature flowers huge reminding me of Georgia O'Keefe's admonition to look, to see the beauty of the infinitesimal detail.

Maude usually comes for a weekend in September. This year she is early. For the first time in 30 years she is not going to school on Tuesday. Last evening we sat and exchanged horror stories. She starts by telling me of a five year old who didn't want to go home from school and what she found when she took him home in her car. I talk about the difficulties I had removing children from abusive situations. It turns out that several times she didn't report the situations to anyone, felt there would be no point. Tomorrow, when I have thought about what she said, I shall write out the exact details of her stories. Too late to rescue those people now. Why do I want a record.

This morning we shall sit over our morning coffee and imagine yellow school buses sucking up the children across the land, delivering them to durance vile. And celebrate that she is no longer waiting in the kindergarten classroom. Not that she disliked it; I did not dislike my years in the slimy heart of social work. Just that we both have other things in mind.

She's getting ready for her first juried show. I'm most of the way through three books. Well, part way through three books. I drew a picture last week of my writer's block. It doesn't keep me from writing, just from finishing Huge mountain, not a square block but a smiling mountain, not smugly smirking, but truly friendly. It lets me get part way through a book and then ....

I write a quotation from Seneca and post it above my desk.

Not because things are difficult do we not dare,
but because we do not dare they are difficult. ⁱ

People think starting is difficult. I get stuck on finishing. I do not dare to finish. Oh, yes. Looking up at the mountain makes it grow. It gets higher and higher as I look. Walking on it, one step at a time, one inch at a time, makes it possible. I must just open the notebook and write the next paragraph even if I have no clue what it will be until it is written; I must rip out the seam on a quilt that's not working and make it possible to begin again; I must unravel the wool from a sweater which is unsatisfactory and redesign it; so I must do this several times, so? So the craft must be practised, revised, changed, re-evaluated, so? I have never expected instant results when working with others, why do I expect instant perfection from myself? The mountain must be visited step by step, changing paths, zigzagging, spiraling around it, searching for other paths. I construct a mantra. Begin; only begin. Begin the beginning. Begin the middle. Begin the end. Begin what is begun. Begin again. Begin. Not starting is a sure way not to finish, not moving on is a sure way to die on the mountain. It stands there, grows, looms over. Loom. What a pun. The web, the weaving. In Morocco the looms sometimes do hang up in the middle of the room and men are seated in mid-air weaving. We get caught in our own web, weaving and then it looms over us, the weaving, the possibility taking on impossible shadows and becoming frightening. The longer it looms the larger it gets. Holding its hand, dancing with it, turning it slowly so that the light shines on its face, climbing in the light, sitting on tree stumps, watching mountain brooks, making friends with our mountain, embracing it makes it possible. Dance with the mountain.

Too high can't get over it,
Too deep can't get under it,
Too wide can't go past it,
Dance with it and turn it around.
Meet it, embrace it ask it to dance.

Emma fell asleep and dreamed she was dancing with More Sinister; he was a puppy still but tall enough to put his paws on her shoulder and slobber on her ear as they danced.   She did not hear her mother come in.

CHAPTER X

FRIDAY, JUNE 5

Waking on Friday Morning Emma was aware of feeling overwhelmed. She had succeeded in finding motive and opportunity for almost everyone. In the normal course of affairs, in the modern world with fast cars and frequent air flights, it is possible to travel quickly and easily, especially if the trip can be planned ahead. Almost everyone to whom she'd spoken could have planned a quick trip to Oliphant on the previous Friday. She thought that her parents were in the clear, but after that she could rule out no one; ruefully she realized that she could have done it herself. She could have obtained the means, had as much motive as most of the others to whom she'd spoken, had the time to fly north and home again on the Friday. Fortunately there were people at her clinic who could testify to her being at work all day Friday. Good. That was one suspect less.

She thought through her muzzy process again. Motive. What motive did these people all have? Did her cousins, or her aunts and uncles, for that matter think that Gertrude's tiny estate would make that much difference in their lives? This was unlikely unless they were insane or desperate. The cousins had even less to gain than her aunts and uncles. The estate went to the older generation. So it was unlikely. Possible but unlikely.

Means. She had the means. Well, depending on how Gertrude had been killed, most of them could find means. If the family were unlikely suspects, in terms of motive and even in terms of means, the women in Gertrude's group were not. They had, perhaps more motive and being of Gertrude's age and having a wide experience with gardens they had easier access to sedatives and poisonous plants. But most of them had, like Gertrude's family, balanced Gertrude's love and generosity against her scathing tongue and overpowering will for many years. If she had been holding over them the peccadillos which she starred in her journal, she had been doing it for a very long time.

Regarded in the light of society at large her grandmother's family and friends were, however, remarkably fortunate and kindly people. What would have sent one of them over the edge on Friday, May 29? What circumstances had lately changed? Whose life had recently been altered by Gertrude. Yes, that was a better route. The journals gave hints of past injuries but those injuries had been long endured. What had changed now?

Emma considered change as she drove north to breakfast with Jean. The rain which had threatened the day before was heavy enough that her windshield wipers were on full and provided a rhythmic background to her repetitive thought patterns. Motive, means, opportunity, change. Change, change, what changed?

Jean rose early and worked each morning on her quilts. The morning light was clearer and her eyes were stronger then. Those tiny wire things used to thread needles were hard to see now that she was in her 80's. So the teen-aged son of her next door neighbor came over most evenings after he'd had supper and she handed him a box of needles and several colors of thread as well as a list stating how many needles were to be threaded with which color. Then the needles with their threads were waiting for her in the morning, hanging from a colorful strip of patchwork which she had framed and hung on the wall beside her easy chair. She still pieced by hand while most young women nowadays were quilting by machine. The meditation of her hands, she called it and could not see why she should give up such an exercise just because it was hard now for her to thread a needle.

She was in her easy chair when Emma arrived. Coffee and toasted English muffins and jam were on a table within easy reach. When Jean had finished eating she wiped her fingers carefully and began to sew. The light from the window beside her was grey; she held the fabric close to her face.

Jean gave substantially the same account as the other women had of the beginning of the weekend. She had been busy with her quilt on the previous Friday morning and had then gone out to buy fruit and coffee cake for the group's Sunday breakfast. She'd discovered a store which had large pans of cinnamon rolls which had been barely cooked and then frozen. You took them out of the freezer and baked them for half an hour and they were as good as if you'd done it yourself. She hadn't gone home for lunch but had soup and salad at a small bookstore which also served light lunches. She did that before she bought the groceries, now that she thought about it, or the bread would have thawed before she got home. In the bookstore you could read and eat and it was very quiet and no one bothered you if you sat for quite a while. She'd read *Alias Grace* though she didn't buy it. Instead she bought a murder mystery on tape – that was what she was listening to in Gertrude's yard when Natasha had come running to the car door gesturing. So dramatic, Natasha. Jean had seen Maude, who had arrived just before her, begin to unload her car and stop to talk to Natasha. Then Maude had run toward the cottage, but she'd not heard anything because she had the windows almost closed and the tape turned up quite loud.

She'd trained as a nurse years before – worked as a nurse too – but her instincts were clouded by the question of who dunit. She was, therefore, not first into the cottage, nor near the living room door when the others peered in. She'd felt very unwell, disoriented perhaps, by being wrenched from a bloody 14th century murder to a calm 20th century death bed. The others said Gertrude was dead.

"Did you actually go into the living room? You were a nurse, surely you'd have felt some obligation to confirm Anna's diagnosis?"

"No. Anna was very certain. I asked her. Besides I retired a long time ago. Playing nurse would be irresponsible and I'd no desire to doubt Anna's opinion. I was shocked though. I think I'd begun to feel we were all invulnerable. Immortal. We'd been together so long."

"So you never went into the living room?"

"I must have, at bed time, crossed the corner to get upstairs; so did Melody and Sarah. I went out to the bunky to go to the bathroom. I did not want to go into the room where she'd died."

Emma forebore to make a comparison with Natasha who'd also felt uneasy but had at last gone to bed, alone, only ten feet from Gertrude's final resting place. Jean's reticence was interesting.

"Why would someone kill Gertrude?" Emma suddenly asked, straying from her usual script in an effort to find a chink in Jean's calm exterior. To her horror she was successful. Jean crumpled over her sewing almost sobbing into it, then catching herself and fumbling for her table napkin. After at least a minute of wordless moaning and sniffing Jean pulled herself upright enough to look at Emma again.

"She was so powerful. You know that, Emma. Often she was calm and powerful and she'd be so far away you'd want to reach her, find what she was thinking. You'd try to talk to her and you couldn't remember what she'd said. Or she would answer by telling a story about someone you'd never heard of. Some literary character, or some sociological experiment. She never spoke in straight lines, only in circles or spirals. Then sometimes she'd be excited and anything could happen. Her sarcasm would fly. It wasn't fair that she could do so many things well. I don't think we understood her. People are afraid of what they don't understand. That's as clear as I can be about your grandmother, Emma."

"Did she ever talk about Roger or George with you?" Emma hadn't intended to ask this question but Jean's outburst had surprised her. Perhaps in her changed mood Jean would reveal something the others had not. But Jean's response was the usual ignorance tinged with annoyance. Was the annoyance jealousy or anger at secrets kept or was it fear? Jean's earlier response had opened a window to the depth of emotion which jealousy might cause.

"No. We rarely talked for long and then usually about art and books. She was really aware of how color and words worked and she could use them. Her sewing and knitting were creative not copied." Jean had returned to her distant analytic mode and was again in the mood to see

Gertrude as superfemale. "She may have been creative about men too," she concluded, nodding wisely, as if agreeing with herself.

On this note Emma left. Jean picked another needle from the wall beside her and went on piecing a quilt swirling with Monet pastels.

*

Melody was surveying fabric swatches and matching paint chips when Emma arrived. Emma had once more lost track of what she wanted to know, was simply muddling around in information. She had a brief view of herself as a small boat swamped by a rough lake of facts, no not facts, perceptions, suspicions. Then she noticed that she was standing looking at herself in the glass of Melody's front door. The door behind the glass was elegantly moulded and sponge painted in blue and aqua, hours of work to create a unique surface which reminded Emma of Jean's quilt. Melody's face appeared at the shiny window and the door eased open. Melody apologized for taking so long to answer. She'd had to put the colored fabrics down in just the right order.

Emma felt huge and horsey beside the infinitely neat Melody. A quick glance showed her a living space as beautiful and studied as the door. "What are you decorating? Everything looks perfect."

"Oh, I just redecorate one room each year. There are other things I like to do but looking for fabric and pictures and interesting touches is an excuse to travel and search through antique stores or garage sales for treasures which can be refinished or painted to suit my project. Shall we sit where we can see out over the garden?"

They sat watching rain make trails down the glass and bend the heads of the daffodils and tulips in the well-regulated flower beds beyond. Over yet another cup of coffee Emma asked Melody for her version of the previous Friday's events. Melody echoed Sarah's account. Emma wondered whether they had rehearsed their memories and supposed they likely had. Why wouldn't they?

However, where Sarah's recollections had been largely practical and auditory, Melody's were more intuitive and visual. She was precise about the position of the cars in the drive, both when they arrived

158

and parked beside Gertrude's little hatchback which was always parked at right angles to the drive and under the eaves of the cottage, and later when the drive was filled. Maude had parked beside Anna's car and Jean had pulled up at right angles to the first three cars and behind them, nosing onto the lawn. Natasha and Edwina had parked parallel to Jean. The police had parked behind the first three cars while the coroner, the sergeant and ambulance had had to leave their vehicles further and further down the drive. The ambulance being almost out to the road had caused the attendants more than a little effort, the wheels on their cart not rolling very effectively on the rough gravel and lawn. She described the open door, the pile of luggage, the food which she put away, the coolers on the steps away from the traffic. She agreed on the order of persons standing in the living room looking at Gertrude.

"I keep seeing her face. She looked alive lying there with her glasses on and her book beside her, neatly lined up with the corner of the coffee table."

"Her glasses on?"

"Yes," Melody paused for several seconds, looking into the garden, concentrating. "Maybe that was why I kept looking at her face. Yes, she had her glasses on and the chain that held them was around the back of her neck. Yes, that's what made it odd."

"Odd?"

"Well, you know when she was having a nap she always took her glasses off. I have friends who fall asleep with their glasses on. They complain about bending the frames in their sleep. I don't recall Gertrude doing that. She'd lie down with the chain already removed from behind her head. She'd read for a while and then she'd put the glasses on top of the open book and go to sleep."

Emma was excited. "Yes, yes. That's what she did. In all the years I visited I never saw her fall asleep with her glasses on and you're right about the book too. It was usually open. The glasses acted as a sort of book mark. I'll check my recollection with Mom, but I think you are right."

"What would that mean to you Emma?"

"It would mean that she hadn't expected to go to sleep. It might mean someone placed her book on the table to make it look as if she'd gone to sleep after reading a bit. It might mean other things too but those are the ones that spring to mind."

"I agree. What have you done about your suspicions so far?"

"I called the police, I think it was on Tuesday, asking them to reopen the case because the dog had died. I don't know how seriously they took me."

"Could I help?"

"If you know someone to call, please, someone who'll listen to suspicions about a dead dog and glasses in the wrong place. It all sounds very slim."

"Gertrude has been cremated, right?"

"Yes. Eric will pick up the ashes on his way north tomorrow."

"Hard to make any but a circumstantial case isn't it?"

"I'm afraid so." Emma did not mention the analysis of the dog's last meal. She was relieved to experience Melody's concern, but also distrusted it.

Emma took Melody on through her recollection of the plate, and cups on the coffee table.

"Were they cups or mugs, Melody?"

"Oh, they were cups, well one was a cup with a saucer and one was a glass mug with a matching plate, the middle size of plate, you know? Not the dinner plates but the dessert plates; she had a set of lovely glass plates. The plate, absolutely clean, was in the middle of the table and a cup and saucer was on each side of the table. It was odd, you know, because there was no chair at the table, but sometimes, if you are across the room and there is no place there to set down your cup, you'd step to the table when you were done. And the book was closed, closed and neatly set at the corner of the table nearest her head. She might have been reading, but if so she had left the book closed which, as we agree, seemed unusual."

No, Melody hadn't noticed the dog but Anna had told her about tripping over it. It must have been completely hidden by the coffee table, in the narrow space between the couch and the table. She'd been offended by the way the police had dumped the dog in the corner of the room. It was ugly and disrespectful. She described digging the hole the next morning and the shifting of the awkward body. Margaret was a great help. Margaret was very strong.

Beyond the recollection of detail Melody was less helpful. On the subject of Roger and George she was downright inventive.

"I find them hard to believe. Perhaps they were characters in her novels. You got the names from her journals, didn't you? Did she write any of her fiction in her journals?"

"I thought about that, Melody. But I'm talking to George this afternoon; so he is real enough."

Melody obviously wasn't about to enlighten Emma as to what she knew of Sarah's relationship with Roger, and had never paid attention to Anna's cigarettes except to sit well away from them when they were lit.

"Did Gertrude ever threaten you or, to give it its proper title, blackmail you with information about your work?"

Melody had been floating along, giving sincere and detailed answers to questions which she had rehearsed not only with Sarah but in her own mind. This question threw her off guard. She sputtered as if there were ice in her feed line.

"Emma. What an improper question!"

"You mean she did?"

"Don't be silly. Your grandmother wasn't like that."

"You mean she was more subtle?"

"I mean she had no cause and I can't see what your question has to do with her death."

Melody scarcely listened to Emma's account of the journal entry with the star beside it, the journal entry which told of Melody's personal involvement in certain cases which had appeared in her courtroom. Melody simply turned her attention to her redecoration project and insisted that Emma follow her upstairs to see the bathroom in question. It was clear that she was no longer interested in answering questions but was too polite to ask Emma to leave. She might bore her to death instead.

*

Driving away from Melody's, Emma realized that it was almost noon on Friday; the vet had said results might be in on Friday. She turned on the radio and listened to the end of the CBC's morning program. But her mind circled. She began by trying to list the things which had changed over the past year. She could think of very little. Then she rehearsed her speech for the memory party. But at the back of her mind was always a question mark. After half an hour on the road speculating on what the report might say while trying to concentrate on tasks she had yet to complete, she could contain her curiosity no longer. She pulled into the service station at Teviotdale, got gas, used the washroom and then gave in and searched for her calling card. She dialed her grandmother's apartment. No answer. There were still five beeps on the machine, though, which should mean that no one had left her a message. She searched through her notebook. She was sure that she'd put the number where she could reach the vet at Guelph in some logical place. What would a logical place be?

Finally she found the number at the beginning of Natasha's interview. Well why not? She called the University. She had to wait a long time and negotiate a series of hurdles, punching in numbers on the touch tone phone. When at last she achieved the correct office the man was out, had left for the weekend. The voice spoke with the bitterness of one who had not yet left for the weekend, was, in fact, tied to the phone talking to someone who wanted to speak to a man who had left for the weekend. Had the professor left a message for her? Emma was impatient. Her impatience slowed the response at the other end of the line. "Yes," the secretary thought he might have. Sounds of papers being shuffled were followed at last by a, "Yes."

The secretary read the information slowly and Emma jotted what she could into her notebook. The vet had left the specific chemical names and numbers and then had translated the science into general terms. The biscuit contained a quantity of what was apparently anti nausea pills, ground into powder, as well as large quantities of barbiturates; the dog had also ingested, though not in the biscuits, bits of

162

plant matter which were not oregano or thyme or any other likely herb. This plant matter, however was high in toxic alkaloids which would have suppressed the central nervous system. The plant matter and its chemical analysis had been forwarded to a forensic botanist but they might not know exactly what plant or plants were involved for some time. Emma said her thanks in distant voice, looking into the receiver as if looking hard enough would permit her to see the biscuit, the pills, or perhaps the secretary, and assure herself that she was hearing correctly. She had suspected this answer but suspicion and confirmation of suspicion are far from the same.

She felt suddenly slightly nauseated and held to the door of the phone booth a moment before phoning the Wiarton detachment of the Provincial Police. That number was at the beginning of Anna's interview. She remembered writing it there, beside Anna's number when she had first called the police. The officer on duty took down her message and said she would get back to her. Emma gave her itinerary for the next 24 hours, and stressed that she would be in Oliphant the next day and needed to see someone before she left for Kentucky on Sunday. Then she hung up and walked slowly back to the car. The rain had stopped but the parking lot was rutted and muddy.

Maude had offered to meet Emma in Elora or, to have coffee in a café above the Elora Gorge or lunch, maybe, in Morriston at Envers. As Emma drove through Arthur she was glad she'd insisted on seeing Maude at home. There was the matter of cigarette butts, of course. There was also the garden.

Maude was the person who had supplied many of the plants in Gertrude's garden. They had traded plants and visited nurseries, shared compost and seedlings. They favoured the naturalized garden, hovering on the verge of chaos, a style which Melody and Margaret and Sarah found distasteful if not frightening. Edwina, having two gardens, had the luxury of controlling one while the other blended into the weeds and woods surrounding her cottage. Emma was hoping that Maude could tell her about the plants in her garden, and in Gertrude's too, of course.

From Melody's Emma had struck north – timing the trip in a serious way once she'd passed Elora. She even remembered to subtract the time she'd used to stop in Teviotdale. From the Gorge north the land slowly flattened, rolled into farmland, curled around artificial lakes and ponds, plunged into the occasional valley but proceeded for the most part serenely.

A long line of pines sheltered Maude's yard and marked the northerly extremity of her property. The sideroad ran southeast to northwest. The entire township had been surveyed at 45° off the straight compass points. This was confusing to those trying to give or follow directions but meant that at any time of year sun entered Maude's workroom for most of the day. Now, approaching the summer solstice, the sun, breaking through the clouds, flooded the sunporch entry with morning light while the afternoon sun warmed the deck on the side of the house farthest from the drive. Cows lounged along the back fence, restrained from grazing on Maude's garden by an electric wire and ancient stone rubble. On the east side of the house two huge beds had been created, one for food and the other, nearer the road, for flowers, although the demarcation was not so clear or simple as that.

Maude's dog, Phoggy, met Emma at the road and succeeded in being on all sides of the car at once as she edged down the drive to the house. Maude rescued her. When the greetings were concluded, but before she allowed Maude and Phoggy to shepherd her into the house, Emma made for the garden. She toured the rows of vegetables, or the rows where vegetables had been last year. They were inches high, at the stage where it is hard to imagine that in less that three months bushels of zucchini and tomatoes will hang from their vines. Now, in early June, rotting cabbage leaves and broccoli only partly dug into the soil were testimony of the previous year's rich crop, while tiny markers heralded the coming season. The raspberry canes at the far end of the bed, already had leaves and promise of berries. Then she wandered along the flower beds and exclaimed over the progress of the peony buds, the fragrant lilacs, the daffodils now past their prime. They admired the herbs sheltering beside the sunny work room, and passed through the space between the porch and the wood shed to reach the other side of the house. Emma wrote the name of each plant on a chart which she drew up in her notebook. She told Maude that she was planning a garden for her home in Kentucky. Maude humoured her.

From Margaret, Emma had a fairly clear idea of where on the west side of the house Anna had sat. There was a chair there, out on the lawn some distance, still. Clearly it had been moved down from the deck, probably so that Anna could sit in the afternoon sun and see the road at the same time. They circled the north side of the yard. When finally they returned to the house, Emma directed her steps, in what she hoped was a casual manner, to pass the chair. There were no butts on the ground and none in the nearest flower border, or in the baskets of geraniums at the edge of the deck. None that Emma could see on a quick inspection anyway. It didn't mean anything. Anna might have kept the messy remains of her habit in her cigarette pack as Margaret suggested. But it was curious. They ate lunch on the deck in the afternoon sun. Birds fluttered around the feeders a few feet away, spitting seeds across the deck, unwilling to forage in the fields as long as there was a ready supply of food available.

"I'm going to stop feeding the birds as soon my supply of food runs out," Maude said as she and Emma spooned fresh asparagus soup across the long distance between the low table and their eager mouths. "But I miss the close company of the chickadees and red polls during the summer months. Sometimes, particularly on dull days in winter, the silly things fly straight into the glass doors. The same glass which allows me to enjoy the birds, kills them. At this time of year I feed the hummingbirds instead, of course, but they are not so messy or noisy as the winter birds."

"I'll miss your grandmother very much Emma," Maude said when they had sat a long time in silence watching the birds." As soon as she said it Emma realized that it was the first time anyone in the women's group had expressed this sort of regret. "I'll miss her place too, almost as much. The fen is so various and so different from the rest of Southern Ontario. I went to Newfoundland ten years ago and there they were, all of Gertrude's plants, not Gertrude's but I think of them as Gertrude's. I don't suppose I shall have much opportunity to go to Oliphant now.

"On the morning after she died, while Margaret was washing up after breakfast, I went out to look for orchids. I'd been down to the beach in the early morning but was too fascinated by the carp to see any flowers. As I was walking I was too preoccupied. Odd isn't it. When we are busy or worried we can't see, or I can't. Just when I most need it, my vision becomes blurred. So after breakfast I took Foggy Dog and we went for a walk up the ski-mobile path into the woods. I was looking to see whether the showy lady's slippers were out. The yellow ones were in clusters along one of the paths and the pitcher plants were nodding slightly in the ditches. I was afraid it would be too windy for good pictures but just at the edge of the trees, where the fen turns into forest it was still and my eyes adjusted downwards to the small things, and there were the deep pinks of Calypsos and the salmon pink of the swamp pinks – tiny perfect flowers, tiny even beside the small purple flames of wild iris. The whole forest floor was alive with flowers when my eyes focused." Emma realized that this woman's words had the lyric quality her grandmother's had when she wrote about the cottage, that of the group Maude most reminded her of her grandmother.

"I took several good pictures. I'll send you some. Then I walked back to the cottage and before going in I sat for a while in the garden. I sat on the wooden seat, near where we buried the dog a bit later, and I realized how poisonous that back corner of the garden is."

"Excuse me?"

"Well, you know the rhubarb is there. Its leaves are poisonous. Funny that every child who has access to a garden has eaten rhubarb, raw and tart. I pulled one of the new shoots while I was there and wiped it on my skirt. It was barely pink and was tender crisp; it tasted almost sweet, offering the promise of tartness yet to come. I threw the leaf over the back fence. How do all those children know not to eat the leaves? Why don't thousands of them turn up in emergency wards every summer? Anyway, beside the rhubarb is the aconite, monk's hood, beautiful but deadly, just leafing out. A painful death I'm told but quick. I was sure that your grandmother had taken a root from my garden, years ago, but mine blooms in August and hers rarely blooms until September. Around the fence in that corner coil vines of deadly nightshade. It's not so deadly really, not the native variety, but what does 'not so deadly' mean? Who tries these things out to find how many leaves constitute 'deadly'? It occurred to me, as I sat there, that your grandmother might have committed suicide. She knew we were all arriving later that afternoon, that we would find her. She had a touch of the dramatic. She and her dog lying there for us to find, scare us half to death. She was capable of that. Don't you think?"

"She didn't intend to die. Not that day. No I don't think so. Her journal gives no hint of such a plan. At other times in her life, at times when she was depressed, she'd write about wanting to die, to punish the people who were controlling or frustrating her, but not the day of the retreat, no.

"Speaking of the journals, I read just last night an interesting journal entry, an entry she wrote when the two of you were here together, celebrating your retirement. She made detailed notes of situations which she felt you should have reported to the Children's Aid. Did she ever speak to you about those again?"

Maude appeared to give the question serious consideration before she answered in the negative. Then she got up and gathered the soup bowls and salad plates together and went in to get dessert. Emma sat and watched the birds.

"How long do you reckon it takes to get from here to grandma's cottage, Maude?" Emma asked when they were settled with fresh cookies and tea on the low white table between them.

"About two hours," Maude replied. "Gertrude used to say that was crazy, that she could make it from her cottage to Orangeville, going down Hwy 10, in under two hours and that's some distance east of my place. However, Gertrude drove quickly, even when she was over eighty. Maybe she'd slowed a bit in the past couple of years. The rest of us took two hours. The shoppers took longer."

"So you left here at about four last Friday?"

"No, I didn't come back here at all. I had an appointment north of here and I packed everything before I went to it so that I could go to the cottage right after I was finished."

Emma did not leave Maude until almost 4 in the afternoon. It had been past noon when she'd arrived and the tour of the garden had taken some time, as had their leisurely lunch. She drove south as quickly as the school buses would let her, conscious that George might not wait if she were late.

*

Standing in the bathroom of Gertrude's apartment she thought how strange it was to be putting on tights and a skirt. She'd retrieved th skirt from the bottom of her suitcase that morning, shaken it out, and hung it over the shower rail in the moist air. Most of the creases had fallen out and the rest she didn't care about. She pulled on a ribbon knit sweater that Gertrude had made for her ten years earlier. It was a pale mix of purple and aqua with a wavy pattern and at the hem a touch of foam rested on about two inches of fantastically dyed blue, green and purple waves. The skirt was blue. She shook her damp blonde hair away from her face and slipped her feet into low pumps. Grabbing her raincoat from the back of a chair where she'd dropped it, she found her keys in the pocket. She was ready for George and the rest. She'd been planning her speech as she drove south.

CHAPTER XI

FRIDAY EVENING, JUNE 5

THE LOT AT THE GOLF CLUB was full. She circled it twice before parking half onto the lawn partway down the drive. As she locked the door a glance at her watch reassured her. She was on the dot of five. Either there were a lot of golfers enjoying the early season, or people were glad to celebrate her grandmother's death. Not that many people could have heard that the bar would be subsidized! Surely. She strode across the pavement as freely as a skirt and pumps allow, wondering how she'd recognize George and what she'd say. She'd been so busy considering her remarks for the party that she'd forgotten to plan her meeting with George. She could have kicked herself, but it would have been dangerous with the pumps on. This was her only chance with him and she was going to have to wing it. She took the steps to the club house two at a time and stopped abruptly at the top. Leaning against the railing of the side deck was a good candidate. The man was wearing neither golf clothes nor formal dress but a blazer and slacks. He was staring out over the course and smoking. She changed course and approached him. He was about her uncle Geoff's age but with less hair. He was taller and blonder than she and he looked somehow unused, as if, despite middle age, he were still banking on his youthful vigor and good looks.

"I'm looking for George Coventry. Would you be George?"

"Why not. It sounds like a good name and if a woman as attractive as you is looking for him..."

He'd begun the repartee, a line which he had practised for years with some success, but realized he had no reason to continue it. She was attractive in a healthy way but he'd met lots of attractive women. His experience with them had not been good and he wouldn't settle for anyone who wasn't attractive. His clothes were expensive. His car was expensive. Only the best would do. Mutual narcissism, however, is not a recipe for good personal relationships. He had one woman too many to look after anyway.

"Shall we go in and get a drink? Then I'll bring my car's trunk to meet your car's trunk, especially if you've managed a better parking space than I have."

He threw his cigarette into the flower bed below and followed her to the entrance holding the door open for her as the stepped out of the afternoon sun into the gloom of the lobby.

"Been here long?"

"No. I haven't been inside to look for you yet. I don't smoke in my car; so I thought I'd have a cigarette and then go in. You must come here often if you can spot me so easily."

"No. I don't live here, actually. I live in Kentucky." His eyebrows moved slightly upward. "I'm from what used to be Port Credit but I practise in Kentucky."

"How soon do you expect to get whatever it is right?"

"Oh, sorry, I'm a vet. I practise veterinary medicine in Kentucky.

At the bar Emma produced her invitation which was stamped twice by the bartender. A crass thing to do at a wake, she supposed, but the only way the Club and the family had been able to decide how to manage an open but limited bar service. The bartender would allow two drinks on each card. Mar and Sue were somewhere handing out cards as people arrived. Emma had grabbed several cards the evening before.

Once again he raised his eyebrows. "You don't live here. You don't belong here but you just hand in a card and get drinks. Wow. I wish I could do that at all the clubs where I'm not a member."

"Oh. That. Well the card is an introduction we worked out for the party. Didn't I tell your I was here for a party? That was why I asked you to meet me here? I expect that's why the lot is so full. We're holding a memorial party for my grandmother and since you knew her I thought you might like to be here too."

"I knew your grandmother?"

"Yes. In fact, as far as I know you were the last person to see her alive." Emma had wondered whether she would tell George this right away but her mouth had made the decision for her.

"I beg your pardon?" George felt the world shift a bit below the chair and was glad he was sitting and glad that his hand was steady as he brought his drink to his lips. He knew his hand was steady because he couldn't hear the ice clinking. He checked. He thought his whole body must be shaking but the evidence of his senses was that he was sitting quite calmly.

"I believe you were the last person to see Gertrude Moseley alive." Emma repeated slowly.

George paused for a long time considering responses. Prove it! sprang to mind. How the hell would you know? What are you talking about? Each response implicated him in some way, either of guilt or of ignorance. He decided to ignore her trap. Or he decided it was time to say something, anything, preferably something distracting.

"So your offer of papers and books was an excuse to get me here, is that it?"

"In part, yes. Though the papers and books are real enough. I wanted to know who you were and see the son of a man my grandmother spent 45 years with, in a manner of speaking. I also thought it appropriate that you be here for her memorial. Find out who she was. I'd like to know about your father too, would like to talk to you about him."

George felt as if he were drowning, his mind whirling. Forty-five years! His father had had an affair for forty-five years? George did the arithmetic automatically. He'd have been a ten-year-old when his father started betraying his mother! It was monstrous. He didn't know what he'd been expecting since Emma had phoned him, but it wasn't this.

To be at Gertrude Moseley's funeral or whatever they were calling it? Appropriate!! What on earth did Emma mean by that? What did she know? He racked his brain to recall exactly what she had said on the phone. What had brought him here? He was glad of a suit jacket which hid the fact that he was sweating; he could feel sweat under his arms and down his back. He finished his drink quickly and asked whether she'd like another. She'd had only a sip from her glass of wine but assured him it would be no problem for her to get him a refill. He watched her cross the lobby and noticed that she disappeared briefly into the cloakroom. Perhaps she was a tense as he was.

When she reappeared she had disposed of her raincoat. She then wove her way through the crowd to the bar. As he watched he considered flight. But he was curious. There were veiled hints in Emma's "Find out who she was" that he felt inclined to explore. And it would be too obvious if he left. Best to stay and talk about his Dad and find out what Emma knew about his visit to Oliphant or what the source of her information was.

He was just making this decision when she handed him his drink and sank down on a low chair at the other side of a small end table. They were close enough to talk quietly but separated by furniture. "Tell me about Roger." She said at the same time that he said, "I guess we've both been doing the same thing."

"What would that be?" she asked.

"Clearing out a lifetime's possessions. Trying to make sense of the junk some stranger has left behind. It's almost an archeological dig, don't you think? Bits of pot and the odd bit of writing but no clue how it fits. Some scholar calls it a temple and another swears its a potter's shop while it might really be a midden, just junk, thrown out by some servant who didn't want to get whipped for breaking the dishes. Who's to say that the books and papers a person keeps are the most precious to him or her; maybe they are the ones they couldn't sell or give away." He stopped. What on earth was he talking about? His drink was getting low again. He'd be drunk in a few moments if he weren't careful. He hadn't eaten since breakfast and he didn't drink any more, not since he'd moved back home.

"I know what you mean. Grocery lists. Phone numbers written on theatre programs. What was saved, the phone number or the program? Did you have other family to help you?"

"No, you?"

"Oh, yes. I'm only clearing out books and papers. My parents and aunts and uncles are taking care of the rest. I'd find that a much larger chore, especially since I've only a week off to do it."

"I just happen to have a box of books in my trunk to exchange. I was taking them to the Goodwill. They are almost the last of the things I have to clean up. As it happens they are your grandmother's books. Now I won't have to go downtown to get rid of them. Sorry." He grinned. He wasn't sorry at all.

After a moment Emma continued. "Your father died in November. When did your mother die?"

"She didn't."

"Oh. You said you were cleaning up alone. I assumed..."

"My mother is an invalid. I care for her. My father cared for her for many years. She becomes very angry if anyone calls her an invalid. She spends hours each day weaving and creating tapestries which are exhibited all over the world but she is often pain and she cannot get around easily in the parts of the house which have not been redesigned."

There was a great deal of unspoken information and anger behind these words but just as Emma was about to ask what care was required, Mar appeared at her shoulder.

"Emma, we've been looking everywhere for you. Come along. The speeches are about to begin."

"OK, Mom. I'll be there in a moment. I do want to say something; so I'll be right there." Emma did not introduce George and her mother did not ask who he was or pause, in that way people do when they are waiting to be introduced. Instead Mar hurried up the steps from the lobby to the banquet room without glancing back. Her displeasure with her daughter was written in the stiffness of her spine and her tightly held elbows.

"Will you stay for the speeches? You might learn about the woman your father knew for so long."

"No, thanks, but no. My mother will be expecting me." He wanted to be away from here. At the same time he was fascinated by the prospect of being in the presence of the person who had sent the rose and poetry to his father's funeral, a spectral presence, but a presence, nonetheless. "I don't want to keep you from your family but I do want to get rid of the box in my trunk. I can stay for an hour. Will that be long enough? My mother expects me for dinner." He was aware as he said it that the last sentence made him sound like a small boy, ruined his macho image. "I do the cooking." As if that helped!

"I'm sure it will be long enough. If you decide to leave, catch my eye and I'll come out with you. I'll try to give my speech early on." The more she thought about that, the less she thought that was likely. She knew that she wanted to speak near the end, to sum up what the others had said but she didn't really expect that there were going to be many people eager to talk about Gertrude.

She was wrong, as it turned out.

There were about 200 people in the large dining room when Emma entered. She hadn't been paying much attention as she and George talked in the lobby, but there must have been a steady progress of people, some dressed somberly for a funeral, some in their work clothes, some in party dress, passing them and proceeding up the stairs. The furniture had, for the most part, been removed from the room. Tables had been left along one wall to accommodate the buffet and on the window side a few tables had been left to provide places for abandoned plates and glasses. There were chairs. The club staff had placed the upholstered stacking chairs in conversation groups, facing the windows which overlooked the golf course and the lake beyond. The guests had had their own ideas about conversation groups and were now seated in clusters randomly scattered across the large floor creating an obstacle course for those wishing to dance.

People had been dancing, Emma surmised. Couples were standing with their arms still around each other, turned to the makeshift podium which had been set up at the far end of the room. She'd heard a Rhumba playing as she hurried up the stairs but the music had stopped now and her Uncle Geoff was announcing the order of events as Gertrude had decreed them. Indeed, he was reading directly from her instructions, partly because they were so Gertrude and partly so that he couldn't be accused of disrespect by those who had expected a more lugubrious affair. He left out nothing and concluded with an invitation for any who wished to join the flotilla of boats which would set out from the Oliphant Marina at noon the next day. He had been informed, he said, nodding in the direction of Edwina, that there would be space in boats for 30 or 40 people; so folks need not worry about driving all that way and not being able to participate in the final ceremony.

"We have now arrived at the portion of the program which Gertrude decreed should be provided for spoken reminiscence or tribute. I must warn you that I will turn off the mike if you speak for more than four minutes!" he said chuckling. "At any sign of flagging interest I shall, as mother directed, turn up the volume on "Joy to the World" and let the dancing, talking and eating, not to mention the drinking, continue. I hope you will circulate, meet others of mother's friends and relatives and celebrate her long and productive life. First I'll ask the DJ to put on the tape of "Bread and Roses" which Mother requested and then I'll hand the microphone over to anyone who wishes to speak."

When the music had died away, a single voice marching into the distance, Gertrude's publisher strode to the podium. He spoke of Gertrude's wry sense of humour and her ability to use it to entertain. He did not sound as if he found her entirely satisfactory, just amusing. Victoria Sellers sold herself briefly and mentioned that Gertrude's most recent book would be on the shelves within a month. Emma noticed that both of these people moved quickly to the back of the room after they had delivered their advertisements and slipped out a few moments later. Gertrude had not been a best seller, but according to her uncle the figures indicated a steady income over the years.

Gertrude's sister-in-law, the only other family member of her generation who could be there, a cheerful little woman who had been driven to the service by her grandson, spoke of Gertrude's parents and brothers and times so far in the past as to seem ancient to most of the crowd. A woman told of travelling to the places Gertrude wrote about and trying to trace the events. Another enjoyed the history and geography which wove through the plots. Then shyly a few clients told of

Gertrude's influence in their lives. They seemed brave, and mystified by their moment on stage.

After the last of these testimonies to Gertrude's determination and understanding had finished, the eight members of her group materialized behind the mike. Across the large space, sweetly and with only a hint of the tremulo age imposes, the words to "The Rose" serenely floated. It was well sung. They remembered all the words and there were very few dry eyes when it was done. The singers maintained their composure through the three stanzas and then could be seen reaching for tissues and hankies as they finished. They did not immediately return to their places but remained together as Edwina, Anna and Melody told short stories illustrating Gertrude's life in the group. They told with special feeling of visiting her cottage in Oliphant each spring. When they had dematerialized, Zack and his mother and Eric spoke. It seemed there could not be many more speakers and, aware that the time George had allotted her was running out, Emma stepped to the microphone.

She'd thought about her message on and off during the previous couple of days but she was still not sure of the words and she was frightened now, looking at all these faces. There was a hint of bravado in her voice and posture as she began.

"Thank you all for coming. Thank you for your memories of my grandmother. You've made her come alive in her work, in her writing, with her friends and with her family. Each of us saw her in only one part of her life and hearing all of your recollections is a wonderful reminder that she was a complicated person. Most of us in the family, for instance, don't think about her books, don't consider that there are people all around the world who know her only as the picture on the dust jacket of a book, the voice of a narrator. Many of us in the family, I suspect, did not read her books. I confess to owning all of them but reading only the first one, the one in which she created a character based on me. On the other hand, probably, most of you, who were her clients, gave no thought to the fact that she had family.

"For me grandmother was a summer presence. We went swimming together, she drove me to riding lessons, we named plants and walked in the woods. She taught me to knit and to crochet and I see her every time there is a brilliant sunset in the west, because we used to sit on the front porch of the cottage and watch the sun go down. One of us would read aloud, usually me, and one of us would knit or sew, usually grandma. We would sit from the time I'd finished washing the dinner dishes – she hated doing dishes – until the sky lost all its color, and then we'd go in. Sunset was my bedtime. I have no idea what she did after that. Wrote I suspect, or edited. As a child I didn't realize she that was writing books. She was my grandmother and she took her note-book with her everywhere, in her purse or pocket if we were travelling, spread out on her desk in the sun porch if we stayed home.

"Hearing your stories of her winter life, the time she spent making your lives whole, the time she spent inspiring you, the time you spent travelling together, the joys and sorrows you shared, introduced a per-son I scarcely knew existed, created a life with which I had no connec-tion. You've provided us all with the sense of a vital living person. Many of you have commented on how full her life was and how blessed she was to die after a full life but before her energy, physical and mental failed her."

Emma took a deep breath.

"I do not think that she was blessed. I've had, during this week, an experience none of you has had, I think. I have heard my grandmother talking to herself, about herself ... and about you. Some of you may know that for about 75 of her 85 years my grandmother kept a journal. I did not know. Clearly in one week I have not been able to read more than a small fraction of her record, but my reading and my research have lead me to be fairly sure that she was not blessed.

Oh, she was blessed more than most people with a full life and many talents and loving friends but she was not blessed in death. She did not want to die. She was not ready to die. That could be said of many peo-ple, but ... I don't believe she died. I believe she was murdered and things being as they are, I suppose, most of her relatives and friends and many of her acquaintance being in this room right now..." she paused for courage.... "it is possible that her murderer is among us."

There had been gasps, when Emma said that Gertrude was not blessed, small intakes of breath. At the first use of the word 'murder' the room became absolutely still. A room where 200 people are absolutely still, holding their collective breath is frightening. Emma's final words were spoken slowly and deliberately. As she said them her uncles appeared, one on each side of her, and escorted her from the platform. It was clear that they were not pleased.

There was a faint scream from Natasha; Sarah and Jean, both looking shaken, helped her from the room. Suddenly everyone was talking at once. Geoff gestured wildly with his free arm in the direction of the D.J. and "Jeremiah was a Bullfrog" at very high volume reverberated against the walls and windows. George put his drink down and headed for the door. Shaking herself free of her uncles' restraining hands, Emma sprinted after George.

Running through the crowd was not easy, though some groups, those who saw her coming, parted before her as if she were contagious. The high heels were a hazard, especially on the stairs, but she made it to the parking lot in time to see George leaning into a gleaming black Acura. He'd removed his jacket and, having hung it over the back of the passenger seat, slid in behind the wheel and reached for the door.

"Wait," she panted sprinting towards him. "Wait."

He rolled his shirt sleeves up over muscular forearms, fiddling with them to make them lie precisely against his biceps. He did not look at her as she approached, but got in and wound the window down.

"You have an interesting take on funeral speeches. I think that you are supposed not only to speak no ill of the dead, but to lie a little, if necessary, to make the living feel better. Real show stopper that was. Got everyone talking I guess," he said, his right hand now reaching for the ignition key and his eyes scanning the instrument panel. The car roared to life.

"If you are really leaving, drive me up to my car and we'll exchange papers," Emma had to shout above the engine.

He indicated the other side of the car with a casual gesture. She thought briefly about what she was doing as she clambered around the car and slid in beside him. This was exactly what she had planned to avoid, arranging to meet in the lobby with lots of company around her. Now she was in the power of a person who might be dangerous. She slammed the door. Her heart stopped as George reversed quickly into the lot and roared up the drive. He grinned at her.

"Here," she shouted a bit too loudly and he hit the brakes as she indicated which was her car. He raised an eyebrow and grinned again.

"Did you know what you were saying in there? Or are you just guessing?" he asked, clicking the lock open. She had not heard him lock her in. He was toying with her. She opened the door quickly and reached into her pocket for her keys.

"Oh, there was a murder all right," she answered. She leaned over and opened the trunk. "Those four boxes are yours," she said. "Where do you want them?" They worked for a few moments in silence.

"But I won't be sure who the murderer was until tomorrow," she said, straightening up and dusting her hands against her thighs, forgetting that she wasn't wearing her jeans.

"Why would that be?"

"Tomorrow we return to the scene of the crime. Murders are always solved at the scene of the crime. At least in the few books I've read they were. I don't suppose I've read more than one or two murder mysteries, come to that, and the only one I remember well is the one my grandmother wrote about me. But that's how it was in her book. I hope you'll be there. You do remember the way don't you?" she said and walked briskly back towards the clubhouse, taking care to stay on the lawn and put the parked cars between herself and George. Walking on the damp lawn was not easy. As she went back up the clubhouse steps she realized that they had not spoken about Roger at all.

*

Facing the crowd would not be easy. Her aunts and uncles would be the worst, but she still needed to talk to Edwina. Edwina was the only one of the group with whom Emma had not spoken. What could she possibly know or say that would help? Except, of course, that she had definitely been in Oliphant on the day Gertrude died. She and George were, if Emma considered opportunity, the most likely to have murdered Gertrude. But of course she'd ruled out opportunity as a major determining factor in her deliberations. Edwina, in her wheelchair, could have pulled up to that place at the coffee table and accounted for

179

the placement of the cup and saucer. Edwina's garden was as likely as Maude's or Gertrude's own, for that matter, to have supplied poisonous plants. With her disability Edwina likely had as much access to barbiturates as George whose mother was an invalid. Emma checked herself again. It was so easy to be tricked into considering opportunity and means. She imagined that was how many miscarriages of justice occurred. The investigators got themselves wound up in opportunity and means and forgot about motive. What could Edwina's motive be? Interesting that George's mother and Edwina were both in wheelchairs. What had that to do with it? Change. What had changed in Edwina's life recently? How could she phrase questions to find out?

Having several times paced the length of the deck surrounding the lower level of the club, Emma shrugged, shook herself and straightened her back. Then holding her head at what she hoped was a jaunty angle she went up the stairs to the banquet room. The free drinks and the band had released any tension remaining after Emma's speech. The party was flying. Conversation was deafening. Fifteen or twenty couples were dancing, still risking their safety as they skirted groups of chairs randomly cluttering the floor. The conversation was shouted above the music and the clatter of plates and glasses. Emma looked for Edwina.

Edwina, Anna and Maude were sitting on the deck, looking out over the golf course, three white haired women: one, the youngest, sitting nearest the rail, smoke trailing from her cigarette looked like a serene Sybil, smiling enigmatically through the smoke; one, her head tilted looked like a stalwart mothering hen, turning first to one speaker, then the other, as if she sheltered whoever spoke in her attention; the third, elegantly upright, long fingers poised on the rims of her chair wheels, could have posed for a seated Nike, had anyone ever carved a seated Nike. They were all dressed in black, not a suitable black but in Anna's case a flamboyantly embroidered black, in Maude's a textured woven black, and in Edwina's a regally glittering black, beads perhaps, which shimmered slightly as she breathed and flowed in medieval curves from her wrists. Had Emma known more about mythology she might have been reminded of the Fates. They were deep in conversation and did not look entirely pleased to see Emma approaching.

Emma began by asking about Natasha and was told that she and Jean had left. No one was exactly sure why Natasha had been so upset, not even Natasha. She had been nervous, excitable, edgy, she said, ever since she'd arrived the previous week. Perhaps she had premonitions. Perhaps the atmosphere was charged. Perhaps coming after all the encomia, the harshness of Emma's accusation had caught her off guard. Once they had eased into the topic of Emma's speech the women were eager to know whether Emma had any basis for her belief. They were polite but firm. She crossed her fingers and assured them that she had. She felt like a little girl being grilled by three teachers. Shrugging slightly she supposed it was fair play, since she had been grilling people all week.

"Edwina, could I see you in the cloak room for a few moments?" she asked when there was an almost suitable gap in the conversation. The three women glanced at each other knowingly. It was obvious that they had discussed Edwina's temporary escape from the attentions of Emma the Detective. There was a hint of mockery as well as satisfaction in the look. Maude and Anna may have been pleased to have their prediction confirmed, though whether they were mocking Edwina or Emma was not clear.

"I have my map of the lakefront in my raincoat pocket and I'd like to talk to you about the boats we're using tomorrow and what place you feel would be best for scattering the ashes." Edwina raised her eyebrows slightly, turned her chair sharply and set off into the dining room and on across the dance floor cutting a swath ahead of Emma.

On her earlier visit to the cloak room, Emma had noticed that there was a small table and a group of upholstered chairs in a secluded area beyond the coat racks and off to the side of the washroom doors. The area faced a small garden and patio at the rear of the club. As she passed her coat Emma removed the map, the sort put out by the Bruce County Tourist Bureau indicating every resort, golf course, restaurant and fishing area along the length of the peninsula. Emma moved one of the chairs and Edwina pulled in at the table. They both sat looking out the window for a moment; then Emma spread the map on the table and pointed to the area between the Oliphant Marina and her grandmother's cottage.

"I'm hoping you'll say that it is not too difficult simply to move out of the harbour and come around to here." Emma indicated a course westward through the breakwater and then directly south towards Lonely Island.

"Edwina looked carefully and frowned a bit. That means we'll have to stay dangerously close together. The water is very shallow in that close to shore. The shoals which you are used to over on the beach side are also in constant motion in that narrow area. If we circle out farther west, between the shore and the islands, it will be safer. Let us say," she continued, noticing the look of disappointment on Emma's face, "if it is very calm we will go in further, but if it is the least bit rough, we'll head to the channel between the shore and Vimy island. We would be just about in line with your grandmother's view to the sunset. Will that do?"

"You're the one with the experience in the boats and I trust your judgement. Now, how many boats will there be? Have you an idea?"

"I have a small one. My older grandson will sail it and we can take five passengers. My other grandson, however, has a big boat. We can accommodate ten to fifteen on that easily. My next door neighbor has another small craft and he came over to tell me, just as I was leaving this afternoon, that a friend of his who owns a good-sized motor launch had volunteered to help out. The big boats are the ones which really concern me in that shallow area. But there is no doubt we'll have considerable passenger space. After that speech do you really think more than the family and the women's group will show up?"

"I'd have said 'no' until today. But look at the turn out. I've no idea who all these people are...but they've all passed Mom's or Sue's gimlet eye; so I imagine they aren't simply golfers hanging about after a round. Thank you ever so much for finding boats for us all. It's really very kind of you. All those years and grandma really never had an interest in boats. Will you all be ready at noon?"

"It's all under control, Emma. I've talked to both of your uncles about it too." Edwina's voice betrayed no hint of irony, but she smiled slightly.

"I'm sorry, Edwina."

"I wasn't in Oliphant last Friday, you know. I wish I had been."

"Oh, I was hoping you'd say you'd driven past and seen something or someone. Silly of me I guess, but I keep hoping."

"You know I was the last to arrive." There was some asperity in the tone of Edwina's voice. "I was last to arrive because I was in Hamilton all day getting fitted for my next wheel chair. I'm getting a very fancy model." Edwina sighed. "You'd think that a person who's lived with my disease for long as I have would not be surprised by its progress. I didn't tell the other women why I was late; I wanted to tell them later during the weekend when I was prepared. I still haven't found an appropriate time." She sighed again and shifted in her chair. "I'm losing strength in my arms but I'm still resisting the motorized chairs; so I was working to convince the doctors that I can handle the racing model. I shall be quite sporty; I'm getting the kind they use for some wheelchair sports, very light and maneuverable.

"Often I arrive at your grandmother's early, I know that, but this time I very nearly didn't get there until the Saturday morning. I couldn't get away from Hamilton until after 3 p.m. and then I had to stop at home for my food and luggage. If I'd known they'd take so long on the assessment I'd have packed ahead of time. I really am sorry. I keep thinking that if I'd been there at the usual time I might have helped in some way. Might have got her to hospital in Wiarton, at least, or got a doctor. Mostly I wonder whether as she was dying she hoped I would arrive. I don't know what I could have done in the circumstances, but I feel terribly guilty about that day."

Emma said nothing for several moments. "Maude pointed out that there were poisonous plants in grandma's garden. I don't know much about noxious plants, outside of the ones which are dangerous to animals of course. Can you help me at all? I'm afraid I've packed up all the books; so that if there was an herbal in the apartment I can't find it now."

"I know that she kept the aconite in the back corner, as far from the children's exploring fingers as possible and that they were under orders not to go into the fenced garden unaccompanied. You likely remember that."

"She said it was because she didn't want us trampling the edible plants or letting rabbits in. Do you mean she was lying to us?"

"Well, I'm sure those were valid reasons also. I think she told us that she used some excuses to keep you out. I suppose if she'd told you there were poisonous plants you'd all have been in there trying them out – daredevils some of you were! Anyway what do you want to know?"

"Do you know what chemicals are in any of those plants? Might she have used them to commit suicide?"

"I thought you told the entire roomful of guests only a few moments ago that your grandmother did not want to die. Are you less sure than you seemed?"

"I'm just trying to explore all the possibilities."

"No I don't know what the chemicals are. I know that the aconite is the most dangerous of the ones that are back there. That's all."

"Hmm. Well, thanks. I guess I'll have to do some research before tomorrow."

As Edwina rolled off toward where Anna and Maude were standing near the dessert table, Emma glanced at her watch. If she hurried she might get to the Public Library before it closed. A survey of the cloakroom revealed in the far corner the phone booth with its book still on the shelf beside it. Emma phoned the Library. A few moments later she kissed her mother and slid out of the club house.

The books on toxicology were easy to find and a quick search assured her that aconite was, indeed, as poisonous as Maude and Edwina had suggested. Its poison was, what was more, the poison which the lab had detected in the material which Sinister had swallowed. She also noted that a lethal dose was just about what the lab had determined was present in Sinister's stomach. The cause of the dog's death, at any rate, was pretty clear. Had Gertrude died in the same way? If suicide were the death of choice, of course, she might have poisoned the dog also, to prevent his harming her body, or attacking her visitors when they arrived later in the day. On the other hand, the dog might have come upon his poison entirely by accident, although the lab report seemed to suggest that the poison was not actually in the biscuit. The biscuit had contained only very strong sedatives. Since the dog had only completely digested one biscuit, this would imply that there was some other cause of death.

*

George drove too quickly. Instead of taking the direct route from the Golf Club to his home he veered left and hit the highway. What did this woman know? She kept teasing him. First it was material of a personal nature. Now it was a solution to a murder mystery. He'd thought his plans were foolproof. Who was to know the old lady would write down her luncheon appointments? Some nonentity, some unimportant old lady and she'd written his name. His mother never kept a list of appointments. She expected him to do that. He had her appointment book and his own. It was one of the many things about his present life that was infuriating. What difference did it make? No one could prove that he'd actually arrived for lunch. It was at this point in his deliberations that the speed began to diminish slightly. About 30 kilometers later he was ready to take the curve on an exit ramp at three times the posted speed and turn around. As he retraced the kilometers towards home he gradually accommodated himself to the speed limit, well, to the vicinity of the speed limit.

Leaving the Library Emma felt as if she'd been awake for a week. She considered going back to the party. Instead she let herself into the apartment and, after phoning the number David Weston had left her and leaving him a message, she got ready to sleep. The journals were conveniently piled beside the bed.

May 14, 1978, Sunday   *Oliphant*
The water is very high this spring. The island really is an island. We must leave the car at the marina and use the boat. Later in the season, when the water is warmer, we will be able to wade across the intervening space. Because it is often exposed, the bottom is not that mucky silt of northern lakes. There are no leaches. Mostly one walks on sand

185

with a bit of clay. Tall grasses are the major fauna and the herons stand almost hidden among them to fish.

I know that other people are used to island living. I'm not. I have an island that is usually not an island. We're used to the water rising or falling an inch or two in a short period of time. Down on the beach visitors put their towels and shoes and glasses safely several feet from the water's edge and come in from swimming, well mostly wading at this time of year, to find them sodden. The water will have run in an inch and then fallen again in the space of half an hour. There seems to be no cause, no tide, no passing boat, just whim which pulls the thin layer of water up and then lets it go. But now that the surface is so high, so much closer to the house, we must keep the boat tied to the front porch.

Last night it, the boat, not the porch, got away from us and Xn, the young devil, swam out after it, unaccompanied, which is against all the rules, especially so early in the year. The water is icy yet. No one is saying who left the boat on the lawn, pulled up almost into the flower bed, but while we were eating dinner the water level rose just enough to float it off. Naturally I found out about none of this until this morning at breakfast when the boys were fighting over who would get the plastic toy out of the cereal box. During the ensuing recriminations the events of the previous evening were dragged in as ammunition.

The water sounds delightful slapping against the rocks right beyond our windows. If I were braver I could enjoy its nearness. However, it will do enormous damage during storms.

My book is half done. On Wednesday I read to R. the sections based on his family. The reading ritual is a part of my creative process. I read each section of my book aloud as I write it. I need to hear it for it to exist. It is enough for him that when he is writing I read and type his script chapter by chapter. He remembers what he has written and does not need to hear himself say it. This time the reading is tense. He has enjoyed hearing passages in which he thinks he recognizes my family or friends but he is dissatisfied with the passages I have written about a person like his son. It does not occur to me to ask whether he is also dissatisfied with his son. First the writing, then the reading, then the editing. The editing moves me forward by tiny steps but is sometimes as interesting as the new sections. When I'm editing I find myself consciously searching for the truth. Whatever that is. The integrity of the story.

When I write new sections I do not consider whether they are true I just get the words onto the page. New sections are remarkable. I never know what will be on the page until it is written. One moment it is a blank page and then suddenly R.'s son or my mother, or an uncle I've not seen in years begins to speak or shrug or move from one room to another. I give them names and they grow into new individuals, like the people who inspired them but also different, as different as siblings or cousins. Amazing really. My characters don't take on a life of their own, not as happens for some writers, but my characters move slightly under the clay.

I remember once in London seeing a production of one of the Mystery Cycles. We were in the balcony of a church. The director began the Adam and Eve scene with a huge basin of kitty litter or bird gravel or some such material on the floor in the centre of the crossing. Then slowly, slowly out of the basin rose the naked figures of Adam first, and then Eve. The figures had grease or glue applied so the clay clung to the skin. An uncomfortable role to play more than once, or to rehearse, I should think, but enormously effective as the clay takes on life – rises and moves in a rough way. When I write, I direct my characters; they are puppets on string. On good days the facility with which they move is astonishing. On bad days the strings are as thick and flexible as lath and the limbs jerk about. I take this opportunity to shape my life, and my children's lives, and my friends too to suit my purposes. How much I change them depends on how powerful I feel as I write. Twice created and recreated. Infinitely recreated, I suppose, in a fiction that is not a fiction or a non fiction that is not a non-fiction. When I watch people, do I watch to see whether they will turn into fiction? If they have secrets in life, in what they think are their real lives, are their secrets fiction? Or do I create secrets for them? I finished reading K.C. Constantine's A Blank Page *last night What a triumph of creating – in 150 pages a town, a community, several lives, intersecting, on a blank page. So undervalued a genre, the murder mystery. Its closure is seductive; its secrets are ours. Its shadows are ours. I named my dogs Sinister, left hand, to remind me of my shadow, my secret self. It turns out my shadow was a writer.*

Shadow artists. Was my whole career a denial of my own artist? Did I use first art and then journals as therapy for my clients because I wanted to do them, wanted an excuse to do them without the risk of saying I was a clothes designer, a cloth artist, or writer?

Did they have cloth artists when I was growing up? I think not. Seam-stresses, usually impoverished gentlewomen or immigrants. I went into social work because sewing and knitting were woman's work, and not well paid woman's work at that. At least social work was paid. Not well paid but secure, a way to support myself when I ceased to rely on my husband. I learned a great deal about my crafts by using them as therapy but without the risk, without the criticism, with no danger of failing. I learned from watching others and reading about life. But I didn't have to do it. If I'd done it, labelled myself artist and tried to earn a living, I'd have learned in a different way, might have been an entirely different writer, had to have been. Instead of learning from my clients' ineptitude, I'd have learned from my own.

Now in my mid-sixties I start from a different place but still I must start. I wrote poetry as a girl. Didn't all girls? Maybe most boys too. Prose. My prose has always been confessional, autobiographical, al-ways. My belief is that everyone else's writing is autobiographical also, unacknowledged, unrecognized, perhaps. But I may be wrong. We write our lives and our fantasy lives and our feared lives. What else can we know but our lives and the lives of those around us. They walk inevitably onto our pages, disguised, amalgamated, improved, deformed but seen and recorded from our own experience and filtered through our lives. How else? Children and beginning writers are told, "Write what you know." How could I write what I don't know? What I imagine is still what I know...even more essentially what I know, more uniquely what I know. That is its danger. Its uniqueness is isolating and alienating. Good therapy but not good literature, not even good entertainment. I write what I know. If it encounters what you know then we will communicate. Hello out there!

CHAPTER XII

SATURDAY, JUNE 6

Cars BEGAN TO PULL IN at the Oliphant Government docks by noon. Emma and her mother had driven north with the early morning light slanting across the fields, glowing in soft green of new leaves and grass. They had not talked much. It had been tough pulling out of bed at six after the events of the previous evening. The apartment was clean and empty, ready to be home to someone else. All of their personal luggage was neatly in the trunk in the event that they decided to stay the night at the cottage and drive directly to the airport the next day. The two of them stopped in Harriston for breakfast and arrived in Oliphant by 10.30.

Emma was driving. She slowed at the SeaDoo dealership. She guessed she was looking to see whether her assistant was there. The place was busy with Saturday-morning, beginning-of-season business. Men were standing about, talking, tinkering, waiting to get their boats into the water. The lot was crowded with R.V.s, vans, Sports Utility vessels and boat trailers, abandoned, not parked. She couldn't see him. She let the car roll on, down the hill, to the corner.

At the corner she paused. She usually paused here, despite the fact that those coming in to Oliphant had the right of way. It was odd really, she thought each time that she took her foot off the accelerator at this corner. Those coming in to town faced a T-junction, faced the lake, and had to turn either north or south. But they had the right of way. She paused because the lake always took her breath away. She'd arrived. It might take another five minutes to reach the cottage, but at the corner, at the lake, they had arrived.

She turned south. The plants, which later would cover the rock retaining walls, the Spotted Knapweed, thistles, Viper's Bugloss and yarrow were just making their spring debut. In the ditches the yellow lady's slippers and paintbrush glowed. At the cottage there were already cars filling the yard. She pulled around her uncle's vehicles next to the house, and tucked her car onto the lawn by the bunky, after reversing so that she faced out. George's car was not there. She wondered whether he would come. Why would he? Of course many people would be parked at the Government Docks, waiting for the boats. The maps they'd given out the previous day all showed the Government Docks as destination. One of her cousins, if any came, could run a van back and forth from the cottage if people needed transportation later.

Inside it was peculiar to see folks wearing jeans and windbreakers but acting as if they were wearing dress clothes. At the party the night before it had been clear that the mood was celebratory; here, it was not so certain. Her aunts were making up plates of sandwiches. The uncles were putting beer into the cooler. Cottage neighbors talked quietly. Several of the women's group sat at the dining room table already starting on a huge basket of Maude's cookies. Emma sampled one. Somehow Maude had created a chewy texture with a shortbread flavor. Caramel chunks added to the decadence. Emma took another to make sure the first one hadn't been a fluke. The second was just as good and her mouth was still full when her uncle suggested that it was time they all move to the docks.

Thus at 11.30 Emma and her mother walked slowly north to the marina. Eric had given his sister the container he'd picked up in Wiarton and was carrying the small box of ashes in the bright orange and yellow and fuchsia canvas bag Gertrude had designed for hiking. Made to hold a water bottle and snack, it was just the right size for the container from the funeral home. Mar smiled at Emma as she slung the bag over her shoulder. She was enjoying the incongruity too. Behind them three or four others also walked while the rest crowded into Geoff's van.

Edwina was waiting in the parking lot, her chair pulled close to a slip where she'd arranged that all the boats could dock for the morning. Emma was startled to notice that her assistant from earlier in the week was at the controls of a rather large and comfortable launch next to Edwina's boat. She would have liked to sit with him but Edwina pressed her to board her small sailboat.

The clouds of the previous day were gone and the wind had died to occasional puffs. The four boats headed out through the narrow channel and south towards Lonely Island. About half way between Lonely and Vimy they paused, rocking gently. Mar passed the box of ashes around, asking each person to take a pinch and sprinkle it over the lake. If words seemed appropriate that would be fine, if not silence was fine too. The box went around one boat and then was passed to the next. When it had gone around the four boats Mar motioned to Anna who began, followed by the other women then Mar and her brothers and a random selection of guests. Emma waited for some time. She was trying to think of just the right words to say about her grandmother, had been trying for most of the morning. It looked, however as if most people had sprinkled their ashes over the lake and the ceremony might be about to end. So she stood up. She wasn't sure why. Several others had, especially if they were not near the side of the two larger boats. In Edwina's boat it was scarcely necessary: Anna had done it to start the whole ceremony off, and being the last Emma thought to bring a similar solemnity to the end of the ritual. There were those who looked a bit nervous when she stood.

She shuffled her feet, turning herself towards the water and said, "Flow with the river; flow with the tide. Dance in the sunlight and rain. Live in our hearts." As Emma swung her arm forward, over the gunwale, Sarah shifted her weight heavily, the boat rocked, suddenly, and jerked, pitching Emma painfully over the side. She had been far enough from the edge that the gunwale hit her just about at the knees and she was aware only of the sharpness of that agony as she went over. It was not for some time, though she calculated when she re played it in her mind later, that it was less than a couple of seconds before she realized she could not move her feet.

In the boat next to Edwina's, the other small sail boat, Natasha leaned close over the side, swinging herself upwards slightly, ostensibly to look for Emma, but in the process clutching for support the side of Edwina's boat. Emma's first thought was the pain in her knees followed by the sheer pain of the cold May water against her skin. Then struggling upwards Emma could see above her the two hulls closing and she launched herself using an awkward butterfly motion to the outside of the gathering. By this time all four boats were in motion, looking for her and substantially impeding her effort to reach the surface. She was so terrified of the propellers and afraid of running out of air that she gave no thought to the rope around her ankles until on the far side of Edwina's boat she realized that she could not get to the surface.

Something was holding her back. Her feet were not only fastened together, the rope was still attached to the anchor in the boat. Pressed against the hull by her own buoyancy she no longer had room to kick. She flailed against the fibreglass with her fists. Exploding into a red world she felt rather than saw a body next to her; she was scarcely conscious of being dragged free of the boat, only that she was no longer hammering against the hull. Just as the blackness and pain in her chest was beyond excruciating she was free – with terrible rushing in her ears and then gasping and gasping for life.

"Here! Here, David!" and a loud voice was above her, hands grasped her arms and pulled her awkwardly upwards as someone steadied her below. She realized as she flopped onto the deck that Margaret's strong hands were on one side of her and that Margaret was wielding a red Swiss Army knife, still attached to her key ring. Margaret bent over her just as someone else threw a blanket towards her face. In a panic Emma flailed at the blanket and wrenched herself away from Margaret. "Stay still; I can't get the rope off your feet."

With a swift stroke the rope was gone and just as Margaret was about to throw it overboard a hand reached out. "I think we'll keep that for evidence, if you don't mind. I think I'd like the answers to some questions before we get rid of it. But I'd prefer to ask the questions in front of the fire at the cottage. No!" this last was in a much louder voice and directed to the other boats, which were veering back towards the public dock, "We'll all dock at the landing next to Ms. Moseley's cottage if you please."

"We'll just get our cars and come back." Voices from the other boats shouted various protests.

"We'll all go directly to the Moseley cottage to get these people warm. There will be transportation to the marina when we are done." The older man who had been steering the launch, the man who'd shouted at David, held up a badge. He had already positioned the boat between the other three and their proposed route to the Government marina. Any one of the boats could have ignored him but they did not. They turned south and were soon tied up. People moved toward the cottage.

David also was covered with a blanket but was staying close to Emma. "What happened?" she asked as they walked up the short path.

"I noticed the rope just as you went over. Too late to do anything but get out my knife and follow you. It wasn't difficult to figure where you'd be. Dad had the tougher job of getting his boat around to pick us up quickly without hitting us in the bargain."

"That's your Dad? Who is he?"

"OPP. When I got home the other day I mentioned my new career as exhumer. When he noticed the message you left – yesterday was it? – he decided to take a look. I guess when he saw them push you over he realized maybe you weren't crazy."

"When he saw what?" Emma's voice rose.

"Shhhh. I shouldn't have said that. That's what he wants to ask a few questions about I imagine. You'll see in a few moments, as soon as we get you out of those cold clothes and into a warm outfit."

"As if you're dry."

"Me too. I've got some spare clothes in the cabin of my boat." Having seen her to the door, he turned and trotted back towards the dock.

Mar materialized at her elbow and put her arms around her before guiding her into the cottage. "Oh, Emma. I don't know what to say. It was like the time you went off over the horse's head and almost hit the jump. Remember? You were riding Snoopy. Here, get into the bathroom and strip off those wet clothes. I'll get the suitcase from the car. That must be why we came prepared to stay over night."

"Never mind, Mom. Grandma's sweat pants and warm tops are right there on the shelf with the towels. I can wear them and be ready in a second."

Mar looked into her daughter's eyes, making that search that mothers make to see whether their children are safe. Nodded and left. Emma hung her wet clothes over the shower rail . She was just pulling the sweat top to one of her grandmother's lavender outfits over her head, when there was a tap on the door and a male voice asked to speak to her. She cracked the door open and peered into the eyes of the man whom David had said was his father.

"Excuse me for a moment." He was almost whispering. "This may be one of the more bizarre places to talk but it's also the only private space available. May I talk to you for a second before you face the crowd?" He appeared to be about to reach again for his O.P.P. identification. Emma shrugged and, with a sweep of her hand indicated that he might enter, though she felt it unlikely that there would be space for him. Pete Weston was a tall, wide man, greying at the top and thickening around the middle. However, easing his way past the towel rack, he hitched himself onto the edge of the vanity. Emma put the toilet lid down and sat there. Their knees touched. They both grinned.

"My son tells me that he explained who I am and why I'm here. It's pretty irregular," his grin widened as his glance took in the interview space again, "but if you are up to it I'd like you to tell me all about what you've discovered."

"Here? Now? All?"

"Hang on. I got your message about the contents of the dog's stomach. But you had called earlier. I take it you have other causes for your suspicions."

"Not much that is concrete but, I've spoken to most of the people who are here today, and I'm suspicious, yes."

"As I say, if you are up to it, I'd like you to go out there and tell your story, step by step. I'll just try to keep order. It's clear to me from what I saw on the lake that something is going on. We might have a better idea what that is if we hear from everyone. If it comes down to it I'll charge someone with trying to do away with you. But first I'd like to see what we can find out while we have all these people" – he noticed her shaking her head, "most of the people?" she nodded – "in one place."

"I'll need my notes. Thank heavens I left my purse and papers locked in the car. Mom will have the keys."

"I'll get them. Will you be alright?"

She nodded again and he slid, though that hardly was the right word, out the bathroom door. She looked in the mirror. The person in the mirror was Emma, but the person looking at Emma was a stranger, a character from a book, playing detective, ordering tests, interviewing suspects, calling police, almost drowning, for God's sake! Leaning closer to the mirror, Emma grimaced. What was she expecting to see? Weed from the lake tucked like parsley between her front teeth? She ran her fingers slowly through her damp hair, turned resolutely and left the room. She felt she'd been making rather a lot of entrances and exits lately.

*

Standing at the bottom of the stairs she looked around the living room.

In the oldest part of the cottage the windows were secured from wind and rain by heavy overhead shutters. These acted as awnings against the sun and were closed down depending on which direction the wind was blowing rain. The big living room was the centre of the old cottage so the overhang of the porch to the west, and the shutters on the north side were cutting out most of the light on a day already dark. Generations of wood fires and wet bathing suits and muddy dogs and mothballs and herbs and sand permeated the air. She could have recognized the smell blindfold.

She'd wondered how they would squeeze everyone in on a rainy day This was how. There were maybe twenty-five or thirty people in the room, seated around the edges waiting for the main event. The eight women from the group were on the couches. The rest of the crowd were on plastic garden chairs or using the brightly colored pillows to sit along the walls and against the knees of those on chairs. Emma, stepping over legs and avoiding crushing fingers, crossed the room and sat at her mother's feet. The coffee table had been removed to the small bedroom and Emma realized with a start that her mother's chair was next to the end of the couch where Gertrude's head had rested just over a week earlier. She herself was sitting where Sinister's head would have been. She shivered.

David's Dad had been standing in front of the fireplace, a position he could not hold for long, and from which he was forced to pace one step forward and one step back in the small empty space in the centre of the room. The movement allowed him to control the room and clearly he had explained how he wished matters to proceed. People who had been talking quietly fell silent when she entered. He leaned down and handed her the papers she'd requested. When Emma had settled herself, and sorted the notes, he nodded at her and moved to stand in the entry to the kitchen.

Emma coughed nervously, looking around at all the faces, and then came up with what she hoped was a brilliant delaying action. She asked people to introduce themselves. There were the eight women whom she'd interviewed; there were also two other women of a similar vintage who had been cottage friends, summer friends for years. Gertrude's children were there and, with the exception of Mike, so were her children's partners. Ailric and Leyland and Zachary were in one corner, together, near the little bedroom. Two of the women had brought partners and Edwina's daughter and grandson were in another corner. George had come and was sitting in the rocking chair close to the kitchen door. Emma noticed that George did not give his name, saying only that Emma had prevailed upon him to come. David and his father also were noncommittal, stating their names, not stating anything beyond their willingness to lend a boat to the festivities. And at the last moment, just as she was again wondering how to begin, a familiar voice spoke from beyond Sergeant Weston.

"And I'm Dan, Emma's brother." Heads turned, the cousins called appropriate greetings while Mar cried out and stumbled across the intervening bodies to hug her son. David and Dan squeezed into the empty space in the centre of the floor. Both reached out and held

Emma's hands for a moment. As order was restored Emma found her starting place. "When did you get here? Where have you been?"

"I picked up your messages two days ago and got here as soon as I could. Hopped about on West Jet and friendly private planes. Drove into the yard, expecting to find it packed with cars. Lots of cars but no people. So I wandered down to the water. Saw boats out on the water. Voices and hand waving. Then that little sail boat suddenly shifted and my sister made a remarkably awkward flip into the lake. Seemed a bit early in the season for a swim. I didn't see you come up. Disappointed. I'd come all this way to see you and was afraid you'd not be available, sunk like a fossil. Your rescuer was changing his clothes behind the lilacs when I came up from the dock and I've been comparing notes with him."

"So what conclusions have you come to? 'Cause I'm really puzzled about what happened out there."

David began. "I saw, the woman opposite you – Anna is it? – moving around a lot while the folks in other boats scattered their ashes. She'd gone first, I believe, stood up too, and then after the others in your boat had leaned over the side and thrown their ashes in all the attention shifted. Dad told me just to keep my eyes on you, otherwise I wouldn't have noticed her bending down to put her cigarettes in her bag, shuffling her feet about for quite a while. I was so curious about what she could be doing and busy keeping my eyes on you that I didn't notice who gave the boat a terrific heave. Someone must have shifted weight sharply just as you were leaning out to sprinkle your ashes. Because I was watching and saw you go off balance, I was ready to grab you when you came up, but the woman in the other boat swung in tight and hung on; so I had to grab my knife and dive over the opposite side of our launch if I didn't want to get caught underneath."

"Anna? Surely you didn't try to drown me on purpose." Emma was horrified to notice that her voice shook. She hadn't had time to realize how the incident had frightened her. Had it frightened her? Yes, perhaps she needed to acknowledge that.

Anna sucked in her breath, slowly, as if she were inhaling smoke and communing with some inner voice. "No. I didn't send you overboard; I had help. However, it happened about as the young man described it. I didn't plan it but when I stood to scatter my ashes I wondered whether others would follow my lead. And a few did. Then when I was reaching down to get my cigarettes out of my bag I saw the anchor rope wound close to your feet. Your back was to me and no one else was watching. I wondered whether I could snare your feet. I got one and then I wondered how hard the boat would have to pitch for you to fall out. I found out, though I must say I was surprised when the side suddenly rose and fell that way. However, I had caught your feet nicely." There was a certain triumph in her voice, a pleasure in accomplishment.

"But why, Anna?"

"To see whether it could be done. To see whether you'd notice you'd been snared. Why were you, Emma, scouring our final memories of your grandmother, turning a nice peaceful death into a melodrama?"

Emma had spent a week, many hours now, believing that her grandmother had been killed and that everyone would share her outrage. The fact that there might be other points of view, that she might be seen as meddling, or simply seeing what she could find out, took her breath away. She could see Sergeant Weston in the doorway waiting for her answer. She decided to explain it all to him. To start over and see where she had gone wrong.

"I arrived here the day after my grandmother's death. I was tired, disoriented, sad. My grandmother is, had been important to me. Arriving twenty four hours after the event, well, almost twenty four hours after you had found her," she couldn't help looking directly at Anna, "put me in a different emotional space from you. You, her friends, had been here for a full day and my uncles had been notified the night before. Mom and Dad had had the long flight on which to talk and explore their feelings. I realize that now. I was a step behind. I suppose that was why I went looking for the dog. Everyone else was talking about wills and memorials and I missed the dog.

"When I asked where he was, I found that he was a body which had got in the way. His body had been a problem to be solved. I was furious. It was so clear to me that he and my grandmother could not have died at the same time without there being some link. If there were some link then at least one of those deaths was not a death from natural causes. But none of you cared. Indeed, you were pleased with yourselves for shovelling the dog into the ground so quickly.

I wondered whether someone, or maybe several of you were equally pleased that my grandmother had been so quickly consigned to be cremated. Melody was the one who had reminded everyone that grandmother had requested cremation. She was also the one who had organized the burial of the dog. I wondered why. I phoned the police. They assured me that the constable and the coroner had handled matters correctly.

"As it happened, the next day I found grandmother's journal and the final week's entries provided no evidence of ill health or suicidal intentions. On the Friday morning she was looking forward to the weekend. She was making preparations. But the last page did reveal that she was expecting George for lunch that day. As I struggled with my suspicions I realized that the dog's body might reveal how he, at least, had died. So I drove up here and, as luck would have it, got David to help me exhume More Sinister.

I decided that I would have to learn more about each of you and reconstruct the events of my grandmother's last day. Scour, if you will. But when I had interviewed only a few of you the report on the dog came in and it was troubling. My interviews were troubling. The timing was becoming clearer, Not helpful but clearer. Anna might have been lying about the time she spent waiting for the three others. Margaret also had time not accounted for. Sarah and Melody might have been to Oliphant together or have been providing alibis for each other. Natasha, of course, was completely unaccounted for. Almost any of Gertrude's friends or relations might have been in this cottage at the crucial noon hour.

Here is my picture of that day. I will talk about Gertrude's friends first, because they saw her first.

"Nine women are getting ready for their thirtieth weekend visit to this cottage. Natasha is in the air flying from Vancouver to Toronto. This can be checked." Emma looked at Weston who made a note. "Her plane arrived early enough for her to phone from the airport at 3."

Mar interrupted. "She couldn't. We took the first plane and it didn't land until 3.15 and it took us at least 15 minutes to get into the terminal. I know it wasn't the same plane but it was the same schedule. They told us that we had made good time; so it's not likely anyone would get in much earlier than we did."

"Ah, " smiled Emma. "I knew there was something about that phone call that bothered me. Natasha?"

Natasha squared her chin and shaped her mouth for maximum accent. "You vant to know vere I vas? Well I was in Toronto. I got here the day before, on the Thursday afternoon. I had an engagement to autograph my latest book in the World's Biggest Book Store on Thursday evening and Friday morning. You can check my alibi if you want but I didn't feel like telling a nosy young person what was none of her business. Then I began to worry when I heard the information from the others that perhaps one of my sisters had been responsible in some way. Or had something to hide. She was so sure something was wrong. So sure one of us – one of us! – had something to do with it. I knew my sisters would not do something like that. My friends, we've been friends for a long time. None of us would hurt each other.

I saw Emma go overboard. I didn't know how it happened but I knew she was making trouble and thought it would be better if she didn't come back up any time soon. So when I saw her go overboard I just moved the boats closer so she couldn't get up between them. I hoped she'd be scared enough to leave us alone. I wasn't aware that her foot was caught. I swear I wasn't."

Natasha's voice rose with each damning revelation. The load of her guilt drove the express of her tongue careening wildly out of control down a slope of self justification.

When she stopped, Emma waited a moment and said, "Let's leave my drowning for the moment and go back to the Friday. So you didn't call Grandmother at 3?"

"Not exactly." Natasha looked nervously at the sergeant. "I did call. But I called in the morning before I went to the signing. I'd been out late the night before and not had a chance to call. When I was thinking about it I could see that if Gertrude had died before we got there, there was time for one of us to drive up in the morning, have lunch with her and still arrive later in the day, even if that meant meeting at Maude's by 3.30 or so. My phone call gave everyone an alibi but Edwina. I couldn't do anything about her. I didn't go to her house that first night though, just in case." Natasha avoided Edwina's eyes, which was just as well.

"Hm. Well, your phone call had really puzzled me. You said you were talking to her at 3. Someone was here with her at noon and maybe later. The doctor suggested that she died around 4. If you had talked to her at 3 she had to die quite quickly and the usual poisons, the usual drugs, the ones to which most of us might have access, don't work that fast. That identified the murderer as having certain expertise or access. On the other hand if you did not call in the afternoon, if none of you spoke to her in the afternoon, she might have been poisoned at lunch and lain unconscious for some time. As Natasha suggests, this means that each of your alibis must be more carefully checked because Gertrude may have been unconscious, but not dead when her murderer left her.

"To continue with my picture of Friday. So far as we know grandmother is here. She goes for her usual morning walk. She writes her journal. Some time during the morning she makes the soup for supper. You phoned, Natasha, and there were other calls. Maude, what time did you call?"

Maude flipped through the pages of the notebook she always carried. She said she could remember nothing without her 'brains'. Most of her writing was done in meetings and while she was taking photos. Otherwise, she said, she wouldn't have any idea what had been said or what pictures she had taken. Emma had forgotten this about Maude. She wondered whether the Sergeant could collect the notebooks as evidence. Emma also recalled that Maude had not used her notebook when they had visited on Friday. Was it only yesterday afternoon that they had sat on Maude's deck and watched the birds feeding?

"I don't have a record of calling, but I have a memo here that I must call. I wrote it on the Thursday night. 'Call Gertrude in am.' I must have called around 9 on Friday morning. Maybe I called to ask whether I could bring the dog. Both Gertrude and I would have been back from our morning walks by then. You either had to call before 7 or after 9 if you wanted to get her. Sometimes she didn't answer after 9, though," Maude answered almost as an afterthought.

"I thought on Thursday you told us…"Edwina whose recall of conversation was often perfect, began and stopped.

"On Thursday? You said what on Thursday?" Emma's voice was growing rough with stress or disbelief. "You've always brought your dog to the retreats. You and grandmother used to joke about making the rest of the women into dog lovers whether they wanted to be or not. So what did you say on Thursday?"

"I remember that I said on Thursday that I'd called at around 11. But I didn't. I called much earlier but I didn't think it mattered at group. I just said a convenient number before lunch time. Emma, I really can't recall what else we might have talked about. I might just have wanted to remind her that I wasn't arriving early because I had an appointment to take some pictures in the afternoon."

"Would you remember where that was, Maude?" Emma looked at Sergeant Weston and suppressed a sigh. The purpose of the appointment which had detained Maude on the Friday afternoon had not been mentioned before.

"Yes, yes. It says here 'babies: 2:00.' I wouldn't usually commit myself on the day of the retreat but a friend in Paisley called and said the baby birds nesting on her deck were about to fly and if I wanted a good picture of them I'd need to get there soon. I already had a doctor's appointment in the morning and I thought I could go from the doctor to the photo shoot and then drive straight north to Gertrude's. Yes, I called just as I was leaving the house. It was about 9 in the morning. I was telling Gertrude I might be late."

"Anna, you called about the crêpe pan, right? What time was that?"

"I called about 11.30. Just before I ate lunch."

"You were not aware of her expecting anyone for lunch; nothing she said led you to believe she was cooking or tidying or in a hurry? Think, please, it's very important that we reconsider every impression."

"No. Gertrude was very much herself: caustic about my requiring a fancy pan, excited that we were all going to be able to attend, pleased that the weather forecast was for sun. She said the soup was made already and all she had to do was pick some greens for salad."

"The soup was ready? Before lunch?" Margaret sounded horrified. "It was going to sit there unrefrigerated all afternoon?"

"Obviously unrefrigerated soup is not a problem if you have all been eating it for 30 years," said Dan, who had never made soup in his life.

"No, Margaret is quite right," said Maude. "On the occasions when I've arrived in the afternoon she'd have the kettle boiling on one element and the soup would just be started. The air would be heavy with the smell of onions sweating and vegetables would be in a huge bowl, all chopped and ready to simmer for an hour before supper. She'd stir from time to time, while we had tea. The pot for nine of us was very large and she tried to leave refrigerator space available for us to put all our salads and desserts in. It would, indeed, have been unusual for the soup to be ready so early."

"But it was ready and it was in a pot in the refrigerator when we got here. I put it on the stove while I was unpacking my cooler," said Sarah.

"So she had made it early," Emma said, almost to herself, wondering whether this suggested her grandmother had made the soup to eat at lunch, or might just have wanted the job done before George arrived.

"Leave the soup for the moment. Go back to the morning. Edwina, you left for Hamilton at 9? 10? And didn't get away until after 3. I think that's what you said?"

Edwina fumbled in a pocket on the side of her chair and produced a card which she passed along to Sergeant Weston. "Please, call the clinic and confirm my attendance."

"Yes, Sarah?" If Sarah had not been close to her, Emma might not have noticed the sharply indrawn breath at the moment that Edwina pulled the card from her appointment book. All eyes turned from the card making its way along the row of people to the policeman.

"I thought…" she stopped.

"Yes, Sarah?" Now Sarah looked awkwardly at Edwina. "I thought perhaps you had … you know. You usually have tea with Gertrude on the Friday afternoon and when I saw the cups on the table, like that, one by Gertrude and the other at the side with no chair near it, I assumed that you'd been there. While Maude and Natasha and Jean were arriving and unpacking I moved the cups and saucers to the bathroom and hid them in the cupboard under the sink until there was a quiet time when I could get them to the kitchen, wash them and put them away. "When I found that Emma was asking questions I called some of you." Sarah glanced around the room. "Perhaps Edwina and Natasha misinterpreted my fears. I was very afraid. I was afraid one of us had killed Gertrude.

"That accounts for the change in cups. We have one mystery solved," said Margaret who had been puzzling over the dishes and wondering whether she had removed a vital clue.

"Why would one of you had reason to kill my grandmother?" Emma tried to sound more surprised than she was.

There was a long pause while Sarah gathered courage and searched for precisely the right words.

"Gertrude had a very good memory. Perhaps it wasn't her memory but her journals. Once in a while she would look knowing, would hint that she knew something about me. If she did that to me I suppose she may have made others feel that way too."

"She was blackmailing you?"

"Oh no. In fact she never said a thing. I knew that she knew, however."

"You thought that Gertrude would talk about something you had done ten…" Sarah nodded and waved her hands twice … "twenty years ago?"

Anna spoke quietly, "Sarah was worried about her marriage. I thought it unfair that Roger's wife might find out about all his years of infidelity. If she hadn't known so far it seemed terrible that she find out now."

"So you were all protecting each other without ever knowing why?" Heads nodded in response to Emma's question.

"Don't you see, Emma, we'd valued each other for 30 years. We'd been fond of each other and to some extent cherished even the faults of our chosen sisters. It's not surprising that we'd protect each other.True, we did not know that Gertrude had kept so complete a tally of our weak moments, but our not knowing about the journals is more evidence that we were not likely to wish to harm her after all these years. She might have used the information to influence our decisions but she'd not used them to harm us, really. Why after all this time would we harm her? What had changed in our relationships? We couldn't be so sure about whether you would harm us, however."

"You're right, of course," Emma sighed. "There were, are so many suspects. I kept suspecting each of you. It seemed no one had an alibi, not her friends nor her family!" Something in what Sarah had said was bothering Emma. She started over again trying to hear what it was as she spoke.

"So the soup was already made when you arrived. Did you have soup for lunch, George?"

"She was stirring it when I knocked on the door."

Heads turned. For some this was the first they'd heard of George lunching with Gertrude and for the rest it was the first solid evidence that Emma's interest in Roger and George was based in fact. The atmosphere changed subtly.

"Ah, yes. We had soup and salad." George's tone left no doubt that he could have done nicely without Gertrude's contribution. "Gertrude had said that she was going to be very busy so I'd offered to bring the lunch. But no. She had to provide soup and salad. I wanted to be considerate and she insisted on providing most of the lunch."

"What was left for you to bring, George?"

"I brought tea biscuits and crème caramel. That's all she'd let me provide!"

Emma looked at David and his father. Then she drew a deep breath and continued.

"I began this search because Gertrude's dog was dead. I thought it unlikely that they would both die at the same time. I was sure that both deaths were unnatural. So I wanted to get to know you. I was looking for which of you was likely to have murdered my grandmother but I found no enemies, only kind and helpful people. Along the way I also found my grandmother. I found a person whom I don't think any of us knew. She gave each of us parts of her, large parts, but mostly the parts she thought we wanted or needed. She kept other parts for herself. One enormous part she kept entirely secret.

"A moment ago you asked what had changed, Anna. Apparently nothing had changed significantly, for us or for her. That was why I couldn't believe she'd commit suicide...her life had gone smoothly, with only minor unpleasantness for years. Barring knowledge of terminal illness and we can check that with her doctor … even then I'd think she'd have waited until after the anniversary weekend..." Emma had been scanning the room, looking faces as she spoke.

The realization surfaced. Anna knew what had changed. Both women looked at George. One by one other people followed their gaze. Emma spoke.

"But there was significant change wasn't there, George? Your father died. Then you found out what your father's life had been like and you found out what had sustained it for all those years. What has your father's death meant to you George? My grandmother had come to terms with Roger's death. Had you? The other night you had to get home to care for your mother. Tell us about your new life.

"Or perhaps you should tell us about your lunch with Gertrude."

*

George had come with the intent to do harm, though without Gertrude's help his plan might only have left her deeply unconscious, or vomiting violently. He had used some of the stock of dog sedative which he'd been accumulating for a couple of years, for an emergency. He'd added in some of his mother's sleeping medication along with sedative for the family's retriever. He'd begun saving pills rather aimlessly, just thinking that they might come in handy, long before his father had died, long before he'd had to care for his mother, had thought that sometime it just might be useful to have a drug which put you calmly to sleep.

He'd convinced the vet that he travelled monthly to Ottawa to see a client and that he stayed overnight at her country home in the Gatineau; so he took the dog. Actually it had begun when his parents had been away and he'd had to take their dog once. He'd forgotten that. The fantasy dog had filled his mind for so long that he'd forgotten he'd begun with the real dog. The vet and he had become quite chatty over the relative merits of flying Rapidair from Toronto and taking the dog

206

who loved the country estate weekends more than he did – or flying Greyhound or whatever small airline was currently using Mt. Hope Airport.

If he did the latter he had an easy drive, free parking, and quick check-in, but because the small planes did not completely pressurize their cargo holds he could not take the dog. That his trips were fantasy did not detract from their interest. He liked solving problems, practical applications, not his father's history and philosophy stuff but how to get to Ottawa with a dog, that was useful.

George had stood at the back door of the cottage and waited for Gertrude to finish seasoning the soup. He had watched her moving firmly around her kitchen and wished that his mother could do the same thing. But mostly he had watched the huge dog which had barked twice and was now sitting on the other side of the screen door staring at him. Gertrude had spoken to the dog before she'd spoken to him. To the dog she'd said, "Sinister, sit!" To him she'd said, "Just one moment and I'll greet you properly."

Here was an interesting development. His father had always named their dog Dexter. Really. He found himself amazed by the duplicity of his father. He leaned down and opened the insulated box he'd brought with him. He reached into the box of biscuits he'd taken from the oven moments before he left home. They were carefully wrapped in foil and still slightly warm. He felt the decoration on the top and brought out one. When Gertrude at last put the spoon down and opened the screen door, George said, "Mind if I give some of our lunch to the dog? I brought plenty." The biscuit disappeared past a frightening array of teeth. The dog sat looking alertly for more.

When George had spoken to Gertrude on the phone she had been brusque. Had not wanted to see him, or to talk to him. She'd said she was going to be very busy all weekend. He'd offered to bring lunch, take only an hour of her time. He had not researched the materials or the doses thoroughly but had relied largely on popular belief. Gertrude was a trial case really. He had more important plans.

Since his father's death George had done most of the cooking for his mother and himself. Had learned a bit about cooking, in fact. If his life was to be circumscribed by his mother's limits, he might just as well do what had to be done well. He'd never be the carpenter or fixer his father was but he could cook. Gertrude had insisted that she would provide soup and salad if he would provide rolls and desert. She said she was making the soup and salad in any case for her dinner guests. George had decided on fresh, hot biscuits, and crème caramel. He hoped that the fast cooking time of the biscuits would keep the extra ingredient from being destroyed in the oven. He'd added some pepper cheese to mask the taste of the drugs. Some of the biscuits he'd marked subtly by pressing an extra bit of dough on top. Others he'd made less desirable by cooking them a minute longer. He placed the darker ones on his side of the serving basket, reserving them politely for himself. The crème caramel was perfectly exquisite, and unadulterated – a sort of final joke.

Gertrude met him at the door. She was not the person he'd expected. He wasn't sure what he'd expected, someone who looked like a mistress. Belle from *Gone with the Wind*, perhaps or someone small and wrinkled with blonde hair and too much makeup. The woman in front of him was as tall as his father had been. She wore her grey hair in a no-nonsense very short cut. Her face and neck were clearly etched by time but not disturbingly wrinkled. She looked vigorously healthy. He realized he was comparing her to his mother and that he had no very clear idea how an 80 year old woman would look.

Gertrude had invited him in. Two individual salads were already made and she simply poured a currant dressing, bright red and only slightly sweet, over them as she put them on the table. She had also insisted on placing a glass plate under his basket of biscuits to keep the steam from marking the table. The plate would be an interesting touch. She had complimented him upon the biscuits and much to his relief, helped her self to a second before he carried in the soup bowls.

Having both salad and soup provided a bit of a problem. She'd insisted on serving the salad first. He hoped they could eat quickly enough that she'd finish before she felt sleepy. The plan had been for them to eat the biscuits with their soup and the salad upset his timing. So busy had he been watching her that as he drove home he realized that he remembered not a word of their conversation. No matter. He hadn't come for conversation. It might have been interesting to hear about his father from her point of view. Not likely though. He'd come to experiment on a person who could scarcely be tied to him. If the barbiturates succeeded on one old lady they might succeed on another.

When Gertrude had slid out of consciousness, George cleared all of his dishes away, wiping finger prints from the table as he went, borrowing Gertrude's rubber gloves to wash her soup bowls and salad plates and put them away on the shelf. The crème caramel he replaced in his cooler and took back to the car. It was too pretty to waste and he decided to serve it to his mother for dinner. When he went to put the biscuit basket in his car he found that the dog had not been completely unconscious but merely sedated beside his mistress. Clearly his opportunistic instincts had not been sedated enough to prevent his finishing the biscuits and knocking the basket to the floor. He must have licked the salad bowls too, George thought. Gertrude had not eaten all the leaves on her plate, yet it was very clean when he took it to the kitchen. He surveyed the room. A book was lying open by the couch. He picked it up and placed it beside Gertrude on the table.

He went to the kitchen, carefully poured the coffee from Gertrude's thermos into the cups which she'd set out on the tray with the dessert, emptied the cups into the sink and placed them appropriately on the table with the glass plate. Margaret's compulsive cleaning or someone else's had obliterated this part of his handiwork. In the kitchen he put the soup pot into the refrigerator which was almost empty and accommodated it easily. Then he rinsed the sink, wiped the counter, put the gloves away and left. He used his elbow to open and shut the screen. He debated closing the glass door but it had been open when he arrived and he left it. He smiled as he drove south.

*

He did not smile when Weston arrested him and charged him with Gertrude's murder. He blustered and protested. There was no evidence to suggest how Gertrude had died. He'd just seen her ashes scattered to the winds and waves. How could anyone prove that he'd killed the old lady (his words).   Like almost everyone else he had forgotten the dog.

January 25, 1998, Saturday   *Wellington*

Cold, icy, typical winter day in southern Ontario. My birthday yesterday. I'm 85. What an age! And no card from R. No phone call from R.

My brother calls. My children call. I restrained Sue who wanted to throw an enormous party for someone who had lived so long. I couldn't. I also couldn't say why I couldn't. I told her to make plans for my 90th. One or two grandchildren called. Zack dropped by with a hug and a kiss and a beautiful pair of purple gloves, fur-lined.

More Sinister and I demonstrated how comforting purple is by wearing the gloves to walk around the block with Zack when he left. It was good to have his arm to lean on. More Sinister is patient with me in this weather but a human arm is comforting. It snowed a week ago and then melted. The result is treacherous. Some sidewalks are clear and others are invitations to broken hips. I lean and slip and hold my breath.

At the door I turn and I wave my purple glove at Zack. It glows against a sky as grey as depression. No cloud shapes break the monotony. An overcast closes down on the city threatening to obliterate all vision. I remember walking in Vancouver during the war, walking on Burrard Street and not being able to see beyond my hands. Once the fog did not lift for nineteen days in a row. Cars would suddenly loom, parked on the sidewalk, abandoned. Some people drove, regardless. The madness of the automobile even then. They had gas – who knows how they'd managed that – and wanted to prove their superiority. What could they see of traffic or of road? I could scarcely see to walk to the stores on Granville, to find the queues. I exaggerate. There were only queues at Xmas and Easter, at the candy stores, or in front of the women's wear if an order of nylons came in. The noise of the horns in the murk remains in my memory.

Depression is like that. One proceeds through the fog – hands in front of face, still moving. We tried to describe how depression felt for each of us in our group, not long ago. I asked. For one it was a death wish, for another an inability to get out of bed in the morning, for another an inability to settle, to concentrate for more than a few seconds. For me it was fog and lack of vision.

It occurs to me that these varied responses are not steps on a ladder to deeper or less severe states, as some therapists might think. The depression is equally severe for each, but wears for each of us the face we've been taught to fear most. So in the jargon, I suppose, depression is the super ego run riot.

I've heard the suggestion that depression is the murk of promises to ourselves, shattered and floating in the air we breathe. Same thing. It hardly matters whether the fog blows in on winds of chemical imbalance or abuse or loss. I suppose chemical imbalance is easier to cure. What a word. The twentieth century is obsessed with curing and ignores healing. We treat ourselves like meat. No wonder we are depressed. Once the fog surrounds us it shouts in the voices of our parents and judges and school teachers. "Cowardly, lazy, stupid! Touch that and you'll die! What have you accomplished lately? Who do you think you are?" We rarely stop, sit down, and look at the drops of moisture, listen to the fog horns; we try instead to move along the dangerous streets in our accustomed patterns, banging into cars parked on the sidewalk.

No call from R. What a great space his passing has left in my mind. Not in my days. He has rarely been present in my days...not since the first years of our affair. But in my mind. Things I do not think; things I do not think to say. I notice that the present book has taken a 180 degree turn. I thought it would be about my women friends but, since his death, R has moved in. Not smashed in the horror of the accident, not dust in a box but nonetheless his passing haunts the pages of my book. His love is there, below the surface. His failures are there. His influence on my life and on his family's life is there, floating, not far below the surface.

He's been present before, of course; so have they, but this time the likenesses are more explicit. For years, for as long as I can recall, I jot down notes as I travel, or reflect on my day. After a group meeting or after a phone call I make a note. Then as I write my journal I transcribe my jottings. The act of jotting begins the fictionalizing.

The fiction grows like a perennial. Roots planted in one border spring up on the opposite side of the garden. Chamomile planted in the front lawn appears in a border of the back garden. This year's purple hollyhock is pink next year. I don't suppose, supposing that they ever read my books, that my friends recognize themselves or their life stories. They recognize the truth of a situation because it is like one they've lived through, but they don't say – oh, Gertrude is writing about me now. I hope they don't. They might be horrified by the notes in my journals though.

I have wondered occasionally whether anyone will ever read these journals. I have left enough clues, should anyone take the time. I think I have lived almost long enough. Better to die while still healthy, and strong, relatively. Better not to be a burden to family and friends. The means are close at hand in the garden. I wonder whether all writers of mysteries toy with the idea of the perfect murder, toy with the idea of revenge, toy with the idea of framing someone. In a sense, they must, but whether they do it consciously is another matter. I think I will plan to die when I am not alone, or not alone for long. I don't want to be rescued, but I don't want to decay and be disgusting either. Time enough for that. A salad should do the trick. I wonder whether I shall recognize the flavor of the aconite, or just think it is a particularly bitter lovage. I wonder who will be blamed?

At the meeting this week Margaret wanted to know how we dealt with phone solicitors. Used to be worried about being nice to door-to-door salespeople. "Ding-dong, Avon Calling." Now it's the phone and the computer. How much does one owe such intruders? What a premium some of us put upon being nice, when we don't enjoy being 'nice' and we don't want people being 'nice' to us. I looked it up when I got home. 'Nice' comes from the Latin ne scire *not to know...ignorant...and in the middle ages meant innocent or foolish...eventually it came to mean precise or picky...following the rules exactly because you are ignorant of what they mean...so doing something nicely has*

It is not known whether Emma ever read this particular entry. The books lay for some years in boxes. It may be that eventually some student discovered what had really happened to Gertrude, and it may be that George was eventually pardoned, though whether he was guilty or not remains unclear.

The author says:

I did what was expected of me, usually. I attended schools in three Canadian provinces as well as in New Hampshire and Massachusetts before attending university until I received a B.A., barely. I married and had three children, parenting them poorly, though loving them dearly. I taught for more than thirty years and actually began to get the hang of it. Going part time to University I added two graduate degrees in English to the original B.A. I retired to live and garden in the chaos of a house which I shared with a daughter, two grandchildren, two dogs and three cats. Finally sanity drove me to the peace of an apartment in Hamilton, Ontario where I research and write self indulgently.

Non quia difficilia sunt non audemus, sed quia non audemus difficilia sunt. (Seneca the Younger, *Epistulae Morales ad Lucilium, 104, 26.*)